Rabbit

Max Ellendale

Cover Artist: Victoria Miller
Editor: Deadra Krieger

Max Ellendale
www.maxellendale.com

ISBN-13: 9781980802471

CHAPTER ONE

"There's a lot more people here than I expected, Porter." I adjusted the cuff of my sleeve while leaning against the brick building of the community center. Dozens of people lined the streets, shouting about immigration reform while dozens more held up anti-immigrant signs. I sighed at the callous displays that read, *White country is our country* and *Send them back*, while trying to focus on the positive displays of, *We are all immigrants* and *We're a nation built on differences.*

"Keep your back about you, Lange," Porter's voice burst into my head through the earpiece.

"My back about me, Porter? Who says that? No one says that."

"We've got some rival activity on the outskirts," he continued over the earpiece clearly ignoring me.

"Not surprised. Uniforms in place?"

"Yes. Shields up."

While scanning the crowd, I thought about the purpose of the operative and the town hall meeting I'd been scheduled to speak at next week. Seattle, despite being one of the most progressive cities in America, wasn't without its bigots. Events like this, since the rise of the former presidential administration, seemed to bring them out of the worst corners of the nation.

The hood-covered head bobbing through the crowd drew my attention right away. I leaned away from my perch and elbowed the uniform standing beside me, nodding in the direction of the figure. "Porter, male in a green hoodie, center left. See him?"

A pause and then, "On it."

"Gun!" someone shouted, followed by varied hollers. I drew my weapon at the same time as the uniformed officer beside me.

"Porter?"

"No eyes, Lange."

"Where's the fucking weapon?" We raced through the scattering crowd. Picket signs hit the soiled streets, tangling with empty water bottles and soggy papers. I crouched behind a unit SUV and shouted to the heavens, "Anyone have eyes?"

People raced around us, hurrying away as the riot team rushed forward. Three heavy pops broke the scramble, sending people fleeing but now with accompanying screams. "Shots fired!" I shouted but no one responded.

Gunfire, now clearly audible, exchanged somewhere to my right. I swung around to see two hooded men, featureless under their black ski masks, firing at each other. Red sweatshirt versus black. They ran crazy, firing wildly at each other. A woman across the street hit the ground while another dove on top of her. Screams and shouts deafened me, closing in on the scene as shielded riot police raced in.

"Drop your weapons!" I hollered, taking aim over the hood of a car. The uniformed officer beside me fired off three rounds at them. Both figures swung in our direction at the same time and began shooting. Rivals became teammates as bullets battered the car we used for cover. I dropped down, hitting the pavement as the assault halted.

When I swung over the hood of the vehicle, both men, their eyes as white as they were wide, shot wildly, guns held sideways as they walked toward us, dead set on slaughter. I took aim in their direction, unloading a clip and hitting one of them in the torso. He spun in a dramatic circle then hit the ground with blood already pooling at his side.

From over the barrel of my weapon, I watched as the red hooded man raced toward us, changing out the clip of his gun, until the rapid fire of a semi-automatic weapon blasted through the scene.

"Get down!" The officer grabbed me, slamming me to the pavement at the same moment a line of holes appeared in the car above us. I cried out when pain lanced through my side, burning me like the hot sear of a branding iron. "Stay down!" Above me, the heavy body of the officer and his breath pressed in on me as I gasped, meeting his gaze as his eyes suddenly widened. His body tensed and shock stole away his terror, freezing his face to stone. A single trickle of blood ran from the side of his mouth, tumbling to my shirt.

"Lange! Answer me!" Porter shouted in my ear but I couldn't. I couldn't move. Couldn't breathe. Black shields and heavy boots stormed the area around us.

"Officer—" I gasped. "Officer *down*!" My breath caught in my throat. "Stay with me, Jenson." I grabbed his face, rolling him slowly onto his back as I slid out from under him. "Officer down!"

"I...please." Jenson heaved for breath as I searched, with trembling hands, for where he was hit. A dark, wet circle formed on the side of his vest. I tore open his shirt to see the corner of his vest where the bullet partially penetrated.

"You're okay. Stay with me, Jenson."

His eyes, murky and terrified, fixed on mine. Someone grabbed me around the middle, dragging me away and forcing a shout from my lungs.

"Easy! We got him," said an EMT, holding his hand up to me.

"Lange. You're hit." Porter tugged me away as shielded officers led us to a black SUV surrounded by a dozen geared-up law enforcement agents. Helmets and body armor covered every inch of them.

"I'm fine. Jenson. It missed the vest."

"They got him! They got him." Porter, with his giant hands, lifted me from the ground and into the car.

***

"I'm fine, guys." I sighed as my team surrounded me while I sat on the edge of the bed in the emergency room, my legs hanging off. Porter and Goldman watched as a nurse peeled back the hem of my shirt.

"Gentleman, if you don't mind. She isn't going to die. Please wait outside." She waved them off, her attitude almost as fiery as her auburn hair as she shoved them from the area, then snapped the curtain shut. Nurse Faye, in all her glory, returned to me with a satisfied smile. "Now, where were we?"

"I believe you were hitting on me. Or examining me. I couldn't tell," I said, smirking a bit as she chuckled at me.

"Well then, aren't you spirited, Detective?" Her eyes remained on the left side of my ribs as she poked it gently with a gloved hand.

"A little." I sucked in my breath when she pressed too hard.

"This is going to be ugly, but you're very lucky. Burns and bruises will heal over time. No evidence of internal injury, but we'll do some more tests, and then the doctor will be in."

"I feel fine, really," I said, leaning back when she nudged me onto the bed. "Other than the topical pain. How's Jenson?"

"He's stable. Now lie back while we take care of you, Detective Lange."

"I don't fair well with being taken care of. I can walk to the x-ray," I said, frowning slightly at the idea of being helpless. Nurse Faye leaned back, cocked a brow at me, and scoffed.

"You're not the first, or last, cop that I've dealt with. You'll behave yourself and get treatment. Got it?" She picked up her clipboard and bopped me on the boot with it. What could I do except laugh at that?

"Got it. Thank you." I nodded and dropped my head back on the pillow. The nurse plopped an ice pack on my ribs and I resigned to dealing with the situation.

While the unexpected events of the day replayed over in my head, I forced the images away and listened to the gentle voice coming from the curtain next to me.

"How long has it been like this, Agnes?" asked the woman.

"Oh, you know, dear. Not very long." By the rattle and twang of her voice, I could only assume that Agnes was rather long in the tooth. "A few days."

"You should've come in sooner. The nurse will take care of your wound and I'll be back to check on you in a little while, all right?"

"Yes'm, Doc."

A soft chuckle preceded the delicate, "Okay. See you soon."

In the quiet, I dropped my head back against the pillow again and listened to the mild sounds of the emergency room. Monitors beeped, feet scuttled, voices murmured. UW Medical wasn't a place I frequented for myself, thankfully, but I often came to talk to victims of violent crimes. The Bias Crimes Unit of the Seattle Police Department wasn't my home when I first arrived, but now, three years later, I called it such. The last time I ended up in the emergency room, I'd been helping a transgender woman file charges against a group of men who assaulted her after leaving a bar. Despite the many SPD Safe Places around the city, hate crimes remained a terrible problem.

The curtain around my bed tugged back to reveal the startling presence of a woman in scrubs. It wasn't the scrubs that set alight the jolt in my chest, but the long brown hair cradling the creamy face of the sharp-eyed doctor. Her cheeks lifted when her smile parted a soft set of pink lips as she extended her hand. "Good evening, Detective Lange. I'm Doctor Corwin," said the familiar voice of the woman who spoke to Agnes a little while ago.

"Hi." I shook her hand as I stared at her pretty face, then forced my gaze away to sweep over the length of her lab coat.

"How are you feeling?"

"I'm fine. Bruised a bit." I lifted the ice pack off my stomach to show her. "But fine, really."

"Let's have a look then." Her eyes fell away from mine to the injury. Delicate fingers poked at my skin in a clinical graze. I clenched my teeth, holding onto my reaction of both pain and interest at the same time. After a few seconds, she released me and met my gaze again. "Your assessment is correct, Detective. You're, at least, *going* to be fine. Have you ever been injured in the line of duty before?"

"This is the second bullet to the vest I've taken, yeah. I know how it'll heal. Burn first, bruise second."

"And some pain, mind you." The doctor leaned her hip on the side of the bed, her hands falling to rest on her thigh. I watched as her face hardened, dampening her features and reactions at the same time. "We've met before."

"We have but superficially. You've treated some of my victims," I said, nodding to her.

"Oh." Her expression lightened a bit. "That makes sense."

I laughed a little. "Why? Did you think I was a freakish long-lost family member or something?"

"Something like that." She grinned then lifted the ice pack from the bed. "Put this back on for awhile more."

"Okay." I let her put it on my side then held it. "Can I go?"

"I'll get the discharge paperwork ready and send you

off. If you have any complications or feel increased pain, or fever, I want you to come back. And I'm suggesting time off to recover." She stood now, pulling a prescription pad from her pocket.

"Doc, I don't need time off."

"You do, Detective."

"I've got cases and after this situation—"

"Detective Lange—"

"Alice."

Her brows flicked upward. "*Alice*, I'm recommending it."

The frown that tugged my mouth couldn't fully manifest because the way she looked at me, with that skulking brow and challenging glare, set fire to my cheeks. "You're very bossy, Doctor Corwin."

She smirked at me, her brow still cocked. "Yes, I am."

"How much time off?"

"A few days at least."

"Fine." I sighed dramatically and she laughed.

"Take care, Detective." She patted the edge of the bed before taking her leave.

It took barely three seconds for her to disappear before Porter busted back in. "Lange, you good?"

"I'm fine." I laughed a little. "Where's Goldm—"

"Alice, didn't I tell you to duck?" Marc Goldman, fellow detective and my resident best friend hurried in after. He hugged me right away and Porter chuckled.

"She sucks, G-man. What can I say?" said Porter.

"How's Jenson?" I asked a second time, giving Marc a squeeze. "He looked bad."

"He's doing okay," said Porter. "Jackson's out front waiting to see you."

"Oh goodie. Everyone wants to see me because I got shot. What kind of weapon was it?"

"They nabbed an AR-15 off the guy," Porter continued to explain. "It was a gang fight in the middle of a peaceful rally that brought out the radical white guy with a semi-automatic weapon. This is the world we live in."

"I can't even begin…" I shook my head, giving up on trying to explain it as I grabbed my shirt from the end of the bed. "Let's just go. The doc is getting my discharge ready."

"You sure, Allie?" Marc asked as I tossed on my shirt.

"Yeah. I'm ready for a drink."

Both guys laughed. "Mine or yours?" Porter asked.

"Yours. You have better junk food."

"Always."

***

"Well, I'm glad that young man is all right as well," my mother said as she set a plate filled with giant sandwiches on the table. Despite the fact that just two of us sat together, it was only a matter of time before the rest of the family came around, bringing their appetites with them.

"Me too." I reached for one of the roast beef sandwiches and devoured it without a second thought. Mom continued to fuss over me, pouring me a glass of soda, and bringing the dish of pasta salad closer.

"All of you in *violent* jobs." Mom sighed dramatically. "What kind of family did I raise?"

"Mom. Evan's a mechanic. That's hardly violent."

"Well you and your father and Ryan." She shook her head despondently.

I couldn't help but laugh. "Mom...Dad's retired."

"But Ryan works with *murderers*!" She flailed about, hopping up from her seat and storming off to the kitchen. "I forgot the pickles."

"He works with youthful offenders. *Youthful*!" I shouted after her, but her theatrics continued.

As predicted, by the time I was halfway finished with my lunch, Evan grumped his way through the front door. "Hi, Ma."

"Lunch is on the table." I heard her smooch his cheek.

"Lunch is always on the table. And none of us even live here."

Evan appeared in the dining room a moment later but Mom shrieked, "Shoes on my carpet, Evan!"

"Alright, Ma!" And off they went, flying toward the front door. "Hey brat. Did you save me any?"

"Nope." I smacked at him as he messed up my hair. "*Gerroff*!"

"Rabbity-roo, didn't hop away from that bullet again, did ya?" Now he had me around the neck.

"Ev! I fucking hate you. Get off me." I punched him in the ribs a few times and he laughed, releasing me to drop down in a chair. His mop of dirty-blonde hair flopped in his eyes. "And cut that hair. You look like a 90s grunge punk band."

"A *whole* band, Rabbit? Come on." He stole the last bit of sandwich from my plate and finished it in one bite, grinning like an asshole when I made to hit him again.

"Jerk."

"Knock it off in there!" Mom shouted down the hall. "Thirty-somethings acting like five-year-olds. *Honestly*."

"You raised us heathens, Ma," Evan called back, brushing some crumbs off his soiled work shirt.

"Stop that. If there are crumbs on the carpet, she'll kill us."

"I heard that," Mom said.

"Jesus Christ."

"Evan!"

More shouting happened in my childhood home than anywhere else in the world. I nabbed myself a second sandwich before Evan destroyed the rest of the food. We finally settled down enough not to insult each other too loudly when Mom rejoined us.

"How's Serena?" she asked.

"She's good, Ma. We're still coming for dinner on Sunday so don't freak out." He held his hands up in surrender.

"Oh, Evan, those *hands*. Did you even wash them?"

"Mom! I fix cars all day. What do you expect?"

"Clean hands! How much grease do you eat in a week?" She scowled, then took a moment to adjust her messy braid. She never seemed to age. Well, at least not to me. She still wore the same cotton house dresses, heels, and hairdo that became her style in the seventies or eighties, at least.

"Six point seven pounds, to be exact."

"Evan!"

"Stop shouting my name, woman!" Evan slammed his hand down on the table.

"Don't yell at Mom!" I reached over and punched him in the shoulder. "Or call her *woman*, you chauvinistic fucktard, like it's some kind of insult."

"Alice! Your *mouth*." Mom slammed the table with both palms.

"Holy shit, I'm leaving. Why does everyone yell around here?" I spat.

"Because we're very fond of each other." Evan scooped himself some pasta salad. "Yelling means fondness."

"Yelling means *psycho*," I said, scowling at the two of them.

"Welcome to the asylum, honey." Mom patted me on the head. "Would you like some more tea?"

"Why does Serena like spending time with us? Is she writing a paper on family dynamics?" I ignored our mother because we weren't even having tea, and looked to Evan.

"She thinks we're endearing. And she's done with her dissertation already, so nope." He shook his head.

"Good. Less ammo." I tore into my second sandwich and continued to glare at my brother.

"Is Marcus coming to dinner?" Mom asked while she stabbed a forkful of salad.

"Not this time."

"I don't understand why the two of you don't just get married. You're so *very* close." Mom sighed, again, dramatically.

"Mom...I'm gay."

"Oh honey…"

"Mom! We've had this conversation about forty times."

"Honey, I know you're gay, but you and Marcus are so lovely together."

"I hate to destroy your fantasy world, Ma, but Marc's gay, too."

"He'll grow out of it—"

"Mom!" I tossed my food on my plate and laughed at her. "You did *not* just say that."

"Ignore her, Rabbit. She has no idea about *the gay*. It's a whole mystery to her." Evan squeezed my hand, but instead of being a jerk about it, it was relatively sincere.

"I understand it, Alice." Mom let out a long, breathy sigh. "But I can still hope for grandbabies."

I just stared at her. "You have two grandbabies, Ma."

"Well, more grandbabies. Ryan can only do so much." Then she glared at Evan. "That witch keeps them from me."

"Give me a minute to get married at least." He shook his head. "And Marisol isn't a witch. She's their mother and they share custody. Amicably, mind you. They're good friends."

"Well, she divorced him."

"Because Ryan needed help. And he got it. And they're happy. So leave them be," I chimed in now.

"Don't worry, Allie." Mom patted my arm. "You won't be alone forever."

"Where did that even come from?" I glanced between them as Evan laughed heartily while he chomped on his third sandwich. "We weren't even talking about me, and how do you know I'm not seeing someone?"

"You're not. When you're seeing someone, you're never here."

"Because the last time I brought my girlfriend over, you scared her off."

"Don't blame Mom for that, Rabbit. She was terrible."

"She was not…"

"She was *terrible*." Mom nodded firmly. "Wrong for you. Not your type."

"I agree with that. Butch never worked for you," Evan said.

"She wasn't butch—"

"She was a *manly* woman." Mom's face screwed up in a grimace. "And not nice to you."

"Mom! That's a horrible description…"

"Rabbit, stick with the pretty girly girls that you like," Evan said, smirking after. "Because you know you like that."

I laughed uncomfortably. "Yeah. I do."

"Well good then, dear." Mom leaned over and kissed my cheek. "Your next girlfriend can be girly. I'll be right back."

"How can you call it a phase one second then talk about my girly non-existent girlfriend the next?"

"I told you." Evan gestured to the kitchen. "She doesn't get the gay."

"She doesn't really think it's a phase, Ev. I mean. Twenty years later…"

"It's her fail-safe. Just ignore it."

"I am." I placed my napkin on my plate then rose to stand. "I better go. I'm meeting the guys for drinks at Jimmy's."

"That stupid cop bar." Evan shook his head.

"Well...I am a cop."

"A cop who got shot. Speaking of, let's see it." He waved at my stomach. "C'mon."

"Jerk. This isn't a raspberry from a baseball slide." I lifted my shirt and showed him.

"Ugh! Nasty-ass, but incredible. My sister is a hero."

"Hardly." I clapped him on the shoulder after letting my sweater fall around my jeans again. "I'm fine, Ev."

"I know." He wrapped one arm around my middle while I stood there, in a strange half-hug. *Brothers*. "See you Sunday."

"Yup." I messed up his hair, making the greasy locks stand on end. "Cut your hair."

"Gah!" He shoved me away and I laughed my way to the kitchen.

CHAPTER TWO

"That's sweet," Marc said as he looked at the card on the flower arrangement I'd left on the hall table by the front door. "Ryan's an eloquent writer."

"I know. He expresses himself much better when writing things down. It tends to be sentimental." My heels clicked on the wood floor as I emerged from my bedroom. "How's this outfit?"

"Good. I like the jeans with those boots. The sweater is a little big."

"I know, but I like it."

"It's not like you're going on a date. Jenson doesn't care what you look like." Marc paused, lifting one eyebrow so high that it disappeared under his well-worn ball cap. "Or maybe he does."

"It doesn't matter even if he does." I laughed a little. "He almost died."

"I'm glad he didn't."

"Me too."

After picking up a few shirts off the sofa, I tossed them into my bedroom and shut the door. The rest of the apartment wasn't nearly as disorganized as my room. I owed that to Marc. "The new sofa looks good."

"Oh yeah." He nodded. "You did good picking out that gray to offset the black carpet. Speaking of…"

"Eh?" I lifted a brow at him as I grabbed my purse, tossing it over my shoulder.

"Saturday night…"

"I know. You want the place to yourself."

"It's just easier…"

"Marc, I don't mind. Really. You live here, too. I know it's easier to bring people home than to go out. At least right now. Is it a hookup or a date?" I asked, taking a quick swipe at my hair in the mirror. Evan wasn't the only one who needed a haircut. Except my darker roots made the growing-out highlights look sloppier.

"Date. Hookups I don't care if you're home." He chuckled, clapping me on the back as he opened the front door. "Let's go."

"Do I know him?"

"Nope."

"Will I know him?" I asked as we walked out together.

"Maybe."

"Have you slept with him?"

"Not yet," he answered, locking up behind us.

"You're going to jizz up the apartment this weekend, aren't you?"

"You know it."

"Gross."

"Lesbo."

"Gaybo."

An *Uber* and a half later, we arrived at UW Medical Center where Jenson recovered in the medical unit. More than the flowers we brought, he appreciated the box of candy bars we'd plucked from the hands of some kids who sold them out in front of the hospital. Jenson was in good spirits when I took a seat beside him on the bed after everyone else left the room.

"You saved my life, rookie." I smirked when he grinned at me. "I wanted to thank you for that."

"Your vest saved your life. I just smacked you into pavement." His pale face twisted into a laugh.

"Well, before you smacked me into pavement, twenty bullets nearly slammed into our bodies so I'm grateful for you. Just accept it." I shoved the chocolate box into his lap. "And the damn candy."

Jenson laughed. "C'mon, Lange."

"Seriously. Thank you."

He nodded, offering me a knowing smile as he pulled out a chocolate and bit into it.

After we chatted for some time, a soft knock sounded on the door. Doctor Corwin stood in the entryway, smiling pleasantly as she entered.

"I don't remember prescribing that." The doctor sauntered over, her arms crossed over her middle, then plucked the candy from Jenson's hand.

"Hey." His eyes widened, but he flinched when he made to move forward.

Doctor Corwin cocked a brow at him and took a bite of the chocolate before sitting on the edge of his bed. "Yum."

A laugh erupted from me at the horrified expression on Jenson's face. I covered my mouth in an attempt to control myself. Jenson gawked at the doctor, unable to speak.

"So I take it you're feeling better." Doctor Corwin, with her face unmoving, took another small bite of the confection and I watched as she swept her tongue over her lips afterward. Her eyes, which I now noted to be blue, never left Jenson's face.

"Er...I was a lot happier a minute ago. What kind of doctor are you? Taking away my happiness." Jenson scowled and finally, Corwin chuckled.

"I'm looking out for your best interest, Officer Jenson." Corwin's gaze flickered in my direction and the faintest hint of a smile made her lip twitch. "How's your injury?"

"Fine if I don't move," he answered, patting his left shoulder where the bullet entered from behind. "Not terrible otherwise."

"That's good news." Corwin stood now as did I. "One of the nurses will be in shortly to change your dressing."

"Okay, cool." Jenson nodded. "Can I have my candy back now?"

"Well, I suppose so," she said, tossing the empty wrapper at him. "But you might need to start over."

Jenson laughed hard, his expression lifting as he met the doctor's gaze. "Worst bedside manner ever."

"I try." She smiled at him, but stepped away when the nurse entered with a tray of equipment. I moved toward the foot of the bed.

"I'll let her take care of you, Jenson. We'll see you tomorrow."

"Take care of yourself, Lange."

"You, too. Don't eat too much candy." I waved at him.

Doctor Corwin exited with me and we walked side-by-side down the hall a few paces. Porter stood at the end of the hall talking to Chief Walsh. I paused, deciding to let them carry on without me. To my surprise, Doctor Corwin stopped walking as well.

"How are you feeling, Detective Lange?" she asked, her gaze flickering to my midsection.

"I'm fine. Nasty looking bruise but fine."

"Let me have a look," she said, waving for me to follow her as she backed into an empty exam room.

"It's not necessar—"

"I insist. Come with me."

"Well, okay." And I did because what else was I supposed to do.

"Hop up," she said, patting the vacant bed.

I listened and pushed myself up to sit with my legs hanging off. Corwin waited while I lifted my sweater to show her the ugly bruise. Her brow furrowed as she leaned forward, cool fingers touching my overheated midsection. Only then did the wafting floral fragrance of her perfume overwhelm me, sending a trickle of enjoyment through my center. My cheeks heated, and I gulped when her hair tickled my arm.

"This looks terrible," she said, leaning up now to meet my gaze. "But healing." Her brow flicked upward again. "Do you feel all right?"

"Yes," I squeaked then cleared my throat as I lowered my shirt. "I'm fine."

"Your face is flushed. Have you had a headache?"

I laughed at my discomfort, shaking my head. "No. Really, I'm fine."

"You say that a lot, Detective. That you're *fine*." She crossed her arms over her middle, watching me with a questioning brow.

"I say it when I mean it." I hopped from the table now. "I better get going."

"Take care then." Doctor Corwin gestured to the door and I led the way back to my partner.

Porter and I headed off to work after stopping for our usual cup of joe. Our boots thudded on the obsidian tile, with me a step behind Porter while I sipped my coffee. My mind wandered back to the hospital, to Jenson, and further back to the onslaught of bullets that could've ended my life or *worse*, career. I brushed my fingertips over my side where the bruise hung out under my shirt. Haunting memories of Doctor Corwin's fingers, like the shrill tickle of a ghost, on my skin set alight a nagging feeling that I couldn't quite shake.

"You're late." Jackson's voice ended my reverie. "On your first day back."

I met his gaze, smirking over the lid of my cup. "Sorry."

"She's always late, boss." Butler's sarcastic tones had me flipping him off. He stuck out his foot to trip me and I narrowly avoided his fat, clunky shoe. I punched his shoulder and he smacked my ass. "Still firm."

I spun around, grabbed his thumb and twisted it so hard that his face contorted. "You're a fucking douchebag, Butler."

"Hey now," Marc spoke up, standing up. "Knock it off.

"Let me go, bitch." Butler laughed, his hair flopping in front of his face like some sort of *Fabio* wannabe.

"Don't fucking touch me again." I shoved him away from me, and returned to sipping my coffee.

"Aw, you say that at least twice a week." Butler chuckled, shaking out his hand.

"If you two are finished—" Jackson glanced between us, his brow narrowed. "I'd like to carry on with something called *work*."

"Easy, Lange." Porter clapped me on the back and I scowled.

"Lange, you're at the middle schools this week, right?" Jackson's shadowed gaze fell on me and I nodded.

"Yeah. But I've arranged for small groups rather than a giant auditorium speech. It works better that way, more personal," I said, dropping down in my chair and propping my feet up on the drawer of my desk. My gear belt dug into my tender side a little, but I tried to ignore it.

"Good. At least that'll keep you off the beat while that injury heels." Jackson nodded, folding his arms over his chest. "Porter and Goldman, I have you working with the Homicide Unit today. They've got a case that they want us to consult on."

"Roger that, sir." Marc saluted him and he chuckled.

"Butler, come with me." Jackson moved away from his desk toward the hallway. "I've got a different assignment for you and your ponytail."

"Should I condition?" He stood up, running his hand through the luscious locks that I fantasized about shaving off. "Or will a usual lather-rinse-repeat suffice?"

"Shut up and follow me."

We watched as the two men disappeared. Most of our team got along well, especially in the field, but Butler took any opportunity to use his masculine wiles to show off his misogynistic bullshit. As a detective, he was great. As a human, I could do without his presence.

"Got plans after work tonight?" Porter asked Marc and me. "I'm thinking of heading to Jimmy's for the *Jets* game."

"Jets." I scoffed. "You're from Seattle and you root for an east coast team."

"Mind you, a sucky east coast team." Marc smirked. "I've got a date. Sorry, man."

"Nice." Porter's brow flicked upward. "How long you been seeing each other?"

"About a month." Marc glanced at me. "Pretty casual right now, but we'll see."

"What about you, Lange?" Porter gestured in my direction.

"Getting my hair done at Jordan's." I sighed dramatically and ran my fingers through my hair. "I need a little *conditioning*. Lather-rinse-repeat just simply isn't cutting it." I turned my voice up pretentiously and the guys laughed.

"Good thing he didn't hear that." Porter cracked up, his hearty laugh echoing in the small room while he shuffled around some papers on his desk. "Looks like I'm on my own tonight."

"You can always come with me and get a primp and curl on that head of yours." I grinned at him, egging on the ridiculousness.

"Oh yeah. Curl up that buzz-cut, bro." Marc nodded firmly as he stood, swiping his badge from the desk and tossing it around his neck. "We better go."

"Later." I dropped my feet and grabbed my bag of educational materials from under my desk.

Lectures weren't the worst thing in the world. After all, without empowering people to report bias and hate crimes, I'd have no job at all.

***

"You're late!" Jordan shouted when I entered the Mermaid Salon ten minutes later than I was supposed to arrive.

"There was traffic," I said, smirking as I set the box of

pastries down on the turquoise counter. Painted from floor to ceiling in an underwater theme, Jordan's keenly crafted salon brought a nautical feel to downtown Seattle. Deep blue floors, soft greenish walls with various sexy women with shell bras painted on them, had the place screaming, *We love women.* Which we did. A lot. All of her stylists had the most amazing hair both in cut and color. Most of them still carried their natural hues with richly painted strands tangled in the mix, however, some of them had their entire heads done in majestic blues, frothy purples, or sporty rainbows.

"You walk here!" Jordan tossed her arms in the air, her luscious curls bouncing with them. "And your hair's a mess."

"I know. Shut up and eat a cruller." I pointed at the box on the counter.

"Don't mind if I do." Jordan bounced over and pulled a dessert cake from the box. "Go get that hair washed already, sexy."

"Oh come on now." I rolled my eyes and shoved her as I walked past toward the sinks in the back. "Hey, Sherry," I said when I greeted the teenager with neon purple hair.

"Hi," she chirped while preparing the towel after I sat. "I'll be fast."

"Thanks."

"Jordan," called a sing-song voice from around the corner. I couldn't see who it was from my leaned back position. "Don't you feel it's poor form to call another woman 'sexy' when your girlfriend can hear you?"

"Nah, babe. It's worrisome if I call a woman sexy when my girlfriend *can't* hear me," Jordan answered and the distinct sound of a kiss had me leaning forward to look. A pretty, copper-skinned woman in scrubs smiled at her. Jordan had her hand on her cheek, and the smile that broke her freckled complexion had me cocking a brow. I'd never seen Jordan look at anyone that way.

"*Touché*," the scrub-clad woman said, grinning.

"Ainsley, this is Alice. Alice, Ainsley." Jordan gestured between us. "Alice is one of my best friends."

"Like Eve?" Ainsley cocked a brow at Jordan as she waved at me. I knew exactly what she implied with the question.

"No. We never slept together," I answered as I lay back in the sink again. Sherry laughed as she sprayed down my hair after removing my ponytail.

"Thanks, Alice. Remind me to return the favor in front of your next girlfriend." Jordan smacked my leg and I laughed. The sound against my jeans was exponentially loud.

"Oh goodie." Ainsley's sharp voice had me chuckling.

"Easy. I'm still bruised." I covered my side while in the vulnerable position.

"From what?" Jordan appeared beside me, her brows lifted under her green and black bangs.

"A bullet to the vest. Again."

"Again?" Ainsley, with her onyx hair and kind green eyes stood beside Jordan, their arms linked together.

"Jesus Christ, Alice. Are you serious?" Jordan's face fell. "Why didn't you tell me?"

Sherry finished with my hair, then wrapped me in a towel. "All done."

"Thanks." I sat up, holding the towel in place. "It wasn't a big deal, Jor."

"Getting shot is always a big deal, Allie." Normally playful, Jordan's worry melted over her features, dampening her gentle brown eyes to a fear-laden wide gaze.

"I'm okay. Really," I said, squeezing her arm as I stood.

"Let's have a look," Ainsley piped up suddenly, releasing Jordan to grab hold of the hem of my sweater and attempting to lift it. I kept my hands over my middle, stopping her.

"Hey. How do you even know where—"

"From how you're walking," Ainsley said, her face

melting to a clinical stillness.

"Ainsley…" Jordan put her hand on her girlfriend's shoulder. "Remember the talk we had about boundaries and touching *lesbians* without asking?"

"Oh." Ainsley leaned back suddenly, releasing my shirt. "Alice, I'd like to see your injury." Her lip twitched as if threatening a smile.

"You're very, *very* strange." I laughed at her, dropping my arms now. "Are you a nurse?"

"A medical examiner," she said, perking up a bit.

"Well, I'm not a corpse." I grinned as I glanced to Jordan whose amused expression returned.

"I'm still a doctor. Let's have a look then."

"You doctors are very pushy." I lifted my shirt a little to show her.

Jordan's face paled, Sherry gasped, and two other stylists leaned away from their charges to have a look. "Jesus Christ, Alice!" exclaimed Jordan.

"That's the second time you've said that. Are you converting, Jordie?" I smirked while Ainsley poked around at me.

"It's healing nicely," she said, standing upright again. "The bruises will fade."

"Well, that's good news that I've already received today. No possibility of putrefaction, M.E.?" I let my shirt fall back down.

"Not a chance, Detective." Ainsley smiled gently, then leaned against Jordan again who wrapped her arm around her without missing a beat.

"Alice, I don't like your job." Jordan reached forward and squeezed my shoulder. "Let's do your hair."

"I like *your* job." I nodded to her as she ushered me over to the chair.

"I better get back to the office," Ainsley said, letting go of Jordan. "I'll see you tonight."

"Be safe." Jordan captured her in a firm kiss, smiling after as she watched her walk toward the door.

When Ainsley was out of earshot, Jordan said, "I love her so much."

"I've noticed. Have you told her?" I pulled the towel off my head and Jordan took it.

"Not yet."

"How long have you been going out?"

"Six months, seriously. We dated on and off six months before that." Jordan began combing out my hair. "Your roots are ridiculous. You should've come a month ago."

"And you've taken this long to tell her how you feel?" I smirked at her comment as I watched her in the mirror. "I know."

"We doing blonde again to highlight your dirty-blonde?" she asked. "And yes."

"Yes. Why so long?"

"She's hard to read sometimes. What if she doesn't feel the same?" She sighed a little, and her combing grew more deliberate.

"Have you seen how she looks at you? *Please*."

"I'm her first relationship with a woman. Not her first crush though. She had a crush on Eve."

"Aww. Medical examiner crushing on the homicide detective. How *sweet*." I laughed hard at the thought. "Like an episode of *Law & Order: Lez-Bo-U*."

Jordan chuckled, smacking me in the shoulder. "Eve's in Sex Crimes now."

"I heard."

"I'm surprised the two of you never hooked up."

"She's not my type, and she's supremely awkward."

"What *is* your type, Allie?" Jordan gave my hair a tug. "Invisible?"

"No." I scoffed, smacking her hand when she made to comb my bangs.

"Vibrator? *Vibrator* seems to be your type these days."

"Shut up, Jor."

"Come to Wildrose on Wednesday. Ainsley and I are going for the band," she implored while primping my hair.

"No thanks."

"You used to all the time."

"Yeah, then I got cheated on and gave up on women forever. I'm asexual now," I said, dryly.

"It doesn't work like that. You're a giant fucking lesbian."

"I'm over it."

"Nope."

"Yes."

"Better concede or I'm going to give you a nice little baby dyke cut." She snapped the scissors in front of my nose.

"Don't you dare." I covered my head, laughing hard.

"Mullet?" She grinned, straddling my legs on the chair rail and moved closer, her nose an inch from mine with the scissors between us.

"Jordan!" I squeaked and shoved her with my knees.

She laughed, and smooched me on the cheek before swinging away to move behind me again.

"Layers!"

She sighed heavily. "Fine. Long sexy layers for one of my best friends."

"Damn right," I said, releasing my hair and relaxing in the seat again while Jordan worked her magic.

We sat quietly for a few minutes while she combed and clipped my hair in places. I watched her in the mirror, contemplating the harsh reality she tossed at me. Since breaking up with Eliza over a year ago, I hadn't trusted a single person with me or my heart. Even though we only went out for a few months, finding out that she'd been sleeping with both men *and* women behind my back destroyed me a little. To think that I allowed her in my bed after she might've slept with someone else disgusted me, and hurt in ways I couldn't express. *Didn't* express, to anyone except Jordan and Marc. Worse, it wasn't the first time someone cheated on me. After college, my first long-term girlfriend did the same after three years of dating.

Eventually, one begins to believe that she isn't worthy of faithfulness. It must've been my fault that I wasn't good enough for them to stay with only me.

"You're thinking an awful lot. Why?" Jordan asked while she worked on my hair from the right side.

"Do you think there's something wrong with me?"

"Totally," she said, her voice perky. I laughed and refrained from tripping her because that might mean baldness for me. "But what do you mean?"

"No one seems to be able to stay with just me."

"Two women, Allie. That's not everyone."

"Two's enough. Maybe I'm terrible at sex."

Jordan laughed hard. "Allie, I've seen you have sex. You're more than wonderful."

"You have not."

"You forget we were roommates for a year."

"Oh." I smirked half-heartedly. "That's right. Creeper."

"And if you and I could've stopped laughing for longer than ten seconds, I would've found out what you were like in the sheets." She snickered hard. "But we're not the F.W.B. type."

"Not at all." I scrunched up my nose and laughed at her.

"There are just some people who are unable to be faithful, Al. Your only fault, in any of it, is giving people the benefit of the doubt. Not everyone you meet is a good person."

"You'd think I'd know that by now, working in the job that I do."

"Believing in goodness isn't a bad thing," she said, moving around to begin clipping the opposite side of my hair. "Blindly believing in it, though…"

"I know." My mind flashed to memories of an uncomfortable place, with two terrible people that I didn't feel like getting into.

"Don't break my chair." Jordan leaned back, her eyes a bit wide as she glanced at my hand that I hadn't noticed squeezed the arm of the chair so hard it creaked. "Are you thinking about—"

"Don't say it, okay?" I let go of the chair and took a deep breath. "I don't want to go there."

"I know." She nudged my chin with the knuckle of her index finger. "I got you."

I nodded as a swell of emotion caught in my throat, but I swallowed it down then met her gaze. "Just...let's talk about something else."

"How's Marc doing?" She rolled with my request and returned to working on my hair.

"He's good. Dating someone seriously now. Hence my banishment from the apartment tonight."

"Ainsley's working late. Why don't you hang here with me at the shop until close, then we can head upstairs and watch a movie? I'll even spring for pizza." She wagged her brows at me. "With pineapple that you like. Weirdo."

I laughed, nodding faintly my agreement. "I'm in."

CHAPTER THREE

"Detective Lange?" One of the seventh grade girls raised her hand while I lectured the group of twenty kids about speaking up and bullying. "What if someone doesn't like, you know, hit you or hurt you, but says stuff like, in your face?"

"Can you give me an example?"

"Like…" She paused to think, her finger twirling one of her braids around her finger. "Like if someone says you're an ugly bitch and women should be on earth to serve men? Is that a hate crime?"

"While saying something like that isn't a hate crime, it can be considered harassment if it continues on," I told her, followed by a long lecture on the definition of harassment, and how orders of protection worked.

At the end of the lecture, I hung back in the room like I did following every talk, in case anyone wanted to speak privately. While sitting at the round table, a legal pad and pencil in front of me, I thought about what Jordan and I talked about at the salon the other night. Had I really been keeping myself out of the dating game on purpose? I knew the answer was *yes*, but it was a harsh reality to face for many reasons.

The door creaked open and a young girl entered. Her tentative steps spoke of both fear and foreboding. When her steely gaze met mine, I made sure to keep myself calm.

"Come on in, Taryn."

"Okay, thanks," the six-grader said, then joined me at the table. She sat quietly for a minute, wringing her hands together. Her body language screamed *pay attention*, and I did, while keeping my movements unassuming. I allowed her the silence. "Um…"

"Take your time," I said, softly.

"What if you think someone else is having a hate crime against them?"

"Can you tell me a little bit more about that?"

"Well…" She glanced toward the door then back to me. "My friend. She lives next door and I think she's having a hate crime against her."

"How come?" I asked, gently, tilting my head.

"Her stepmother hates her because she's not her daughter. She treats her really mean. Her dad doesn't know." She glanced to the door again then back to me. "You can't tell her I told you."

"Taryn." I leaned forward, resting my elbows on the table. "Remember when we talked about good citizenship and if you know about someone being hurt, it's part of our responsibility to speak up for them because maybe they can't speak for themselves?"

She nodded, reaching back to toy with her ponytail. "Yeah, that's why I came here. She'll be mad at me if she knew I said, but what if she kills her?"

"What exactly is happening to your friend?"

"She said that her stepmother puts glass in her food so she's afraid to eat it. I bring her lunch at school so she doesn't have to eat at home." She took a deep breath. "And sometimes, from my window at night, I hear her stepmother yelling at her when her father isn't home."

"Have you told your parents?"

She shook her head. "No, but Mom lets me invite her

for dinner a lot."

"Do you think she'd like to talk to me?"

"I don't know…"

"Want to try and ask her?"

Taryn grew quiet for a moment, then nodded. "I can try."

"Okay. Let's do that together. What do you think?"

"Okay."

Either way, with a report like that, Child Protective Services would have to investigate. However, I wanted to at least have the chance to help empower the girl to speak up for herself. That's what I'm there for, isn't it? To help people find their voices.

Taryn took her leave and I waited there, like she asked.

Twenty minutes passed and as my hope began to fall while I looked up the number for CPS on my phone, the door knob turned. This time, Taryn returned with more confidence and, behind her, a scrawny-looking *boy* with bright green eyes nestled in his ebony complexion, stared at me. His lips pursed together as he entered the room, his fists clenched tightly at his sides. Taryn was clever enough to elude me by reporting her friend was a girl. Clever kid. But the neighbor comment was the true giveaway.

"You can talk to her," Taryn whispered. "You have to, Daniel."

"No, I don't," he spat, his voice soft.

"She can't treat you like that anymore." Taryn put her hand on his shoulder and the two of them held each other's gaze for quite some time.

Eventually, the boy looked at me again and conceded.

***

"You think he ate glass?" Doctor Corwin asked me as we walked down the hall of the hospital. She'd just sent Daniel off for some tests.

"It's possible. CPS is here now and I wanted him medically cleared before they take the next step."

"They'll have a case. He's worse for wear, for such a

young kid."

"His father had no idea. He's heartbroken." I sighed as we stopped by the nurses' station. This late at night, only a few people buzzed around during their shift. Doctor Corwin handed Daniel's chart to a woman who took it and turned toward one of the computers.

"He's not the only one," Corwin said. When I looked back to her, the intensity of her gaze startled me.

"What?"

"You look a little heartbroken to me, too, Detective Lange."

"Alice."

She smiled gently. "Alice. Is your partner here?"

"He's with the family. I usually deal with the victims."

"The victim is getting the help he needs. As is the family." She gripped my forearm and I glanced down at her hand. Warm and firm, even against my sweater-covered arm, the gesture stirred up emotions in me that I'd been holding on to all week. "Alice?"

"I have to go," I said, turning away from her. "Thanks for your help, Doc."

"You can call me Stella."

"Okay." I broke away from her and moved past Porter who'd been standing in the doorway. His startled expression was the last thing I saw before heading down the street.

At home, Marc sat on the sofa, beer in hand while watching a Seahawks versus Jets game on our big screen. He wore nothing but a set of basketball shorts and his burly, muscled chest hung out for the world to see. I dropped down beside him and he offered me a sip of his beer which I gratefully accepted.

"Let's order takeout," I said.

"I'm in the mood for barbeque." He nodded toward the television. "This is gonna be a long one."

"I'll order it."

"You *manly* hunter-gatherer, you." He flexed his chest

muscles and I chuckled, then stood to retrieve the phone.

Half an hour later, various meats filled our coffee table. Wings, ribs, and pulled pork packed in tightly between dishes of fries and mashed potatoes.

"We're fatties," I said, licking the barbeque sauce from my fingers.

"This is not news."

"So how's the new beau? Did you wash the sheets?" I laughed at him when he kicked me under the table.

"He's good. I think you should meet him," he said, tearing into a meaty rib.

"Yeah?" My brows flicked upward. "He's meet the BFF material?"

"He is." He nodded, his pale cheeks reddening a bit.

"What's his name?"

"Gavin." He didn't look at me when he said it, which only told me of his shyness.

"Nice." I smiled, my insides fluttering with happiness for my friend. "Can't wait to meet him."

"Think he could come to Thanksgiving?" he asked gently. For the past five years, Marc came to all the holidays at my parents' house. We'd always laughed about Mom's desire to shove the two of us together. Dad was the easier sell. He understood both of us, and his hopes weren't marred by our sexuality.

"I think he should if you think he can deal with my mom believing we're all still going through a twenty-year phase."

"She doesn't really mean that." He laughed hard at the notion. "She's nuts."

"Can he handle nuts?"

"He can handle me." Marc shrugged, finally meeting my gaze.

"Invite him." I smiled, leaning over and squeezing his shoulder.

"I will." He perked up and grinned. "Say, where's Butler been?"

"No idea, but I think he's on an undercover op. Walsh alluded to something in our department meeting this week."

"Ah. Figures. Maybe he's undercover on a porn shoot."

I snorted, shaking my head. "Wouldn't he love that."

"Your hair looks amazing, by the way. I never told you."

"Thanks." I laughed, shaking it out a bit obnoxiously. "I got to meet Jordan's girlfriend. She's an M.E. for the county. Ainsley Monson. Know her?"

"Oh yeah." His eyes widened a bit. "I met her when I was in homicide briefly."

"She's so weird." I chuckled at the thought of the quirky doctor. "But suits Jordan perfectly."

"I bet. Jordan's pretty eccentric."

"She is. You gonna come to her dinner party next week?"

"With ten lesbians?" He grinned, then took a swig of beer. "No way."

"Bring Gavin." I cracked up at him. "Come on."

"Hmm. I'll think about it."

"Marc...We really should talk about—"

"No, Allie. Not yet."

"But what if things get serious with Gavin? Like really serious…"

"We'll cross that bridge when we get to it."

"Marc, we can literally *see* the bridge." I gestured wildly at the nothing in front of us. "It's right there."

"Still. You have no idea." He shook his head. "It's different for guys. People look at you and see a sexy, beautiful woman and imagine you with other sexy, beautiful women. When they learn a guy like me is gay…it's just different."

"Why? Because you're not *obviously* gay? Because you live life on the downlow like it's some sort of underground embarrassment?"

"Yeah. And it is. It *is*, Allie." He dropped his rib and

wiped his hands on a napkin.

"It isn't, Marc. It's who you are. You're not an embarrassment any more than I am. Gavin is lucky to have met you, and you him. There's a reason why we celebrate *pride*. It's time to start being proud of who you are," I told him, sincerely, reaching over to squeeze his shoulder. "I'm proud of who you are."

He said nothing, but when he reached over and squeezed my hand, I knew I'd hit a nerve.

We finished our dinner in relative quiet, then sat together on the sofa while watching the endless football game. By the time the fourth quarter began, seemingly hours later, Marc put his arm around my shoulders and I found myself leaning in to the security of him.

That week had been one of the shittiest in a while, tangled with getting shot, a colleague injured, exposing child abuse, and emotional issues rising up. At the very least, I had a best friend to come home to and, no matter what, I'd always have that.

The week that followed was much less exciting. I'd finished the education programs in the middle schools, and moved on to high schools, which was inordinately challenging. Turns out, teenagers are pretty hateful people. Most of them. Not all.

Darkness fell early in the weeks before the holidays, making my usual walk to the train in downtown Seattle more annoying. Brisk air squeezed my lungs, and I tugged my jacket tighter around myself. My phone rang as soon as I got to the platform. I pulled it from my pocket to see Jordan's name on the screen.

"Tell me you're coming tonight," she said as soon as I answered.

"Jordan, c'mon—"

"No whining. Meet you at Wildrose in an hour."

"Jord—" And she was gone. I sighed and pocketed my phone.

Jordan and I used to hang out at Wildrose, the local

lesbian-friendly bar, all the time but over the past year, I'd faded from that scene in favor of my own. Holed up in my apartment doing nothing, usually with Marc...until recently anyway.

"Right on time," Jordan said as I found her seated in a corner booth at the dimly-lit bar. Dark pink couches, pretty drinks, and an all-girl band filled the room with familiar experiences. I smirked when Jordan gestured for me to sit beside her. Ainsley scooted over when Jordan did.

"She's quite late," Ainsley said, perkily. "Missed the whole first set."

"Allie's always late. Which is why I book her appointments for half-an-hour later than I tell her," Jordan said, grinning at me when she offered me a French fry.

"Very funny."

"What are you drinking tonight, Al?" Jordan asked, picking up her empty glass. "Fancy pants here wants more Pinot Noir." She nodded toward Ainsley who smiled cheekily.

I laughed a little. "What are you having?"

"Did you really ask me that?" Jordan scoffed. "Beer, Allie. *Beer.*"

"Then bring me beer." I waved at her like she was a humble servant, then crossed my legs as I leaned closer to Ainsley. "So...while she's gone, tell me all her secrets."

"Don't you dare." Jordan pointed at her girlfriend. "That's a hypothetical taunt."

Ainsley laughed, her mischievous gaze falling on me. "I'll start with the secret box under her bed."

"I hate you both," Jordan called out behind her on the way over to the bar.

"She doesn't hate us," I said.

"I know." Ainsley smiled, her eyes lingering on Jordan's ass in her leggings.

"I see what you're looking at."

"Hush up now." She drew her gaze back to me. "How

come you never hang out with us?"

"I haven't been going out much lately. Tell me, how do you really feel about Jordan?"

"She's the best thing that ever happened to me," Ainsley said with earnest.

I glanced to the bar to see Jordan chatting away with the bartender who fixed our drinks, then back to Ainsley. "Do you love her?"

"Of course," she answered without pause.

"Tell her." I spoke quickly when Jordan carried two bottles of beer and a glass of wine our way.

"It's not too soon?" Ainsley hissed under her breath.

"No." I smiled when Jordan handed me a beer. "Thank you."

"Welcome. And for fancy pants." She sat and offered Ainsley the wine at the same time.

"Thanks."

"Now drink it and relax, you ladyless recluse." Jordan sipped her beer, then saluted me while Ainsley laughed her head off.

"I'm not a recluse and you're a douchebag." I flipped her off and they both laughed.

We watched the band together and, despite my efforts to ignore it, Ainsley's affection toward Jordan unnerved me a little. Not because of my feelings for either of them, but rather, the keen awareness that no one had ever treated me that way before. Part of the reason I spent so much time alone or with Marc was to avoid situations like this. There I was, sitting in Wildrose, envying one of my best friends and feeling lonelier by the minute. Sometimes, staying away from all of it was so much easier.

When the last set was over, I placed my empty bottle down and turned to the women beside me. Ainsley, with her chin on Jordan's shoulder while Jordan had her hand resting between her knees, furrowed a brow at me.

"I'm gonna get going," I said, standing and pulling on my jacket. "I'll see you next week for dinner."

"Are you sure, Al?" Jordan asked, turning to face me.

"Yeah. I'm kind of tired. Thanks for the drink." I offered her the best smile I could. "See you."

"Take care of yourself, Alice." Ainsley smiled, a kind and knowing one, and I waved to them before taking my leave.

The worst part about living in Seattle wasn't necessarily the overcast or rainy days, but the frozen mist that happened during the in-between time during fall and winter. Icy spittle covered my cheeks as I shoved my hands deeper into my jacket pockets. My apartment, although not far from work, was a fair distance from Wildrose. I sighed as I gripped my phone, pulled it from my pocket, and flipped through to the Uber app. *Twenty minutes, great.*

By the time the black Corolla pulled up, my fingers were ready to snap off.

"Hey, thanks," I said, as I slid into the backseat. To my surprise, another passenger took up the spot next to me. She gazed out the opposite window with her purse in her lap. "Sorry, didn't know this was a group ride."

"No worries," said the driver. "You're both headed in the same direction."

"All right," I said, rubbing my hands together in the warmth of the car.

Familiar fragrance met my nose at the same time that the woman pulled her gaze from outside to me. She started, her shadowed expression widening. "Alice," she said, her voice a pitch higher. Doctor Corwin's posture relaxed and I couldn't help but laugh a little.

"Hey. Sorry. Didn't mean to spook you," I said.

"You didn't—I mean." She chuckled. "Hello."

The driver pulled away from the curb, and headed north toward home. I tugged my coat tighter around me and leaned into the comfort of the warm vehicle.

"I didn't expect to share an Uber tonight," I said, nodding toward the driver who snickered quietly. "He better not charge us the whole fee." I raised my voice at the end. "Trying to rip off a *cop* is poor form."

Doctor Corwin grinned, wagging her brows at me.

"You're not a cop. Don't even play," said the driver, glancing to us in the mirror.

I yanked my badge from my pocket and shoved it in his face at the next traffic stop. "Bam!"

"Shit, *psycho*. Sit down." He laughed hard, swatting my hand.

Doctor Corwin's laughter rang out fully and brought a sharp twinge of enjoyment to my center. I dropped back in my seat and grinned while pocketing my badge.

"I'd say you're going to get us pulled over but—" Corwin shrugged. "I don't think that will matter."

"Not one bit." I smiled at her and, in the dim of the streetlights, her bright expression warmed my insides in ways the heated car couldn't. I noticed then that she wasn't wearing scrubs but a pair of black jeans and heeled boots. Her black pea coat covered the rest of her outfit. "No work tonight?"

She shook her head. "A coworker had a bachelorette party tonight."

"Bachelorette party? Kind of early for the end of a drunken women fest," I commented, smirking.

"I left early." She shrugged, pulling her bag closer to her. "Not my thing really."

"I get that." She didn't need to know that I'd left somewhere early, too.

"First stop up in three, ladies," the driver called out.

"Thanks," said Corwin, tossing her bag over her shoulder. "Nice sharing a car with you, Alice."

"You, too. I'm sure we'll run into each other again."

"Perhaps." She nodded, her gentle smile broadening as the car slowed to a roll. "Hopefully, not as a patient the next time."

"Hopefully not." I laughed, waving to her as she exited the car in front of a tall apartment building with a doorman waiting out front. I glanced up at the huge *Ivory*

Tower and smirked, wondering what the rent would be in a place like that.

"Keep dreaming, copper. Neither one of us is gonna live there," said the driver as he pulled away again.

"Tell me about it. Onward to the land of the middle class, fair coachman."

"Aye Aye, matey."

"Not even close." I shook my head, laughing at him.

"Damn skippy."

***

"You don't look like you had a good time last night," Marc commented as we sat in Jimmy's bar with the team. "Or today."

"Last night was a bust, but today I met with some refugees at the resettlement place. It was really hard and I'm tired." I downed the rest of my beer and knocked on the bar counter for another. Jimmy poured another icy pint and slid it down the counter.

"Aw, c'mon, Lange." Porter clapped me on the back. "You're good at talking to victims. We—" He gestured between Marc and himself. "Suck."

"No, you don't. Butler sucks," I said, cocking a brow at Porter.

"Well… yeah. He does." Porter shrugged. "But he's a great investigator."

"If you mean intimidator, then yeah. We work in Bias Crimes, not at Gitmo," I said.

"Jackson and Walsh seem to think he's effective." Porter argued his point between swigs of Guinness.

"Maybe. But what do you think?" Marc asked, glancing between the two of us.

Porter paused, running his hand over his stubbly chin. "I think that, although effective, his technique isn't the first line of attack."

"At least we can agree on that." Marc nodded, lifting his beer bottle unceremoniously before taking a drink.

"Since the twenty-sixteen election, almost ten years ago,

hate crimes in this country have risen exponentially. Violence, of any sort, even if it's to get information, isn't something I'm ever going to agree with. There's a reason why war crimes are prosecuted, and torture is in that line. Butler smashed a suspect's face into a table, shattering his eye socket. Yes, he confessed to purposefully attacking People of Color afterward, but smashing his face?" I shook my head. "How does that make us any better?"

"I don't know, Al." Marc squeezed my forearm. "You're really intense tonight."

"Sorry. I'm tired. And I drank too much," I said, shoving my glass back down the counter. Jimmy caught it, cocking a bushy brow at me.

"You're still paying for that, kid," he teased.

"Yeah, yeah." I flipped him off and he laughed. "I'm going home," I said, drawing my attention back to Marc.

"We might as well call it a night, Al." Marc stood from the barstool then nodded to Porter and Jimmy. "Later."

"See you tomorrow," Porter said. "Take it easy, Lange."

Marc and I didn't talk much on the way home but by the time we got to the apartment, he found his courage. "Alice, what's gotten you so edgy lately?"

"I'm not sure. Maybe getting shot a second time did it. Or knowing my two best friends are in good relationships and I'm a chronic third wheel. Or…" I tossed my hands in the air as I kicked off my shoes. "I don't even know." Anger bubbled inside me, untethered and useless in its own right.

"Allie, come on…"

"No, Marc. I'm just...I'm just done."

"Done with what, Allie?" He followed me as I stormed into my room and flopped down on the messy bed. "You're drunk."

"So what."

"You're a grumpy drunk." He pulled the blanket over me and then sat down. I looked up at him, frowning away. "And your room is a disaster." Marc laughed then bashed me with a pillow.

"This is not news at all."

"Go to sleep."

"You go to sleep."

"Fine." He flopped down on the bed beside me and snuggled into the purple sheets, bouncing around in exaggerated fashion. "Sleepover! *Squee*!"

I laughed and punched his shoulder. "Don't even. That's terrible."

"We're girlfriends now. Paint my nails?" He held his hand in the air and flexed his fingers. My laughter expanded to hysterics as he grinned, pulling me into a hug.

I snuggled into him, sighing heavily. "I'm not painting your nails."

"Then shut up and sleep."

"You shut up and sleep."

"Fine!"

"*Fine*."

The blaring ring of my cell phone screamed in the middle of the night, jarring me from sleep. Marc's phone demanded his attention and we both sat up at the same time. He reached toward the nightstand and I searched the sheets for my phone. We both answered at the same time.

"Lange, we need you at the hospital to interview a vic," Walsh's raspy voice burst through the line.

"What? Now?"

"I'm afraid so," said Walsh.

"No, we'll get there in an hour. Thanks. Bye." Marc rolled out of bed and picked up his shoes from the floor.

"Okay. I'll meet you there." I hung up and grabbed my towels off the bench at the end of the bed. "Some shit went down."

"Sure did. Can't wait to find out what." Marc's sarcasm dripped heavily from him as he exited my room.

Marc dropped me off at UW Medical, again—my new home away from home it seemed— while he headed to the department. My footsteps echoed through the empty halls at nearly four in the morning. I ran my fingers through my damp hair as my muddled, slightly hungover brain tried to catch up with me. Immediate regret weighed in on me as I considered how I acted last night; like a pathetic, angry mess.

Walsh waved me over as he stood beside Jackson in the emergency room. Two female nurses and a male doctor joined them.

"What's going on?" I asked, glancing over the group.

"We've got Sex Crimes on the way. Figured you and Grant could interview her together," Walsh said, gesturing to the closed door.

"Is she stable?" I asked the doctor now.

"She is, but Doctor Corwin is with her now," he said, nodding toward the door. "And the rape-trauma nurse."

"Okay," I said, shoving my hands deeper into my pockets. "Has she named a suspect?"

"Not yet. We haven't been in there yet," said Jackson, his steely gaze on mine.

"Well, first, we should all probably move away from the door. I'm sure she can see our shadows or at least hear murmurs." I nodded toward the waiting area.

We stood around for a good ten minutes before Eve and Stiles showed up. Eve, in her too-tight black jeans, and long, thigh-length sweater appeared way too put together at nearly five in the morning. She approached, smiling faintly as she ran her fingers through her auburn bob.

"Hey, Eve."

"Hey. Sorry to see you under such shitty circumstances," she said, nodding toward the closed door. "Just the two of us?"

"It's best to send in female investigators at this time. The doctors are recommending it," said Walsh, clapping Stiles on the back. "You good, Stiles?"

"Yeah. You woke up the kids, by the way. Katie might kill you," he said, his deep, husky voice a reflection of his burly physique.

"Let's take a walk," Eve said, gesturing down the hall. "Until they're ready."

"Fine," I agreed and we walked quietly beside each other for a few paces.

I hadn't thought of Eve in any particular way until Jordan said something about hooking up with her. There was no doubt that Eve was a strong, sexy woman but we just didn't see each other that way.

"How's Ciara?" I asked after a while.

"She's great." Eve's expression lit up with a smile that reached her eyes. "We're moving in together next month."

"That's awesome, Eve. I'm happy for you." I offered her a genuine smile and she chuckled, shrugging a bit as we paused in the empty corridor.

"Thanks." She leaned against the wall, folding her arms across her middle as the awkwardness that was Eve returned. She never could take a compliment. "So, how do you want to go at this interview?"

"Do you normally lead? I'm not even sure why they called me."

"She was targeted, allegedly, racially motivated crime," she explained. "And normally, Stiles leads, but I'm okay leading an interview. What about you?"

"I usually lead, but not often immediately following a rape," I admitted.

"All right. I'll lead with questions and you be you, Alice." Eve smiled gently, reaching out to squeeze my arm.

"What does that even mean?"

"You're gentle, and you care."

"And you don't?" I cocked a brow at her.

Eve gave pause, her gaze flickering pensively to the floor then back to me. "Not with the same intensity."

"You hardly know me." I laughed at her strangeness which reminded me of the doctor that helped the dead.

"I know you enough."

"I met your girl-crush a few weeks ago for the first time."

"My who?" Eve started, shifting her weight from left to right in line with the nervousness I'd evoked.

"Ainsley." I laughed harder. "She's a strange little buttercup."

Eve waved me off. "She is. But she suits Jordan."

"They're definitely a pair; I'll drink to that."

Doctor Corwin emerged from the patient's room. Her normally pale complexion appeared slightly flushed as she approached Eve and I. "Two nights in a row, Detective Lange."

"We've moved to a new level of our relationship, Doc." I smirked, gesturing to Eve. "This is Detective Grant. She's from the sex crimes unit."

"Well met, Detective Grant."

"You as well. How is she?"

"Stable, traumatized," said the doctor.

"Do you think she can tolerate questioning?" Eve asked.

"Perhaps at the moment. She's comfortable and resting, but not dysregulated. She is in some opiate withdrawal so the medication we've given her has helped keep her calm," explained Doctor Corwin.

"We'll be cautious," said Eve as she led us toward the room.

"I'll wait outside." The doctor motioned toward the door.

Again, Eve led and I followed as we fell into our pre-planned roles. Dimmed lights met our presence and the nurse sat quietly beside the woman in the bed who rested with her eyes closed. Her black hair and olive skin stood out against the white sheets that surrounded her. Under her left eye, her cheek swelled with a bruise that spoke of a firm object striking her face. The nurse, with reddish hair and a round face, ushered us in.

"I'll take my leave then," she said softly, reaching out to squeeze Eve's elbow. I cocked a brow at her and she offered me a half-smile before turning to the woman who opened her eyes to us.

"How are you holding up, Ms. Morales?" Eve asked, moving to the side of her bed while I remained at the end.

"Shitty," she said immediately.

"Understandable. I'm Detective Grant and this is Detective Lange. We're here to ask you a few questions, if you're feeling up to it." Eve leaned her hip on the edge of the bed as the woman's gaze flicked between us.

"Might as well get it over with." With the longer sentence, her voice cracked with raspiness.

"Okay." Eve's gentle voice coupled with her relaxed posture soothed me more than anything else. "First, do you have any questions for us?"

"Yeah. Did you catch them?" Dark eyes glanced between us. "I told them who it was."

"I'm not sure." Eve glanced to me.

"Me either, but we can find out for you."

Ms. Morales nodded, dropping her head back on the pillow. "Okay."

"Let's start at the beginning." Eve drew her attention back to focus. "What happened to you?"

Ms. Morales took a deep breath, her fingers digging into the sheet over her stomach. "We were at a party when—"

The door opened suddenly, swiftly even, and Doctor Corwin appeared. "Detective Lange, we need you out here, please."

"What? Why?" I moved away from the bed, motioning toward Ms. Morales.

"Right away." Doctor Corwin glanced to Eve then back to me.

"I'm sorry," I said to the woman who stared, wide-eyed at me. "I'm sorry."

She nodded and I hurried toward the door with the doctor's urging, leaving Eve alone until the nurse swept in after me. The door swung shut and Doctor Corwin ushered me the few steps to where Walsh and Jackson stood, both of them with furrowed brows. Stiles, on the other hand, looked about ready to kill with his balled fists and narrowed gaze.

"What's going on?" I pressed.

"Lange, you're off this case immediately. The whole unit is off." Walsh nearly growled when he spoke it. "Get a hold of this shit, Jackson. I need to get back for I.A." Walsh stormed off, his phone to his ear in a second.

"I.A.?" My voice raised an octave. "What the hell for?" I rounded on Jackson now. Sweat beaded along his ebony brow, dampening the roots of his dreads. He glanced at Stiles who offered him no out, but his anger was unmistakable. Corwin remained standing beside us, her gaze fixed on the two men in front of us.

"That girl in there just named Butler's undercover alias as her rapist." Jackson pointed at the room door. "And his partner."

"What?" Horror gripped my torso, tangling my lungs in barbed wire. "Are you kidding me?"

"No," Stiles answered for him. "He isn't."

I clutched my chest, gripping my jacket as I considered the news. "Is it true?"

"We're leaving that up to I.A." Jackson's phone rang and he turned away from us to answer it. I looked to Stiles who made to grab my shoulder when I took a step forward, but I shoved him off.

"Answer me. Is it true?"

"Jackson said—"

"I don't fucking care. *Did* he *do* it?" Rage tangled with disgust and forced spittle from my teeth with the intensity of my question.

War waged in Stiles' eyes, darkening his resolve and his pupils. "Yes."

Every ass slap, every comment, every violent interview, bleeding suspect, and sexually-charged comment he sent my way flooded my mind as I stared into the eyes of the detective in front of me.

"Alice." A soft voice drew my attention away from him. "Come with me." Doctor Corwin grabbed me by the elbow and led me away from Stiles and the booming voice of Jackson in the hallway. I followed her down the hall, around a bend, and into a different part of the hospital that appeared much less busy. Corwin used her key card to swipe a digital lock, then we entered a pristine office.

Dark wood, black leather upholstery, and perfectly neat shelves filled with books adorned most of the room. Corwin guided me to the sofa and I sat. She offered me a tissue then took a seat across from me. I snatched it from her, holding it in my fist as I stared at the hem of her scrub top.

Neither of us spoke for some time and she just sat quietly with me. She didn't question me or offer somber platitudes. My mind stilled, in time, and I leaned my elbow on the back of the sofa, my head in my hand.

"That kid...she's barely eighteen. How could he do that?" My words came out softer than I'd intended.

"I don't know," Doctor Corwin said, her palms pressed together as she held her hands between her knees. "Butler is someone on your team?"

"Yeah." I lifted my gaze to meet hers. "There's four of us on Bias Crimes. He's one." I sighed, running my fingers through my now dry hair. "I fucking trusted that bastard."

"I'm sorry, Alice."

My eyelashes fluttered as a single tear slid down my cheek. I swallowed the rest of my emotions and took a swipe at it. "I should go."

"Where are you going to?"

"Back to the unit. Home. I don't know."

"I think you should figure that out first. Before you leave, I mean."

"Yeah." I closed my eyes and just listened to my own breathing, eventually focusing on hers, too. She let me just sit there. *How could he do this? How could… He's supposed to protect… I don't understand.*

"Were you close with him?" Corwin asked delicately.

"We're all close in our own way." I took a deep breath, fighting the anger that forced its way to my chest again, rolling over my shoulders like hot ash tumbling from an erupted volcano. "How could he do this?"

"I don't know. I've asked myself that question often."

"Me too." I met her gaze again, only then noting the sharp blue of her eyes. Astonishingly blue, like the way the sky looks on the first cool autumn day. Crisp, sharp, clear, but intrinsically warm. Her brows, soft and concerned, settled me in knowing that someone else gave a shit. "I really should go."

"All right." Corwin nodded and we stood together. I moved to the door, gripping the handle until she called out, "Alice?" I turned around and Corwin approached, holding out her business card. "If you need to talk, my cell number is on it."

I took it, glancing at her name, embossed in silver, *Stella Corwin, MD*, and pocketed it before looking back to her. "Thanks."

"Take care of yourself."

"You, too."

CHAPTER FOUR

Internal Affairs spent the next five days combing through every inch of our office, every nook of our desks. Butler hadn't just forced himself under the microscope but the rest of us as well. His desk, turned upside down and inside out, along with every case file he'd ever worked on, thrust into the open and scrutinized for every mis-crossed *t* or undotted *i*.

Walsh was worse for wear and Jackson presented as the angriest human in the universe. Porter, shell-shocked to say the least, hadn't said more than two words all week. Marc wasn't any better. He sat quietly at his desk, writing up our reports and avoiding the gazes of everyone.

It took Walsh two days afterward to gather us in the conference room, and tell us the whole story.

"They were undercover with the D.E.A. on a combined task force with Bias Crimes. Dealers targeting the Latino community with tainted dope. Fourteen overdoses in a week." He sighed, messing up his oily hair. "The girl, she was part of the shakedown on a drug den. The way she tells it, as the others moved in, Butler and the other undercover, promised safety after flashing their badges. She was under the influence of narcotics. They took her into their surveillance van and assaulted her."

"Have they, at least, denied it?" Porter asked, his face ashen with disgust.

"Neither of them have spoken a word. They have lawyers. I.A. is on it," Walsh explained. "Nothing we can do, boys, until they finish."

I leaned forward, pounding my elbow on the table. "Firstly, I'm not a boy. Second, this is fucking insane, Walsh. How could you two *allow* him undercover when he was a runaway fuse in a mine full of dynamite? You knew he could go off at any moment. Any *fucking* moment."

"Calm your crazy, Lange." Walsh held up both hands. "He was requested. We didn't volunteer him." He gestured between himself and Jackson.

"Bullshit. You had to approve the request."

"I second that." Marc spoke up now, his anger bringing tight lines across his forehead as he looked at me.

"Regardless, the whole unit is under scrutiny," Porter said, motioning around the room. "We're all suffering for your lack of judgment, sir."

"Butler has never demonstrated inability to do his job, Porter," defended Jackson.

"Bullshit, again! Roughing up suspects? He's been written up half a dozen times and psych eval'ed twice." I pointed a finger at both of them. "Don't even deny it. We're not stupid."

"Go home, Lange." Walsh looked between us. "Go home all of you. Cool off. Clear your heads. We're frozen until I.A. releases us anyway. Don't talk about the case."

"You'll be lucky if we come back." I snatched my jacket off the back of the chair and stormed out of the room.

For the next four hours, I walked the streets of downtown Seattle. My gear belt dug into my hip annoyingly after a while, but I ignored it. I contemplated calling Jordan, but what would she care about this? I couldn't exactly tell her. Or Eve. What was the point?

I stopped beside a set of flat screens playing in a

department store window. Two of them on separate news stations with marquees that read, *Two Undercover Seattle P.D. Officers Accused of Sexual Assault.* They didn't name anyone, but I'll be damned if they didn't sensationalize every bit of it.

With my hands shoved deep into the pockets of my jacket, I jerked away from the screens and stalked off down the street. My fingers collided with the card I'd tucked in my pocket after leaving Doctor Corwin's office last week. I pulled it out, pursing my lips as I considered calling her. Why would I? What would she care?

But before I could think too much about it, I'd already plugged the numbers into my phone.

"Hello?" she answered, her voice a perky question.

"Hey. It's Alice."

"Oh, Alice. I didn't recognize the number, I'm sorry."

"It's okay. Listen...do you want to grab coffee or something?"

"I'm on until eight, but then yes. I'd like to."

"Meet you at Allegro?"

"You got it. See you then," she said, ending the call after.

I spent an hour or so wandering the busy streets while lost in my thoughts. Everything seemed like such a mess.

A little after eight on a weeknight, the quaint cafe was relatively quiet. I picked the table farthest in the corner after ordering a vanilla latte and cinnamon bun. I barely touched the latter while I sipped my coffee, and flipped through the news articles on my phone. A text from Eve came in while I waited.

Saw the news. You good?

Fine. How'd you know?

Pulled you from the interview. Figured it out. I'm livid.

Me too.

See you at Jordan's on Saturday?

Yeah.

We'll talk.

K.

"Sorry, walking would've been faster than that Uber." Corwin announced her presence then shook the rain from her long black jacket.

"It's okay. Haven't been here long."

"Let me grab a cup and I'll be right back."

"Okay."

I watched as she approached the counter. No longer clad in scrubs, but in a loose-fitting pair of yoga pants and a t-shirt that hung off her in all the right places, I found myself drawing my gaze away to stare at the pastry in front of me.

Corwin returned with a steamy mug of something a moment later and sat, crossing her legs then sipping her drink. "That's better."

"Coffee makes things better. Wine makes them fine." I raised my cup in mock cheers and took a sip. Corwin chuckled lightly, shaking her head.

"Couldn't agree more." Again, the rim of her drink met her lips and I noticed myself paying attention. That was the third time in as many weeks that I caught myself admiring the gentle doctor and suddenly I began to question my motives for calling her. "What's the matter?"

"Huh?" A jolt hit my gut and my gaze shot to hers from her mouth.

"Your expression dimmed suddenly, like you'd just thought of something horrible."

"Maybe." I shrugged. "Lately, all I think about is horrible."

"I saw the news tonight. How are you holding up?"

Her delicate question reminded me of the way Eve spoke to the victim. "I've had better days. Internal Affairs is all over everything. None of us can get any work done and a coworker, who I spent dozens of hours with a week for years, just raped a woman." I glanced around to make sure no one was close enough to hear. "And I can't help wondering if he's done it before."

"Must be weird thinking about how much you'd been around him."

"Yeah. It is. Like it could've been me. Or someone I knew. A friend who I invited to a dinner party with him there. Anyone."

"Even a teenage girl."

"Even that." I paused to sip my coffee. "What's it like working in an emergency room?"

"Similar at times. Considering how much you've been there. Emergency medicine is all fine and good when you're treating accidents or injuries, but when you get a rape victim in the E.R. or mentally ill person, it changes things," she said, again, delicately.

"How long have you been there?"

"About five years. Did my last residency then fellowship there and stayed."

"Fancy." I smirked, lifting a brow at her.

"Me or my job?" Her cocked brow mirrored mine and I laughed.

"Both, actually."

"Tell me that when you see me elbow deep in a thoracic cavity sucking out fluid."

"Ew." I scrunched up my face. "I don't even know what a thoracic cavity is, but any place you're sucking fluid from sounds gross."

"My sentiments exactly." Her laugh, relaxed and genuine, brought out the deeper tones of her voice. It made me smile and the warmth it brought to my face offered mild relief from the anger that'd left me nothing but cold over the past few days. "What's bias crimes like in general?"

"A mix. Sometimes I'm visiting schools, refugee centers, or events and lecturing on what a hate crime is and how to report it. Sometimes I do bullying prevention. Other times I'm talking to victims or interviewing suspects."

"Getting shot, you know, the *usual*." Her lips curved

into a smile as she looked at me from over the rim of her mug.

I laughed softly. "Yeah. Though to be fair, the first bullet to the vest I took was when I was a beat cop. I've had a few years in between."

"Well, that's hopeful."

"Definitely."

"Is there a certain population you work with? Like the Latino community or women, etcetera?" She set her mug down, blue eyes twinkling a little in the dim overhead light.

"Not particularly, but I tend to favor cases involving women and crimes against the LGBT community. I'm particularly sensitive to that and feel my best work happens there," I told her, cupping my hands around the warm mug when the opening and closing door brought in a damp, chilly draft.

"Oh." Corwin gave pause, her gaze flickering to the window beside us then back to me. I watched as moderate tension narrowed her posture, bringing her shoulders up slightly. The pause in our conversation soon became awkward, which brought a sense of confusion to the table.

"Does that bother you?" I asked, finally.

"What?" She started, faintly, with her eyes widening a fraction under her controlled expression. "No. Not at all. Why do you ask?"

"You got really quiet for a second there." I smirked, leaning back in my chair. "Noticeably."

"It just surprised me, that's all." She waved her hand dismissively, smiling immediately after. "I'm sorry."

I couldn't help laughing a little bit. "For what? You're not a radical right-winged Evangelical, are you?"

"*What*?" Her voice lifted an octave. "God no." She chuckled, her gaze falling to meet mine again. "I just didn't expect you to say that, that's all."

My laugh broadened with hers and I shook my head. "You mean you didn't think I was gay. I mean, not everyone who works with the LGBT community is, but..."

"Well, no. But that's not what I meant either." She took a deep breath, setting her mug on the table and leaning forward on her elbows. "I'm really mucking this up, aren't I?"

I nodded, getting my jollies off on her discomfort. "It's mildly entertaining watching you flounder about, I have to admit. Next time I'll wear my lesbian identification badge." I pointed to the pocket of my jacket. "Normally, I clip it there."

"Alice." Corwin laughed, her cheeks reddening with amusement or embarrassment, I couldn't tell which. "You don't really have that."

"Nope." I cocked a brow at her. "But wearing it might help my sex life a bit."

"I'll have to try that some time." She continued to chuckle, seemingly relaxing at that point back into her eased posture.

"Try wearing a lesbian identification badge?"

She nodded gently. "Might've made this conversation less flounder-filled."

"Are you coming out to me, doc? I'm not good with subtleties," I teased, shaking my head at her.

"It seems that way." She nodded again, sucking in her breath then smirking as the energy suddenly fell to seriousness. I sat forward in my chair again, holding her gaze in an attempt to read her minimal facial movements.

"For real or are you kidding?"

"I'm not kidding," she said, sighing faintly. "But what you said is true. I didn't think you were gay."

"Right back at you."

A thick, pregnant, pause followed the disclosure. We watched each other for a moment until the jingle of the door chime drew my attention. The mane of a tousled blond mess attached to the man who entered had me starting when my brother waltzed in, soaked from the rain and still clad in oily coveralls. He looked to the barista then did a double-take when he saw me.

"Rabbit! What are you doing here?" Evan swept over, grabbing me into a brotherly hug. Which meant he nearly spilled my coffee and left a blob of rain water on my shirt. "And hey," he said to Doctor Corwin when he stepped away. "Who's this, Rabbit?"

I thwapped him on the shoulder, and looked to Corwin. "Doctor Corwin, this is my brother, Evan. Evan, Stella Corwin."

"*Doctor*? That's fancy." He reached out to shake her hand.

She took it, laughing hard after he spoke. "So I've heard. Just Stella is fine, and nice to meet you." She smiled, her expression brightening to her usual confident, practiced one that I recognized from her greetings at the hospital.

"*Stella* works at UW Medical. We've shared a few cases," I added quickly before my brother asked something embarrassing. "And she fixed up my injury a few weeks ago."

"Well, then I'm grateful to have met you." He glanced between us, grinning like the towheaded goof that he was. "I'm just picking up the coffee order for the shop. We're all working overtime tonight."

"That's nice of you, Ev."

"I better run though, Rabbit. See you Sunday?" He messed up my hair, then shoved my forehead. I swatted at him like a maniac.

"Quit it! Yes. Get lost."

He laughed hard, turning to Corwin again. "Nice to meet you, Doc."

"You, too." She chuckled at us as I tried desperately to fix my hair back to normal. "Take care."

"Later."

We watched as my brother grabbed two trays of drinks that waited for him at the counter then nodded when he took his leave.

"I'm sorry. He's insane," I told her when he was out of

earshot.

"He seems nice." She chuckled, leaning back with her cup resting in her lap. "Why does he call you Rabbit?"

"Both of my brothers do." I smirked, shaking my head. "From *Alice in Wonderland*. The white rabbit. The one who's always late."

"Are you always late?" Her brow furrowed as she fought the extended chuckle rising in her throat.

"Chronically, but that's only part of it. They're both older than me and they used to chase me around the house when we were kids. They said I was hard to catch, like a rabbit." I shrugged, smiling at the thought of our childhood shenanigans. "The name just stuck. Only Mom calls me Alice, really."

"Do your friends call you Rabbit, too?"

"Nah. Allie or Al."

"Well, they're all endearing. Alice is a nice name. Not very common now."

"So is Stella, mind you," I told her.

"Thanks. I've always liked it." Her smile, genuine and soft, elicited a similar response in me as our gazes lingered longer than normal. Again, I caught myself relaxing into it and, when she bit her bottom lip in a swift, faint gesture, my insides fluttered with something so familiar, so strong that I gripped my coffee mug harder than I should.

Corwin took a deep breath, setting her cup down before reaching for her coat. "I have to go," she said. "But this has been nice."

"Yeah." I cleared my throat, standing with her as she rose from her seat. "Thanks for meeting me."

"Of course."

We both adorned our jackets and, with the faint jingle of the door chime in the distance behind us, headed toward the street corner.

"You have my number now so, if you ever want to grab coffee again or whatever, let me know," I said, swallowing the rest of the sentence that nearly spewed itself out of my mouth.

"I will. I'm sure I'll see you soon." Again, she smiled gently and gestured down the street. "I'm that way."

"I know. Take care." I waved as she walked backward a few steps, offering me a simple two-finger salute before turning and heading down the street.

***

So tell me about this doctor, Rabbit? Evan's early morning text message made me smirk.

Nothing to tell. Heading to work now. See you later.

Aw come on.

Love you.

Alice!

Bye.

Jerk...bye.

"You good, Lange?" Porter asked when I dropped down into my desk chair. "Where's Goldman?"

"We came in separately today. He'll be here."

While spending the morning working on reports, Evan's text message lingered on my mind. And so did Doctor Corwin. It was no secret that I lacked the keenly coined *gaydar* that most people joked about. Never in a million years did I think she was gay. Her way-too-feminine nature, flawless confidence, and general demeanor didn't allude to anything at all. At least not to me.

More importantly, when she suspected that I was of the lesbian persuasion, it didn't seem to bring her comfort at all, rather, it freaked her out despite her tempered reaction. Maybe she felt the same way and her sixth sense for gayness was just as broken as mine.

Porter and I worked together on a report involving swastikas painted along the wall of a school, while Marc finished the rest of the report from our incident at the immigration reform rally.

"You ready for that big lecture at Washington U?" he asked after we were nearly bored to tears.

"Yeah. That stuff is easy. Talking about hate crimes against the transgender community, stats." I shrugged, leaning back in my chair to prop my feet up on the trash can under the desk. "Easy peasy lemon squeezy."

"Suave, Allie. Suave." Porter rolled his eyes at me and I laughed. "You pick up women with lines like that?"

"Always. They sweat my style." I brushed off my shoulder and he smacked my boot.

"What style is that? Pretty blonde harpy who wears the same clothes two days in a row?"

"Yup. Just that."

"Alice, you're gross," Marc called out and I laughed harder.

"I change my under clothes!"

"Ugh. You're like a boy. A hot boy that looks like a girl." Porter scowled, rolling his chair away from me.

Our ridiculous banter continued well into the afternoon. At the end of the work day, Porter left and Marc wandered off with Jackson to meet with Internal Affairs in their *super secret* conference room down the hall. The office space grew chilly under the early darkness of November. No one worked late that night. How could they when our activity was restricted to report writing and paperwork? Who was actually doing the police work for our unit under those circumstances?

I rose from my seat and headed down the hall to where our closed case room held the rest of the paperwork that I needed for the swastika case. My footsteps echoed louder than usual with the general emptiness of the office.

A familiar chortle rang out behind me and I turned around to see Butler standing there, shaking the hand of a man in a business suit. The man walked away, and Butler turned in time to look at me. His expression fell from jovial to annoyed in a heartbeat.

"What the fuck are you doing here?" I called out, stalking down the hall in his direction.

"It's called bail, Lange. Thought you were at least smart

enough to figure that out."

"You're suspended." I stopped in front of him, glaring up at him with the inch he had on me.

"Yeah but I still have to meet with I.A. and get my shit. Back the fuck off, you beast."

"Beast?" I nearly spat at him. "You're the goddamn *rapist*, Butler."

His face contorted and he adjusted the ugly blue tie against his collar. "It was consensual."

"Is that the story you're telling?" I took a step toward him again. "That a teenager consented to have her face smashed and insides torn out by the likes of you? Sure. Most women *consent* to being destroyed, you ugly pig."

"Back the fuck up, Lange." He moved toward me, his shoulders posturing aggressively but I didn't care. I didn't give a flying fuck what he did. Rage boiled my blood, setting my pulse to slam in my ears as my fingers balled into fists.

"Bet she wasn't your first either. Woman-fearing bastard." I turned my back on him, resigning to the higher road as I attempted to storm off down the hall. "Get out of my sight."

A jolt hit me from behind, shoving my shoulders forward and causing me to stumble a step. I swung around only to face the dark-eyed, hateful gaze of my *former* partner. "You did not just push me, you fucking piece of shit."

"You asked for it." The smile, his fucking piss-drinking smile did me in and I lunged, landing a double-fisted shove into his torso. He stumbled back, his Oxfords sliding against the floor as he made for me again.

"Just like that kid, Butler! Right? She asked to be tortured by your sorry ass excuse for a man?" I shouted at the top of my voice as I charged at him, throwing a punch at his square jaw. He dodged, grabbed me around the middle, and a full on brawl ensued in the confined hallway.

Butler lifted me off my feet, his arms around my waist

as I swung my elbow, aiming for his face wildly. I connected with his cheek and he nearly growled, shaking me violently before he tossed me like a sandbag. Hollers and shouts echoed around us as my body collided with the fire extinguisher mounted on the wall. A sharp pain snagged my middle and I crashed to the floor along with the heavy metal canister that clipped the back of my head on the way down. Nausea tightened my stomach, squeezing it as twinkling lights circled my field of vision. I sucked in my breath, holding down my reaction to the double assault.

"Jesus Christ, Butler!" Walsh wailed, and from my heap on the floor, I looked up to see Jackson wrestling with Butler as he pinned him to the wall. "Get him out of here!" Walsh demanded, pointing down the hall as Butler screamed like the psychopath that he was.

In the doorway of the conference room, two Internal Affairs agents stared, wide-eyed at the scene as Marc rushed over to me.

"Easy, Allie." He grabbed my elbow, helping me stand but the minute my feet hit the floor, I noticed the spattering of blood on it. Marc's hand cupped the back of my head. "You're bleeding."

"I'm fine."

"No, it's a lot of blood." His face paled and his greenish eyes shrunk under his widening pupils

"Here." One of the I.A. agents, an angry-faced woman with dark hair and chocolate skin, approached with a handful of paper towels. She pressed it to the back of my head, and I watched as her brows flicked upward. "Someone grab a first-aid kit."

The agent and Marc walked me to a chair in the conference room where I sat without complaint as my vision continued to swirl a little. Only when stillness found me did I notice the blood trickling down the shoulder of my white blouse. "Shit."

"It's so much blood," Marc repeated.

"Head wounds bleed a lot, Goldman," the woman said. "She needs to go to the hospital."

"I'm fine," I told them though my throbbing head and aching side, yet again, seemed to protest. The badge dangling from the woman's neck read *Sarah Ramos, Internal Affairs.*

"No. You need to go," she insisted as she poked around at my hair. "You're going to need a stitch or two."

"How can you tell?" Mark asked.

"By the fact she's bleeding like a maniac." Ramos nodded toward the doorway. "Grab more towels then we'll take her to the car."

"On it." Marc complied and rushed off to grab more supplies.

She stood there, quietly for a moment, before lowering herself in front of me while I took over holding the towels. "Are you okay? For real?"

"Yeah."

"A man just threw you down the hallway. Do you realize that?" she asked to which I nodded, glancing away from her as she stood again. "Let's go to the car."

I stood, slowly, and walked with her to Marc's car parked out front. Walsh met us just as I climbed into the passenger seat. "Lange."

"I'm fine," I told him when Marc started the engine.

"Call me later," Walsh said, his grumbly voice controlled as he fought to modulate himself.

"Okay."

Marc and I drove off, leaving him and Ramos behind.

CHAPTER FIVE

"You again?" Corwin's voice announced as she entered the exam room. "I thought you were a hard to catch *rabbit* and yet, here you are."

"Very funny," I said, sighing while Marc continued to hold the bloody rag to my head. I reached up once I gave my arm a rest and he let me take it from him.

"Let's have a look then." Doctor Corwin moved beside me and I lowered the towel to let her see. Her gloved fingers, gentle and faint, moved through my hair as she examined me. Quiet fell in the room and I listened to her soft breathing, while her fragrant, sweet-smelling perfume wafted up my nose. I closed my eyes but gripped the table when my head spun a bit. "Whoa. Easy. Are you dizzy?"

"A little."

"We're going to need to clean that up and stitch it," she said, taking a step back and peeling away her blue gloves. "I'll grab the nurse and—"

"Can you do it?" I asked her, avoiding her gaze as a sudden surge of emotion struck me.

"I can." Corwin stepped in front of me, her middle an inch from my knees. She waited but I still didn't look at her. "Alice?" I shook my head, pressing my lips together defiantly.

"Al?" Marc put his hand on my shoulder and I recoiled under his touch, jerking my arm away.

"I'm fine."

"Detective Goldman, can you give us a minute?"

"Yeah. Sure." He hesitated at first. "I'll be outside waiting, okay, Allie?"

I glanced at him, nodding faintly as I watched him leave the room. The door clicked shut behind him and finally, I looked up to Corwin. Her eyes, as kind and gentle as the rest of her, evoked the emotions that I'd kept under wraps for the better part of an hour or two. She smiled faintly, her gaze flickering between my eyes in a clinical manner only for a second before she placed her hand on my shoulder. "Lie back. Carefully."

I listened to her, scooting back on the exam table after she placed a blue and white medical pad under my head. I watched her as she moved around me, both of us quiet as she pulled on a new pair of gloves.

"You'll have to turn on your side slightly," she said, returning to my side with the medical tray filled with the supplies she needed.

I made to move but hissed as soon as my hip pressed the table.

"What is it?"

"I don't know." I gripped my side and she moved to pull up my shirt. Sure enough, a deep gash near the top of my pants made itself known. Blood dried around it and it clearly soaked the corner of my pants as the metallic sheen lingered on my belt. "Shit."

Corwin said nothing but she picked up square gauze from the table and covered it, tucking it into the waist of my pants. "We'll take care of that after we stitch you up."

"Okay."

She rolled the stool to the side of the bed and sat, her hand falling on my head as she looked at me. Again, the swell of emotion strangled my throat, but I fought it and looked away from her, turning my head to the side and shifting so that my back was to her.

I listened as the wheels of the stool squeaked and she began working on me. Warmth met my hair as I imagined she washed the wound, and I felt her fingers pushing my hair aside. I listened to her movements but we didn't speak. That didn't mean my thoughts turned off at all. In my mind's eye, I kept seeing Butler's ugly face and feeling myself flying like I was a weightless piece of nothing.

"Small pinch," she said, and I started when something poked me. After that, I felt nothing against my scalp but the dull sensation of pressure that occurred every so often.

Barely ten minutes later, the clink of metal on metal broke the quiet. "All done."

"Thanks," I said, rolling onto my back again. "At least you didn't have to shave my head."

"Just three stitches is all, and some antibiotic." Corwin rolled backward a little then stopped at my hip. "On to the next." I pulled my shirt up again, and she shook her head. "Can you take your belt off, please? And unfasten your pants. I'll need to look around that wound."

"Fuck, my shirt is a mess," I called out, finally noticing what I looked like when I reached down to unbuckle my belt.

"Most of you is," she said, her hand resting on my hip. When I laid back again, she tugged down my pants and nudged my panties down a little, too. Her gaze fixated on the wound, her lips pursing as she poked around a little while I held my breath. "Painful?"

"It's definitely going to bruise," I answered, avoiding her question.

"I see that. Let's clean it up at least."

"Okay." I folded one arm behind my head, avoiding both my stitches and looking at her while she did what she needed to.

While she tended to my injury, my thoughts became more bothersome. My throat tightened but I couldn't fight the pressure that built against my eyelids. It sent a quiver to my bottom lip and I bit it to hold on to myself.

"What happened, Alice?" Corwin asked softly as she dabbed something against my skin. It burned and ached worse than my head. Worse than the bruise from the bullet to the vest I took, if that were even possible.

"Nothing."

"Alice. Come on." She looked up from her work to me. "You realize I'm in a position to torture you with medical equipment until you talk, right?"

"Are you a *Harold Shipman* kind of doctor?" I teased, sniffling as I wiped my eyes with my sleeve.

She laughed softly, shaking her head. "You'll never know."

"You know who that is?" I drew my attention her way finally.

"British serial-killing doctor, yes indeed." She smiled genuinely and winked at me before returning to tend to my injury.

It took her longer than my head and, when she was done, I watched as she taped a gauze pad over it. Her fingers tickled along the waist of my panties, way too close to places that no one except me had been in a long time. When she was done, she carefully tugged them over the bandage, and fixed my pants back in place. She rolled closer to me after removing her gloves, then placed the palm of her hand on my stomach.

"What happened?" she repeated her question, soft eyes boring into me.

"Butler is out on bail. I saw him at work and we got into a fight." I breathed slowly, purposefully, to control the onslaught of tears that pushed their way to the surface again. "He picked me up and threw me against the wall."

Corwin's expression didn't falter, but she watched me with caution. "I'm sorry, Alice."

"It's not your fault. Only his."

"I know, but this situation has upset you profoundly and, from what little I know of you, it takes a lot to push you to that point," she said.

"Yeah." I smirked, taking a swipe at my eyes. "You're right in that assessment, Doc."

"Stella. Okay?"

I nodded faintly. "Okay."

"I'd like to make sure that you don't have a concussion. The dizziness is a symptom."

"Whatever you want to do." I shrugged a little and slowly made to sit up. She rose with me, her hand gripping my elbow firmly. My head spun again and she squeezed my arm.

"Change of plans. Lie back down." Corwin cleared the medical pad and adjusted the bed so that it was half way up. I settled back against it with her help and she put the rails up on both sides of the bed. "Is your stomach sick?"

"Not much."

"It will all fade but let's check you out anyway. Marc can stay with you though I have to step out to get everything ordered. Okay?"

"Yeah, it's fine."

"That didn't sound too convincing." She leaned on the edge of the bed the same way she did the first time she treated me. "Is there someone else you want me to call?"

"No. Don't call anyone else. My parents will panic."

"What about Evan?"

"He'll freak out, too."

"Isn't Marc a good friend?"

"Yeah." I covered my face with my hands and took a few deep breaths. "I think I feel weird."

"You have a concussion, I'm pretty sure of it. Sometimes feeling weird is part of it."

"Like overly emotional?" I dropped my hands again with a sigh.

She nodded. "Sometimes, yes."

"Okay. Just do whatever."

"I'll come back and check on you when I'm done. Okay?"

"Yeah. You can send Marc in."

"I will."

***

"Hey bum," Marc said as he entered our apartment with bags of groceries. "How do you feel?"

"Fine," I said, leaning over the back of the sofa. "What'd you get?"

"Junk food like you requested."

"Yay."

"Three days home and you killed every bit of food we had."

"I'm a hero." I laughed at him when he flipped me off. "How's work?"

"Walsh is pressing charges on your behalf against Butler and he's back in jail. They had the whole thing on video. Him pushing you first and then throwing you. It makes the other case against him look horrible."

"It is horrible."

"Well, more horrible."

"He's horrible."

"Agreed."

I rested my chin on my hands, not offering to help him put anything away at all.

"Are you okay alone tonight? Gavin wants to go out to dinner…" His gaze flickered in my direction. "I tried to convince him to order in."

"Just go, Marc. Men share meals all the time. It won't be any different."

"We'll see. You okay if he comes back here after?"

"Of course. Quit asking. I'll clean up the house and stuff while you're out," I promised.

"Are you sure that concussion didn't fuck up your brain?" He laughed hard and this time I flipped him off.

"I'm sure. Thanksgiving is next week. Is Gavin coming?"

"He said yes." He nodded, smiling faintly though I knew he was tickled pink about it.

"Mom will be happy to inform him about his *phase*."

"He's prepped and ready."

"Awesome."

Hours later, with the bathroom clean, the living room tidy, and my room less disorganized, I lounged on the sofa and watched reruns of an old show about superheroes. My head felt fine, but the bruise and gash on my hip ached worse than anything else.

Half an hour into the third episode, my phone rang. I picked it up to see *Stella Corwin, MD*, on the screen.

"Hello?"

"How are you feeling?" she asked right away.

"Better. A really nice doctor excused me from work for a few days so I'm enjoying the lush lazy life. How about you?"

"Sounds like a great provider." She laughed softly. "Are you home?"

"I am."

"Want company?"

"Is said company bringing coffee?" My lip twitched, threatening a smirk.

"Said company is very able to bring coffee."

"Then said company is welcome."

"Text me your address."

I chuckled before answering, "I will."

Corwin arrived half an hour later with two hot lattes and pastries.

"Best house call ever, Doc," I said, ushering her inside.

"I'll write you a prescription for snarky pills before I leave," she teased as I took her coat and gestured toward the living room.

"Very funny."

"Nice place," she said, setting her purse down on the table. "Love the color scheme."

"Thank Marc for that. If it were up to me, everything would be white and vacant." I dropped down to sit on the sofa after we took a brief lap around the house and she joined me. I sat cross-legged facing her while she angled herself toward me, crossing her legs.

"Not a fan of decorating?"

"I just don't think that way really. I grew up with two brothers. Nothing was ever color-coordinated or orderly. And they used to steal all my stuff so I didn't get too attached to material things," I told her, sipping my latte after. "This is perfect. Thank you."

"Welcome. I never had siblings so I was used to orderly and quiet."

"That sounds divine."

She chuckled, tugging her sweater down over her hips when she shifted her position. "It was at times." Her smile, coupled with her perpetual gaze on mine as she sipped her coffee, sent a shudder of something up my middle, reminding me of the fragrance of her perfume when she examined my head the other day. "How do you feel?"

"Okay, generally. My hip hurts more than my head."

"Is it bruised?"

"Oh yeah. Super ugly."

She laughed hard. "Let me see." I lifted my shirt and tugged down my sweatpants a little. "Nice. It's healing okay though."

"You've said that to me a lot lately."

"You get hurt a lot."

"It's been an unusual month," I said, smirking along with it. "Otherwise, it's been almost ten years since my last on-the-job injury. Though the latter wasn't exactly because of my job."

"No, it wasn't." The mood dropped from playful to serious in a heartbeat. "How are you doing with that?"

"You mean with being man-handled, again, and thrown around like a weightless piece of shit?" I shrugged dramatically. "I'll get over it."

"Perhaps, but still." She sipped her coffee then paused suddenly, a single eyebrow lifting. "What do you mean again? Has it happened before?"

"Not in the same way." I cursed myself for even mentioning it, but now that I tossed myself into a load of cow dung known as history, I was left to reap the shitty consequences.

"With him?"

"Butler?" I shook my head. "No. Nothing like that. In college I didn't have the easiest time."

Corwin watched me, her eyes soft and knowing. "You don't have to get into it if you don't want to, Alice. You don't owe me anything. Not even a story."

"I know." I rested my elbow on the back of the sofa while watching her. She tucked her legs to the side and settled in more comfortably. "Thanks for checking on me."

"Of course. And besides, I like talking to you."

"Ditto." I smirked, running my fingers through my hair. "Do you like talking to your friends as much?"

"Not many friends to really talk to. Just to some work folks that I'm closer with."

"You seem like someone who would have a lot of friends."

"Why?" She tilted her head, a tendril of her long, dark hair tumbling over her shoulder.

"Because you're kind and caring. People usually like that."

"Perhaps. Doesn't mean I'm vested in sharing anything with them though," she said, running her finger over the lid of her cup.

"True. Have you ever gone to Wildrose downtown? A few of my friends go on Wednesdays or when they have events. You can come with us if you like."

"What's Wildrose?"

"A lesbian bar. Though they have other LGBT events now and then. We go on Wednesdays because they have live music and decent food," I told her.

"Not sure I'd be into that scene. I'm not the greatest in social situations."

"You seem okay to me."

"In larger groups." She smiled though it wasn't a comfortable smile at all.

"Think about it. The offer stands."

"I will." She grew quiet for a moment, looking down at the figure-eights she drew on her coffee cup. "Maybe, if you wanted, you could come to my place for dinner some time. I like to cook. It's kind of my thing."

"You mean doctoring *and* cooking?" I grinned at her. "Good thing I need both medical attention and food almost daily lately."

Corwin laughed softly, her gaze flickering in my direction. "That's the truth."

"I'll come for dinner. You like cooking, I like eating. It's a good match up."

"It is."

Voices carried outside the front door and we both looked over to see Marc enter with Gavin. The two of them chattered spiritedly about something, but I was pretty sure I heard *Seahawks* spewed out more than once.

"Hey," I said, drawing Marc's attention.

"Hey, Al. Oh...we have company. Did you need more stitches?" Marc teased, smiling as he set down a plastic bag on the table.

I laughed. "Not yet. Hey Gavin. This is my friend Stella, Stella, Gavin. She already knows Marc."

"Nice to meet you." Gavin, unlike Marc, was of a more slender build but still muscular like he'd spent a lot of time working out. The managing his own body weight type of working out, rather than pumping tons of iron. He shook Corwin's hand and removed his ball cap at the same time. Tawny hair tumbled all over the place and he pushed it back.

"You, too." Corwin smiled, releasing his hand after.

"Stella brought pastries." I gestured to the coffee table. "If you guys want."

"I'm good," Gavin said, glancing to Marc.

"Me too," he said. "Help yourself to my leftovers, Al, if you want."

"Thanks." I nodded to him. Stella and I watched as the guys disappeared into Marc's room down the hall. She looked to me, her brow furrowed. "Marc and I are roommates. Did I not mention that?"

"I don't think you did." She shook her head.

"Oh." I paused, took a breath then said, "Marc and I are roommates."

She laughed a little, and continued toying with the plastic cover of her cup. "Good to know. Rooming with a handsome man who brings over other handsome men."

"You're missing an adjective in there." I wiggled my finger in the air and she cocked a brow at me.

"Just what is that, exactly?"

"Gay. *Gay* handsome man bringing over other *gay* handsome men. But I never told you that so if you say I did, I'll deny it."

"Is he not, you know, open about himself?" She glanced to the closed bedroom door then back to me.

"Not out at all. I, on the other hand, am very out. I'm out all over the place." I waved my hands around in an expansive gesture and she laughed.

"Also good to know."

"Are you?"

"I used to be. People have probably forgotten by now." She shrugged, smirking slightly afterward.

"Why would they forget that?"

"It's been five years since I've been in a relationship. Couple that with staff turnover and no one bothers noticing."

"Ouch. Yeah. I see what you mean." I turned the volume up on the television just in case Marc decided to get noisy with his man. "You haven't dated or anything?"

"No," she said, her voice stilted. I watched as the confident, open doctor tensed and tumbled away like she had the moment she found out about my sexuality.

"We don't have to talk about this either, you know. I am capable of shutting up...sometimes."

She laughed softly, glancing at me again. "It's okay." A quiet followed again until she asked. "Are you dating?"

"Not currently. It's been well over a year since I've been in a relationship. Hard to get over being cheated on. Twice."

"Ouch." She scrunched up her nose and shook her head. "Yeah, I can only imagine."

"Doesn't help my confidence any. My friend Jordan gets on me about it sometimes," I said.

"Jordan." Corwin gave pause. "Does she run the salon downtown? Blue hair streaks."

"Yeah." I perked up. "She's one of my best friends."

"I've gone there before. It's a great place."

"And full of lesbians. I think it's the hub of everything. Do you know her girlfriend? She's a county M.E."

"Ainsley Monson?" She nodded, her smile brightening a bit. "I know Ainsley's mother better though. She's a nurse in my E.R."

"Oh right! Shit. Our world is tiny."

"Very." She smiled softly as she sipped her coffee again, but the way her eyes never left me sent a shiver up my spine. "What?" Her brow lifted again, the way it usually did when she caught me thinking.

"Nothing."

"Uh huh. You know, Alice, I'm beginning to think that you don't talk much about what's really going on in your head." She set her cup on the table near us, then pulled a pillow into her lap after.

"Neither do you," I shot back, a trickle of anger tightening my chest. "What do you think is going on in my head then, Doc?"

"That you were really bothered by what happened to you a few days ago. That you haven't spoken a word about it to anyone. And I'm also pretty sure you haven't left this apartment either." Her calmness unnerved me and annoyed me at the same time. "Thought so."

"Did you come here to aggravate me or hang out? Because the former is happening right now."

"Both, actually." She gathered her hair and pulled it over her shoulder. The glow of the television in the darkened room emphasized the sharp curve of her jaw.

"Of course it bothered me. A fucking rapist, who I thought was, at best, a guy who I trusted, who I had drinks and dinner with as part of our team, hurt me. Someone who used to bring in bad guys, not actually be one." Tears tumbled down my cheeks and I sent a punch into the back of the sofa before shoving myself up to stand. Corwin rose with me, blocking my path when I made to storm off.

"Alice, stop."

"Why do you even care?" I clenched my fists as my breathing picked up. My refusal to cry only fueled my anger, but the tears that betrayed me made it worse.

"Because I do. Because you need someone to care. Okay?" Blue eyes bore into me, cooling my anger and setting alight something far more dangerous.

"Yeah." I swiped at my tears and when I looked up again, Corwin reached forward, gripping my shoulders.

"You're a messy rabbit," she said, smiling gently when she guided me to sit down again.

I laughed. "You should see my room."

"Noted." Her chuckle rang out, lifting my spirits exponentially.

"Want to watch a movie?" I asked, gesturing to the TV.

"Sure." She nodded and we settled back into our places on the sofa.

I let myself relax into the comedy that Corwin picked and, for the first time in a long time, shared a couch and a movie with another woman.

***

"The fresh kind, Alice, not the canned!" Mom's screeching voice burst through my phone as I pushed a grocery cart down the aisle of the store.

"Ma, I got it. Heaven forbid a dish of canned cranberry sauce make it to the table. Call the FBI." I rolled my eyes and purposely pushed four cans of canned crap into the cart.

"Alice!"

"Mom! I'll get the fresh cranberries."

"And orange peel."

"Fresh oranges with peels or the dried jar kind?"

"Both!" She panicked, or at least it sounded that way, and hung up. I laughed as I pocketed my phone and made my way to the produce section.

Marc met me there with arms full of groceries, most notable, big bags of stuffing mix. "Okay. Got it."

"Did you notice that every year, Mom forgets the same thing? Stuffing and cranberry sauce?"

"I did. It's how she keeps you out of her hair while she's cooking. And here I thought you were a great detective." He dumped the ingredients in the basket and grinned.

"Great. Just great. What tasks does she give my brothers?"

"Nothing. They sit there watching football while you insist on helping." He clapped me on the back so hard it made a nice thwapping noise. I laughed and punched him in the shoulder. "I also found someone wandering aimlessly in the dairy section."

"Who?" I cocked a brow, glancing behind him.

"A hot doctor who, just a few nights ago, spent hours on our sofa with two feet between you." He wagged his brows at me. "And I may, or may not have, invited her to Thanksgiving."

"*What?*" I spat, shoving the cart into his leg. "Are you serious?"

"Ow!" He laughed hard, his deep tones drawing attention from the other same-day-as-the-holiday shoppers. "Come on. You know she's hot."

"Her hotness is not the question. You invited her to my

parents' house? Have you *been* there? My mother will rake her over the coals. Dad will destroy her with tales of football games that he's still bereaving."

"Yeah. Pretty sure *bereaving* isn't a word." He grabbed the cart, turned it sharply, and headed off toward our next venture.

"Marc!" I chased after him, skidding to a halt when he stopped in the spice aisle. Sure enough, Corwin stood at the end of it, perusing some kind of jarred ingredient.

"Hey, Doc. Look who I found," Marc called out then pointed at me like an obnoxious fool.

Corwin laughed, tossing something in the basket she had on her arm before approaching us. "Is he always like this?" she asked me, her eyes seemingly twinkling under the fluorescent lights.

"Always. Shopping for forgotten cooking ingredients like us?"

"A bit. Making my dad some apple crisp for today," she said, smiling half-heartedly.

"Is he coming to your place?" I asked, but Marc shook his head at me.

"I'll get the orange peel." He pointed down the aisle and slipped past us.

"Nah. I stop by his. He's in an assisted living place."

"Oh." I started, gripping the handles of the carriage tighter. "I'm sorry."

"Don't be. He's not. He loves it there." She smiled, though it didn't exactly meet her eyes.

"Well, that's good at least." I glanced down the aisle to see Marc flailing his arms, as if pushing me toward Corwin. I looked back to her and she fiddled with her fancy little coach bag. "So, um, I know Marc invited you to my parents tonight if you're up for it. I mean, that's assuming you don't have any other plans."

"I don't." She shifted her weight uncomfortably. "But I'll think about it."

"Okay. But...just so you know. My family is insane,

Mom thinks being gay is a twenty-year phase but other than that, she's accepting. Dad and Ryan are football junkies who suck at holding conversations, and Evan, well, you've met him. Plus, my six-year-old nephew is an uber nerd, and my niece is probably going to want to paint your nails. Other than that, it's a totally normal, calm, quiet experience."

Corwin laughed hard, shaking her head at me. "Well, I suppose that explains your put-togetherness."

"Oh yeah. Totally explains my entire life."

"I'll think about it," she repeated, her smile soft. "I better go."

"Me too. I'll text you the address in case you decide to."

"Okay. Bye, Alice."

"Bye."

It took Marc and I an hour to fix the stuffing and cranberry sauce, and when we arrived at my parents with Gavin, the three of us stood outside the front door. I took a deep breath, glancing at the guys.

"Are you sure you're ready? Gavin, armor up?"

"Aye aye, Captain. Shields activated. Gay phase in full effect." He saluted me and both Marc and I cracked up.

The second I opened the front door, chaos slammed us in the face. Evan chased Nathaniel around the living room while he screeched and held his glasses to his face. Tabitha, in her fairy wings, brought up the rear while shouting, "Halt in the name of the law."

Ryan and Dad shouted at the television while Mom set the dining room table. None of them noticed us and I just stood there, holding the bowl of cranberry sauce and sighing. Hopefully, Corwin would decide not to dive into the absolute mess that was my family. Marc tugged Gavin and me into the dining room, narrowly avoiding a foam dart that went flying in our direction.

"Evan! No weapons near the table. Keep it in the den." Mom pointed and he led the kids away. "Hello dears!" She rounded on us, kissing our cheeks then grabbing both of

Gavin's hands. "This must be Gavin. Lovely to meet you." She leaned over to Marc and whispered, loudly, "He's very handsome."

"I know." Marc grinned proudly while Gavin laughed. "Thanks for having us."

"Every year, every holiday, my boy." She placed her hand on Marc's cheek then tugged both of them toward the kitchen, leaving me behind.

"Hi, Mom! Nice to see you, too." I rolled my eyes and set the bowl down on the dining room table.

"Auntie Rabbit!" Tabitha ran at me, leaping into my arms as I swept her up into a hug. "Do you like my wings?"

"They're amazing, kiddo. Are you a fairy?"

"A tree fairy!" She shrieked, her blonde ringlets bouncing all over. "Mommy said to say hi."

"Is she coming today?"

"For dessert." She wiggled so I set her down, then watched as she tore off to destroy something a moment later.

I joined Dad and Ryan in the living room, leaning over the sofa to kiss both their cheeks. Dad hugged me around the neck then Ryan grabbed me by the jacket, pulling me over the pillows in a harsh flop. "Ack." I guarded the tender spot on my hip with my arm.

"What up, Rabbit? You're late. As always. The game's half over."

"Good." I laughed as I landed beside him, and he caught me around the shoulders. "How are you?"

"Good. Shh." He pointed at the screen.

"Hopeless," I said.

"Don't try to help your mother. She has a knife at the ready," Dad said, still staring at the TV but taking a moment to pat me on the head.

"Thanks for the warning. How's the leg? Mom said it was bothering you." I tapped his knee which wasn't actually his knee but part of his prosthetic.

"Beer makes it better. Shh." Again, he patted my head and I just gave in to flopping on the sofa with them, my legs across Ryan's lap. He might not have looked at me much, but the hand he kept on my ankle was enough acknowledgement.

Marc and Gavin joined us a few minutes later and, in typical fashion, I lost them, too. Dad and Ryan didn't even bother introducing themselves to Gavin but sure enough, they offered him chips and beer in between shouting at the television.

"It's been over ten years since they won a Super Bowl guys, calm down," I said, which earned me a round of boos.

"Alice, come here," Mom beckoned and I joined her in the kitchen. "Gavin is lovely."

"He's perfect for Marc." I smiled when I thought of the two of them.

"Marc mentioned that you invited a friend. Should we set a place?" She kissed my cheek then handed me a basket of rolls. Tabitha came screaming into the room, ran around the island, then bolted again. "I'm going to kill your brother."

"Which one?" I laughed as I dodged the kid. "I'm not sure if she's coming. Set one anyway."

Dinner went over as it usually did, with everyone talking over each other. Except me because I didn't have much to talk about. Not anything good anyway. Gavin caught my gaze from across the table and grinned around a mouthful of turkey. "I like your family," he mouthed and I laughed.

"They're nuts," I told him.

"But the good kind. Like pistachios."

I cracked up and glanced at Marc as he and Ryan bantered about football. Gavin looked on at him and smiled, his light eyes twinkling under the yellowed light of the chandelier.

Evan clapped me on the back, drawing my attention to

him. "So...the doctor."

"What about her?" I took a bite of potatoes while watching him. My heart sunk a little bit when Corwin hadn't shown up. Part of me expected her to, but the realistic part told me that we were barely friends and not many people would be comfortable going to a stranger's house for a holiday.

"You like her," Evan accused, jabbing his fork in my direction.

"I do not."

"You do. Don't even lie. I've seen you look at women before and the way you were looking at her that night…" He nodded, nudging me with his elbow. "Is she gay?"

"Yeah, but I didn't know it until that night." My face heated and I took a giant gulp of my wine to hide the flush that I knew would expose me.

"She's hot. And your type," he said, grinning after. "Sexy, femme, motivated."

"What are you two whispering about over there?" Dad asked and I started, dropping my fork like a clumsy fool.

"Nothing—"

"Women. Rabbit has a crush." Evan's perky announcement earned him a punch in the thigh. "Ow!"

"Alice! No hitting at the table." Mom gestured to my niece and nephew who giggled at me.

"Only at the table?" Ryan laughed, waving at the two of us. "Go hit each other outside."

The whole table erupted with laughter and Gavin's hearty laugh had me glaring. He snorted, attempting to hide his amusement. Marc was already in hysterics so there was no hope for him.

"Who's this crush?" grumbled Dad, eyeing me from over his thick-rimmed glasses.

"No one. He's just teasing." I sighed, shooting a glare at Evan.

"Is it the friend you invited?" asked Mom, her voice laden with hope and fear. If that were possible anyway.

"No—"

"Yes." Gavin nodded hard.

"You guys suck," I said, huffing and puffing out frustration. "I'm always the brunt of the teasing."

"It's because we love you, Rabbit." Ryan grinned a goofy, food-laden grin.

"Gross," I said.

"Ew, Daddy." Tabitha giggled, covering her mouth with her tiny hands and pink fingernails.

It took hours for Mom to fix dinner, and about fifteen minutes for us to devour it. I helped clean up, just like every year, then set the table for dessert. Ryan's ex-wife joined us just in time for coffee and I sat there with my cup in its saucer, saddened by the notion that Corwin didn't show up. Or text.

Tabitha climbed into my lap without warning, a bottle of purple nail polish in hand. "Your turn, Auntie Rabbit."

"Oh boy. Are you going to do it neatly?" I asked as she grabbed my wrist and plopped my hand down on the table.

"Pro'ly not." She shook the bottle while I laughed, resting my chin on top of her head while she had at it.

By the end of the night, my purple fingernails became a badge of honor that I would wear until the color faded a week from then. Mom handed me two containers of leftovers and some other yummy homemade delicacies to fill my fridge as I stood by the front door, pulling on my knee-high boots.

"Why two?" I asked, shrugging on my jacket.

"Take one to your friend," she said, her brows lifting with her smile.

"That'll be rude if I just show up…"

"I doubt it. Just take it to her."

"Mom...I know you're thinking—"

"Just do it, Alice. It's good for you."

"Bully. If it blows up in my face, it's your fault." I accepted the packed bags and kissed her cheek. "Thank you."

"Welcome."

After tons of kisses, a few hugs, and a smattering of punches later, Marc, Gavin, and I loaded into the car. Marc drove and Gavin road shotgun as we made our way home.

"Can you drop me in Belltown?"

"What?" Marc glanced at me in the mirror. "Why?"

"I'm going to bring some food to Stella," I said, gnawing on my bottom lip while awaiting his reaction.

"Smooth moves, Alice," Gavin commented first.

"Mom's making me," I muttered, glancing out the window.

"Uh huh…"

Getting into Corwin's building wasn't easy. I had to flash my badge twice to the security officers, the second time when they threatened to take my gun. I hadn't messaged her to warn her of my arrival, and there weren't any mailboxes at the ready in the fancy foyer so my hunt for Corwin's apartment took a lot longer than expected. Fancy carpets, sleek gray walls, and a security system right out of a sci-fi movie greeted me at every turn. Finally, after two floors of fruitless searching, I ran into a man who told me that Doctor Corwin lived on the sixth floor but he didn't know which apartment.

By the time I made it up the stairs, foregoing the elevator like an idiot, I was nearly out of breath. Beside the luxurious seating area in front of the elevator, I found the floor's wall of mailboxes and Corwin's name beside box number 605.

Halfway down the row of twelve doors, I knocked on one marked with a zero-five. I stood there, holding the cooled container of food, catching my breath while waiting. A good thirty seconds must've passed before I heard the chain on the door releasing. When the door opened, Corwin appeared windblown with surprise. She wore a pair of floppy scrub bottoms, untied around her hips, and a white tank top. Her sock-covered feet soundless on the marble tile. Her eyes, wide with surprise, set alight a newfound nervousness to my gut.

"Alice. What are you doing here?"

"Bringing you food because my mother made me." I smirked and offered her the container. She accepted without complaint and I crossed my arms over my middle.

"That's sweet of her. And you," she said, pushing the door open wider. "Do you want to come in? I've just opened a bottle of wine."

"I was about to decline until you said the magic word. Yeah, I'll come in."

She chuckled and ushered me inside, securing the door after. Unlike my apartment, hers wasn't quaint or cozy. Marble floors covered the foyer straight down to the living room where plush white carpet met a giant full wall of windows. In between, a black stone fireplace sat in the middle of matching leather sofas. A huge flat screen television mounted on the wall above the hearth drew my attention to the screen where the paused image of two women facing each other, one with a brunette bob, the other with long blonde hair, looked about ready to cry or kiss.

"Did I interrupt your foray into lesbian indie films?" I gestured to the television.

"What?" She started, swinging around and laughing. "Oh. No. That's *Supergirl.* Old show from twenty-seventeen."

"I vaguely remember that in my youth." I tapped my lip and again she laughed.

"Youth. Please." She waved her hand at me as she set the leftovers on the kitchen counter. Everything was stainless steel and absolutely spotless. Our voices echoed when we spoke. Corwin poured out two glasses of white wine and offered one to me.

"Thanks." I took a sip and closed my eyes, pretending to die from happiness. When I looked back at her, she laughed softly, her glass pressed to her lips. She pulled her hair from a messy ponytail and I watched as it fell over her shoulders. No doubt, I preferred her hair down.

"Welcome. Did you eat dessert?"

"I ate *everything*," I confessed, laughing afterward.

"Hmm. Too bad. I have tons of ice cream." There it was again, that playful smile that made me want to…

"There's always room for ice cream. What kind?"

"Chocolate or mint chip." She swept to the freezer and pulled out both.

"Both. In the same bowl." I nodded and she chuckled, taking two bowls out of the cabinet and setting them on the counter. "Where are the spoons?"

"There," she answered, pointing to the drawer at my hip.

I tugged it open and grabbed the spoons. Corwin scooped out two bowls of both flavors, then put the cartons back in the freezer. We swapped a spoon for a bowl and both of us dug in together. The second the icy confection met her lips, she wagged her brows at me, grabbed her wine, and turned away, heading toward the living room.

Like the lost rabbit that I was, I followed her. She led me to the sofa, piled with fluffy blankets that smelled like fresh fabric softener, and we settled in. We both set our glasses on the sleek black coffee table, then faced each other while we ate.

"Good idea," she said, tucking her feet on the sofa with the rest of her. "Mixing them."

"It's the only acceptable way to eat ice cream, mixing flavors." I licked a mouthful from my spoon and grinned at her. She laughed at me and pulled a bite into her mouth. "My second favorite to this—" I lifted the bowl. "—is pistachio and black cherry."

"That sounds good, too. Are you a foodie, in general?"

"Not really. I just eat everything."

"Good. Picky eaters are annoying." She pulled the spoon slowly from her lips that were now a shade darker under the cold. "How are your stitches?"

"Not bad. They tug a little."

"They can probably come out soon. Let me see." She set her bowl down on the table and I did the same, scooting closer. "Tilt forward."

I moved my hair to the side and leaned my head forward. Corwin shifted her position, her knees pressed against my thigh as she ran her fingers through my hair, nails tickling along my scalp until she found what she was looking for. Her body leaned over mine, and the heat of her burned like the fire of a thousand blue stars. I dug my fingers into my knees, closing my eyes when the scent of her leftover perfume struck me. My insides clenched and my mouth tingled with desire. I didn't want to feel like this. I didn't want Evan to be right or my feelings to be twisted for the one person who showed me a different kind of care.

"It looks good. They're dissolving well." Her fingers ran through my hair again, this time in a less clinical caress. Slowly, I leaned up to meet her gaze again. Without the excuse of an injury examination, our proximity to each other grew more uncomfortable by the second.

Corwin's gaze darted back and forth between mine, finally flickering to my mouth. We hung there, in stalemate, two inches from each other until she closed the distance with a soft, tentative kiss. Her lips on mine set off a landmine of sensations, pouring through me like molten liquid. It screamed, seared, and tore at places long lifeless. Emotions caught in my chest, tightening my breath and forcing my heart into a fury.

My return was less tentative, more eager and she leaned into it, her palm hovering, barely touching my cheek. In our laps, our hands moved at the same time until our fingers tangled together. She squeezed mine, her hand trembling until I poked my tongue against her mouth. Vigor met our connection and she gripped my thigh, squeezing as her hand moved upward. My core ached and my stomach shuddered with possibilities.

Without any warning, Corwin broke away from me, crying out as if in pain as she shot up to stand, the back of her hand pressed against her mouth. "I can't," she said, turning away from me as the crackle of emotion wrecked her voice. "I *can't*."

"What? Why?" I rose, approaching her from behind. She shook her head, cupping her hands over her mouth when she turned to look at me.

"I can't. I can't do this. You have to go." A sob caught in her throat and tears tumbled from her blue eyes, sharpening their color. The pain, *grief* that lingered in them brought a surge of emotion to my throat, choking me up as I reached for her.

"Stella, I thought you—"

"Please. You have to go," she croaked, jerking away from me and rushing off to, what I assumed, was her bedroom. The door shut with a bang, and the last thing I heard was the sound of her stricken sobs.

CHAPTER SIX

"What the hell happened?" Marc asked me as I stepped out of the shower, snatching the towel he offered me. "Allie…"

"Leave me alone," I spat, wrapping it around me as I shoved past him.

"Allie, what the hell happened?" He followed me right into my bedroom where I pushed some clothes off the bed then dropped down on it.

"I fuck everything up. That's what happened. Everything, Marc." I tossed my arms up, then let them flop down beside me. "I make one new friend. Someone who I actually enjoy talking to. Who isn't hanging on the arm of her girlfriend or fuckmate of the week, and actually seems to genuinely give a shit about my existence. And I fuck it up."

"I thought she kissed you first…"

"*Obviously*, I did something wrong afterward." I scowled, shoving away from him and getting into bed properly. Marc crawled up next to me, dropped down on the pillow, and lay on his side to face me.

"It doesn't sound like it. She was the one who said she couldn't. For whatever reason—what is this?" He smacked his hand around the pillow then reached under it to pull out my pink vibrator. "Oh my God, *ew*."

"Marc." I punched him hard before I snatched it from him. "Asshole."

He laughed and pretended to freak out, making a gag face. "I touched something that was in your *vagina*."

"Marc!" I joined his laughter and rammed my fist into his shoulder again. "It doesn't go in my vagina. I'm a lesbian. It lives on my *clit*."

"Oh my God. I'm dying. I'm going to die from the images your terrible words are causing me. The horror." He continued his pretend gag, gasping and hacking afterward.

"Better knock it the fuck off before I flash you my real vagina. Which is a credible threat considering I'm naked under this towel and you're in my bed," I threatened and he stopped immediately.

"Wait...I've never seen one. Let me see." He rolled onto his stomach, grabbed my towel, and I freaked out immediately. Shrieks left me as I cracked up and beat him with a pillow.

"Get away from me, you psycho!"

His heavy laughter, deep and guttural, lifted my spirits exponentially. I smiled at him when he settled down, his arm draped over my middle almost protectively. "Made you grin," he said.

"Yeah, you did." I sighed, leaning my head on his shoulder. Quiet fell for a moment until I asked, "Have you really never seen a vagina?"

He chuckled, his body bouncing against mine. "Not up close. High school sex was a lot less looking, a lot more finding the hole."

"Ew."

"My sentiments exactly."

***

Four days passed before I received an, *I'm sorry*, message from Stella. My response, *What's going on, Stella?*

went unanswered.

"Lange, get in here," Walsh called out from his post in the conference room. I sighed, pocketing my phone that I'd checked for the tenth time today.

"What do you want?" I asked as soon as I stepped into the room. Ramos and her partner sat at the conference table. Walsh closed the door behind me, gesturing for me to sit. "What do *all* of you want?"

"Detective Lange, we'd like to talk to you about your run-in with Detective Butler," said the man beside Ramos. He folded his hands on top of a legal pad while looking at me from over his skinny, unusual glasses.

"My...run-in? He pushed me then threw me into a wall. Did you forget about that part?"

"This isn't an inquisition, Detective Lange." Ramos gestured for me to sit. Slowly, I did and glanced at Walsh who joined me. "Our concern is that if Detective Butler were to return to duty, how the two of you would get along."

"Return to *duty*?" My fingers dug into the table. "He's in jail for *rape* and *assault*, if you haven't forgotten."

"There is due process, Detective Lange. He hasn't been to trial yet and, considering the circumstances of the victim, there is the possibility he will be found not guilty," the other I.A. agent, whose name badge I could not read, said as he squeezed his hands together while speaking.

"Are you kidding me? From what I understand, his DNA was all over her, as was that of the other accused." My voice trembled with fury. "Not to mention the level of pain inflicted on that girl—her bashed up face, to name one."

"A drug-addicted teenage prostitute's word against his. Couple that with a jury of his peers, not hers, and the odds aren't good," Ramos admitted. "He'll get probation and suspended, but if he comes back—"

"Then I won't be here, Ramos. It's bad enough I've endured his sexual harassment for years, without complaint, mind you, because I know how to hang with the boys. But this?" I shook my head. "Is unacceptable."

My phone buzzed in my pocket and I ignored it the first time. But by the third, I pulled it out and saw Jordan's name on the screen and the missed call icon on top. "I need to take this. We're done here anyway." I stood, swiping the answer button and taking my leave without a glance back in their direction.

"Jordan, what's—"

"Allie." She seemed to breathe out my name. "You need to get to Wildrose now."

"What? I'm at work."

"I know. That's why you need to get here." Her voice cracked and she sniffled. "Please."

"Okay. I'm coming. Are you okay?"

"Yeah, but Kari isn't."

My heart skipped a beat. "Okay, Jord. I'll be right there."

"Okay."

Porter caught me by the elbow as I rushed toward the front entrance. I jerked my arm away and looked at him. "I'm coming with you," he said. "Patrol's just called."

"How bad is it?" I asked as we piled into his car.

"Not good."

With our sirens on—a rare thing these days—Porter swung through the busy, rain-laden streets. Neither of us spoke but the way Porter kept flickering his annoying, steely gaze, in my direction, pissed me off.

As we pulled up to the slew of marked cars with their lights flashing, the sight that was Wildrose flooded my senses. Across the brick face of the building, the spray painted, tagged words *fags* and *dykes* scarred the front of the formerly pretty, flower-filled welcome sign. I jumped out of the car, slammed the door, and raced up the steps only to find Jordan surrounded by a half-a-dozen uniformed officers. Between them, Kari, the owner and operator of the bar, stood wrapped in a blanket and leaning against Jordan.

"What happened?" My words tumbled out in a breathless gasp as I took in the damage. Every table, every chair destroyed. Homophobic slurs covered every inch of the walls, all the photos and band posters were now all over the place and the band equipment had holes or sat in a shambles on the floor. Liquor bottles and glass littered nearly every inch of the floor.

"My God," Porter said, moving around us as he covered his mouth.

"Allie," Kari called to me and as soon as I met her gaze, she started crying. I moved to her and she hugged me right away, the blanket tumbling from her shoulders to reveal the bruises that covered most of her torso, neck, and arms.

"I got you, Kar. Who did this?" I rubbed her back as cautiously as I could. Jordan's eyes welled with tears and I held an arm to her. She joined us in the embrace. "And you need to go to the hospital. You're bleeding, Kari."

"I wanted to see you first." She leaned back to look at me and I tucked her messy hair away from her face.

"I'm here."

"We should go to the hospital, Kar." Jordan gripped her hand and she nodded finally.

"Catch who did this, Allie. Please?" she begged, going with Jordan when she led her away.

"I will," I promised, tightening my resolve as I watched her go.

***

"How bad is it?" I asked Jordan hours later while we sat together in the waiting area of the emergency room. At this point, I might as well move in.

"She has broken ribs and a lot of bruises," she said, leaning her head on my shoulder. "Ainsley went back to talk to them."

"Must be useful dating a doctor in this situation." I wrapped my arm around her shoulders.

"Yeah." She sniffled, swiping at her nose with a tissue

while I stroked the purple streak in her hair. "Do you think they raped her, Allie?"

"I don't know. She didn't tell you?"

"No. She said she was in the back cleaning up after last night and they busted in. Two of them in masks. Definitely men." Jordan sat up straighter when Ainsley appeared, clad in full-on scrubs and a lab coat. She appeared markedly different and much more professional. She held her hands to Jordan who rose and took them immediately.

Seeing the two of them together strangled my heart and I couldn't help glancing around us for Stella. She hadn't made an appearance at all and, despite the circumstances, part of me believed she would.

"How is she?" I asked as Ainsley urged Jordan over to sit again. She fussed over her, smoothing her hair and touching her face gently.

"Recovering. She has multiple contusions and fractured ribs." Ainsley's soft voice did little to soothe me. Her face was even more frozen than Stella's in her most clinical moments.

"Did he...they, rape her?" Jordan asked her, her gaze fixed on Ainsley's.

"No, love. They didn't." She cupped Jordan's face. "Come on. I'll take you to see her."

"Okay." Jordan cried harder with relief as she stood with Ainsley who held her hand as she led her down the hall. My heart ached for my friend and for Kari—who once was more than a friend—and the place we called our safe haven.

I breathed out the air I'd held onto in order to fight my upset and checked my phone. Porter messaged me updates which right now included literally nothing. In my defiance, and anger, I approached the nurses' station, attempting to push away my pain with the ultimate distraction.

"Excuse me," I called out, and the young nurse at the desk turned around.

"Can I help you, Detective?" Her brow furrowed with

concern under her dark curls.

"Is Doctor Corwin here tonight?"

"Yes." She nodded, tapping something on the computer screen. "She's just finished with a patient and is probably in her office. Do you want me to page her?"

"No." I began, holding up my hand to stop her from lifting the phone. "But can I just go back there?"

"Sure. It's on this floor, end of the hall." She pointed to her left and offered me a polite nod.

"Thanks." I took a deep breath, and headed off in pursuit of the answers I had some power over at two in the morning.

On the door, *Stella Corwin, MD*, glared at me from its etching on the gold embossed plaque. I took a deep breath and knocked. The distinct sound of a drawer rolling shut emanated from inside the room before the doorknob turned. When the door opened, Stella's expression went from neutral to despair in a heartbeat. In her lab coat and scrubs, with a stethoscope around her neck, she was the epitome of presence and strength. It took my breath away.

"Alice."

"Surprised?" I smirked, folding my arms over my stomach. Without a jacket, my gear belt stuck out past my elbows.

"Partially yes, partially no. Did you get shot or thrown around again?" The corner of her mouth twitched as if threatening a smile.

"Not today. My friend's bar was vandalized by some gay-haters that roughed her up and I have zero leads on it so far. Also, you kicked me out of your house and haven't spoken to me since. It's been a bad few weeks." I let everything tumble out of my mouth without much hesitation.

"Kari's your friend?" She folded her arms, noticeably not offering me entry into her doctor cave.

"Yeah. And former girlfriend." I shrugged, meeting her gaze when she looked at me.

"I'm sorry." She looked at me, holding on longer than usual.

"Me too."

Finally, she stepped aside and gestured for me to enter. She closed the door behind me and made her way to the desk. Her body leaned against the large oval desk though she never dropped her arms from around her middle, a gesture of restraint and limits at the same time. In her perfectly manicured office, not a single item appeared out of place. Oak bookshelves, clean brownish carpets, and a leather sofa offered absolutely no insight into the fact that someone worked here or even existed. To me, it seemed like a catalogue-decorated, way-too-good-to-be-real setup.

"Look, Alice...I can't do this. I just can't."

"Do what, Stella? You keep saying you can't but what, exactly, can't you?" I stepped toward her, letting my arms drop to my sides. "You're the one who kissed me first."

"I know, I just—"

"Just what?" Exasperation tangled with the painful images of Kari and Wildrose. "Just what…" Emotion choked me, but it wasn't my eyes that cried tears.

Stella's face, frozen and unmoving, spoke nothing to the tear that trickled down her cheek. A silent, single tear that had her pushing away from me, her hands cupped over her mouth as she peered out the window that faced the darkness of the night.

"Stella…"

"Just leave, Alice. Okay? Just leave."

"Let me tell you something, *Doctor* Corwin." I stalked over to her, shoving my way between her and the window so that she was forced to face me. "No one in my life has ever been upfront with me. Has ever told me the truth. My parents and brothers kept me in the dark all the time because I was the youngest. My job treats me like I'm lesser-than because I'm a woman. My girlfriends cheated on me, one with men, mind you, and the one place in this entire city that I felt I could be safe at and be myself, has just been destroyed. You don't owe me anything, Stella, but the least you could do is tell me the truth about why kissing me makes you cry." My hands clenched to fists as I stood there, fighting the anger and rejection she brought me, and the sadness that lingered over the exposition of some of my deepest pains.

"God," she said, looking up at the ceiling before turning her attention to me. "It's not you, Alice."

"A few weeks ago, I would've believed you. But that doesn't make this any easier. Don't you understand that?"

"I do, I just." She covered her mouth again and turned toward the window. Her chest lifted with rapid breathing as she seemed to fight any sounds from making it to her throat. "You're the first woman I've kissed in *five* years." The soft-spoken admission barely made it to my ears. "Five years."

"Okay…" I turned around and leaned against the window sill, listening to her with my palms pressed together between my knees.

She sniffled, turning to look at me as she swiped at her eyes. "I can't do this here. I'm on shift until morning. I can't stand here and tell you everything and expect to function for the next six hours."

"All right," I said, nodding as a wave of fatigue pressed in on me. "I didn't come here to upset you." I rose again, adjusting the holster against my hip. "I'm going to visit with Kari then I'll leave."

Stella nodded, sucking in her breath as she walked me to the door. "I'm sorry."

"I know." Despite my better judgment, and the warning lights that screamed inside me, I reached out and squeezed her hand gently. "Bye."

Her fingers twitched in my hand before we parted ways. "Bye."

***

Kari left the hospital a few days later and in between working on catching the vandals, I spent most of my time down at Wildrose with Jordan and Ainsley, cleaning up the mess in shifts. Eve and her girlfriend, Ciara, joined us twice, but today, six women, who I recognized from the club but didn't know, helped us. Jordan and I worked behind the bar, sweeping up glass and scouring countertops while two others replaced the band equipment after clearing off the stage. Our only goal was to put the bar back together before Kari healed up enough to return to work. In her typical way, she was adamant about coming back. To further piss off the vandals, or community at large, we made sure to hang giant rainbow flags out front with a banner that read, *Under Reconstruction and Resisting Hate. Grand Reopening Coming Soon.*

Marc helped on the third day, painting over the graffiti on the outside of the building with the help of Gavin and Ciara, who turned out to be quite the artist. After the initial base coats, she painted a mural of a rose so intricate and unique, it presented as photorealistic. It took my breath away when I arrived Saturday morning.

"It's incredible. Kari is going to love it," I said, smiling at Marc when he hopped down from the ladder.

"She will. Ciara's really talented," he said.

I folded my arms, taking in the sight with a surge of pride racing up my spine. The flags, the flower, everything.

"I admire you showing up to help, Allie." Marc wrapped his sweaty arm around my shoulders. "For Kari."

"Yeah, well, lesbians and being friends with your exes and such." I waved him off with a smirk.

"Yeah, but she cheated on you like three times. That changes things," he said, tugging a strand of my hair.

"I know. She still didn't deserve this. No one does."

"Are you annoyed that Jackson won't let you on this case?"

"He won't let me on any case right now." I shrugged, shifting my weight to step away from him.

"What did you do now?" He laughed, his hands on my shoulders.

"Lost my shit with I.A. Nothing new." I made to continue telling him but my phone buzzed in my pocket. Tugging it out revealed Stella's name. I turned it to show Marc before answering.

"Hi."

"Hey…" Awkward pause. "I was wondering if you were busy."

"I can be unbusy. What's going on?"

"I owe you a conversation," she said, her voice soft.

"Okay…"

"Can you come over?"

"Yeah. I'll be there in half an hour."

"See you then."

"See you."

"Well?" Marc lifted both eyebrows.

"I'm going to talk to her." I pocketed my phone, and let out a long-drawn breath.

"At least you'll talk to somebody because you haven't said a word to me, a real word, in weeks. And I suspect you haven't said a real word to anyone at all." Finally, the truth poured from his lips.

"I'm sorry." I shoved my hands into the pockets of my jeans. "I just…"

"I know, Allie." He gripped my shoulder again.

"See you."

"Later." He kissed my cheek and I took my leave.

The walk to Stella's apartment was longer than I thought and, in typical fashion, half an hour turned into almost an hour by the time I knocked on her door. When she pulled it open, the sight of her, as usual, left me aching for breath. Leave it to me to fall for someone who wasn't willing to fall back. I suppose it's better than falling for someone who would cheat on me. Honestly, I didn't know anything at all.

My gaze wandered over her in sweeping appraisal of her leggings, fluffy socks, and long tunic. It wasn't the outfit that killed me, but that hair, in soft, loose tendrils that moved like feathers on a breeze whenever she turned her head. "Hey," I managed to muster up.

"Hi," she said, her lips curling into a soft smile. "Come in."

I followed her, like a lost puppy aching for a treat. A sweet, floral scent met my nose as soon as I entered the living room and, the strength of it told me she'd recently spritzed perfume. Instead of sitting on the sofa, she brought me to the dining room table off the side of the kitchen and we sat at the sleek black granite table together.

"Can I get you tea or coffee or something?" she asked, gesturing to the kitchen.

"I'm okay. I'd rather just...hear what you have to say." Honesty dripped from my lips and she looked at me, sapphires pouring into mine.

Before she even spoke, shimmers of emotion twinkled in her gaze and she tucked her hair behind her ears. "I don't know where to start."

"Why not start with 'you're the first woman I've kissed in five years.'" I leaned my elbows on the table, folding my arms on top of one another. With nothing to fiddle with, I had no distractions to help subdue my feelings.

"Yeah." She laughed a little and again, she brushed her hair behind her ears. It made me smile, noting her nervous habit. "What?"

"You put your hair back when you're anxious," I said, nodding in her direction.

"I do not." She did it again.

I laughed hard, thumping the table gently. "You just did."

"Alice! It's not funny." Her laugh only egged me on more. "Maybe a little…"

"A smidge." I nodded and she swatted my hand.

Her eyes twinkled and, the moment she relaxed into it, her laughter faded. "Sorry."

"Don't be. Just tell me…"

"Okay." She glanced away, her gaze falling on the fire

flickering in the hearth as she rested her chin on her hand. I waited, impatiently, but I waited until she was ready. She turned back to me finally, again, her eyes shimmering like crystals in the sun. Her expression dimmed and so did the light.

When I realized how much pain this caused her, it slowed my need and allowed me the peace of mind to open to her experience. "Take your time, Stella."

She took a deep breath, and again with the hair. "Ten years ago, when I was in medical school, I met this girl." She smiled when her attention shifted to my left as the memories seemed to fall over her, replacing her pained face with smoothed features of contentment. "She was beautiful, and strong, and courageous. And a teacher in one of the middle schools in central Seattle." She paused, staring down at her hands. "Does hearing this bother you?"

"No. It's important to you," I told her, watching as she squeezed her hands together tightly. "And I asked to know."

"Okay." She sniffled a bit. "Her name was Clarissa. Like from that television show from the nineties. Do you remember?"

"No." I laughed a little. "I was like two in the nineties. So were you."

"Reruns." Her chuckle lifted the mood only a fraction. "But I digress. Her name was Clarissa and I fell for her, and her me. And we spent four amazing years together until the day she proposed to me on the same day I was hired on full-time at UW Medical." Tears brimmed her eyes and she swiped one that tumbled down her cheek. "I was so happy that day, Alice."

My heart simultaneously broke and soared for Stella, for something called happiness. I watched as it lingered in her gaze, on her lips, on the way her cheeks lifted when she smiled. Wasn't that what we hoped for in life every day? "Did you break up?"

"No." Her smile morphed into something more twisted, sinister almost as she fought whatever else tortured her. "We spent the next year planning our wedding. Who we would invite, where we'd have it. On the beach and we'd take an Alaskan cruise for our honeymoon." More tears tumbled down her cheeks. "On her birthday, I reverse proposed to her and we had matching engagement rings. It took the jeweler two months to recreate what she'd done for me. And of course, she accepted." She dropped her head in her hands and choked on a sob. Only then did I reach across the table to offer her my hand, our angled seating making it easier. It took her a moment but she took it, and I squeezed hers gently.

I waited quietly until she stilled herself enough to continue. "It was the best year, planning all of that. And then one morning, I woke up to breakfast she'd made. School was on break and I was so overwhelmed studying for my boards." Again, she tucked her hair behind her ear with one hand but allowed me to hold on to the other. Her left hand, which no longer bore the ring she talked about. "But she always made time for small things like that."

"Sounds like it was a big thing," I said softly, to which she nodded.

"Yeah," she said, sniffling as she took a deep breath. "We had breakfast, and made love, then I went to work after she dropped me off. I remember…" She paused, her voice catching in her throat. "I remember the way her lips felt against mine in that car. I remember that every day and sometimes in my dreams." She dropped my hand and covered her mouth as a heavier sob caught her. Her eyes, wide and filled with panic as she looked at me.

My stomach lurched as worry for her struck me like a jolt of icy water. "It's okay, Stella." I held both hands to her this time. "It's okay."

"I haven't told anyone this, Alice. I mean, my family knew, but I haven't ever." She grabbed my hands as if desperate for an anchor.

"You don't have to—"

"I do. My God, I do." Her desperate cries broke my heart and I moved from my chair to kneel in front of her. Hot, horrible tears brought pressure to my eyelids, but I fought their tumble.

"Okay. Okay. Look at me," I beckoned and she did. "What happened?"

"She died." Her cries tore me apart but I stayed there, holding her hands while I let her pour out her memories. "I didn't know it was her."

"What do you mean?"

Her bottom lip trembled and I watched the strong, confident doctor that I'd known only a month or so crumble in front of me. "We said goodbye and she left. I worked a double and on my second shift, we got a call that a trauma case was coming in, motor vehicle. Head trauma. They rushed them in, four people, one child. I worked on them all. Two were D.O.A. and one, the adult female, we didn't know who she was, Alice. There was so much blood, all over her face, and glass." Her voice was barely a whisper. "Until I saw her ring. Her *ring*! I just started screaming. So loud and I couldn't help her." She fell forward now, tumbling toward me. "I couldn't help her, Alice. And she died with my hands covered in her blood."

I caught her before she hit the floor. "I'm sorry, Stella. I'm so sorry. I'm sorry for making you tell me this." My tears were a beat behind hers as I wrapped my arms around her shoulders. "I'm sorry Clarissa died."

"I can't do this," she repeated her mantra of days ago. Cries wracked her body as she dropped her head on her knees, her hands held out in front of her as if she'd just touched something horrible or contagious. "I *can't*."

"Okay, you don't have to do anything. I'm sorry." My apologies tangled with a sob of my own as I held her frozen body against my chest. "I'm so sorry."

A deep, primal scream left her and finally, she dropped

against me, her face hidden on my shoulder as I cupped her head against my chest.

What have I done? What have I done…

CHAPTER SEVEN

I watched as Stella slept, or passed out, I wasn't sure, for a few hours after she told me what happened to her fiancée. Knowing the pain it caused her to recount it, and the fact that she recounted it for me, both destroyed me and worried me at the same time. Tucked in her bed, curled up on her side with the blankets to her shoulders, she rested peacefully it seemed. I kept an eye on her from my perch in the armchair beside the nightstand.

Occasionally, I'd wipe a stray tear from my face as I was forced to face everything the last few weeks had brought. First, getting shot, then Butler raping that girl, then Stella, then getting assaulted by said rapist, then Wildrose, now this. It was so much and I never felt more alone in my life, and it made me wonder just how alone Stella truly was. I might've felt alone, but I wasn't. I had my family, and Marc, and Jordan. She had a father in an assisted living home. I never bothered to ask about her mother.

Stella stirred, her lashes fluttering when her eyes peeked open. It took her a moment to orient herself and, when her gaze fell on me, she stilled and a single tear trickled down her cheek onto the pillow. I moved from my chair to kneel at the side of the bed and, without thinking much about it, ran my fingers through her hair. She let me and closed her eyes. Her fingers tangled with the cuff of my jacket, holding me in place in front of her. I listened to her soft breaths and occasional sniffle.

"I'm sorry," I whispered, resting my chin on my arm. She opened her eyes, searching my face before grabbing a fistful of my hair that hung between us, again, holding me in place.

"You're the last person I kissed now. Not Clarissa."

"I know. I'm sorry, Stella. I didn't mean to… to erase her." It killed me to say it, but I did.

"You didn't." Her hand fell to my cheek as she watched me for a minute, her gaze darting all over until she rolled on to her back to look out the window where daylight began to fade.

"I'm so sorry," I confessed again, as terrible guilt still weighed in on me like wilted grave moss after a heavy rain.

"It's not your fault," she whispered, her lips pursing after.

"It's not yours either, Stella. You weren't driving either car."

"The other guy, he was drunk with his two kids in the car. Killed Clarissa, himself, and his oldest son. The younger child survived."

"You saved him?"

She nodded. "But not her."

"Something tells me she was beyond saving then…"

Again, she nodded, pressing her lips together even tighter before speaking. "Her skull was crushed."

"I'm sorry you're plagued by these images and that someone you loved so much was taken from you. I can't imagine what that must feel like, or how badly you're still grieving."

"I never stopped grieving."

"I know—"

"Until I met you." She turned back to look at me now. "And you made me smile with your snarky comments, and *stupid* ice cream mixing." Despite her tears, her laugh made me smile. "And your proclivity for nearly-mortal wounds—"

"Hey." I chuckled, reaching over and brushing away the tears that gathered at her jaw line. "Those were *accidents*."

"And how you're late to everything—"

"Not everything—"

"*Everything*." She smiled at me now, a genuine one. "And your brown eyes that don't match your blonde-ish hair at all."

"It's just highlights."

"You're blonde like that towheaded brother of yours."

"You flatter me now, Stella." I laughed harder, though it only brought more tears down my cheeks.

"And how you cry for me." This time, she reached over and wiped my cheek with her thumb. "Because they certainly aren't tears for you. Not in public anyway."

"Maybe they are."

"Not today."

We grew quiet after a while, both of us calming away from our crying to the vacancy of release that followed. By the time darkness settled around us, Stella scooted over and patted the bed beside her. I climbed up, letting my boots hang off the edge as I lay on my side facing her. She made to put her hand on my waist but paused when she hit my gear belt.

"Gun," she said, simply.

"Sorry. Hazards of inviting cops into your bed." I released the holster and set it on the nightstand. Her silence scored me as she stared at my belt way too long.

"I couldn't take it if you got hurt at work. I couldn't."

"Well...if I.A. has it their way, that worry won't exist much longer."

"Why?" Her brow furrowed now.

"Because I pitched a fit over the possibility of Butler returning to work if he's found not guilty and honestly, I don't even care. I don't care about anything anymore. Can't do a job like mine without caring."

"You care, Alice. Or you wouldn't be bothered by it," she said, reaching to touch my face again, but she stopped halfway there. Though the giveaway of her intention lay in the way she bit her bottom lip for the briefest second.

"You can...I mean, if you want to."

"Can what?" She shifted her weight until she was fully on her side again, facing me with her head resting on the pillow beside mine.

"Touch me. You stopped yourself twice now."

Silence found her for a moment, until she tentatively draped her hand over my middle. No movement followed, but she left it there for the time being. "I miss her…"

"I know."

"How can I like you so much when I miss her?"

"I'm not sure but I like you, too."

"Why? I'm a mess." Tears welled in her eyes again, though she swallowed them away.

"I'd be more worried if you weren't in this circumstance. And generally, you're not a mess. You're amazing, and funny, and flirty, and you don't even know it."

"I am not—"

I laughed softly. "Yes, you are. It's all in your eyes. The way you look at me while doing little things like sipping coffee or licking ice cream from a spoon. You don't even know you're doing it."

"What do I do?" She cocked a brow at me and it made me grin as her usual self peeked through the grief toward playfulness again.

"Your biggest tell? When you bite your lip every time you're trying not to do something like stare at my tits, or touch me, or kiss me. Because you like looking at my mouth."

"Alice! I *don't* do those things at *all*." The laugh that left her made my insides leap with excitement and joy.

"Yeah." The word tangled on a chuckle. "You do."

"I don't know if I'll ever stop feeling like I'm cheating on her…" Seriousness broke our reverie. "I don't know if it'll ever go away."

"You can always ask her." I shrugged, glancing around us. "See if she answers you."

"Ask her?" She scoffed. "How?"

"I dunno. Do you pray or anything?"

"I'm an atheist. So...no."

"So you believe that when people die, they just die and that's it? No messages or signs or anything?"

She quieted again after my questions, though her fingers on my waist moved slightly in a thoughtless caress. "After my mom died…" She shrugged. "I never got any signs or messages either."

"What's your dad think?"

"He's a bigger atheist than me. Science proves existence and that's it."

"Well, I like to believe in everything equally. One of them has to be right." I shrugged. "Or more than one, and I think that if Clarissa had something to tell you, she would find a way. Because our loved ones can't ever really leave us, not as long as we remember them. Know how I know?"

"Not a clue…"

"Dreams. Has she ever been in your dreams?"

"All the time. But she's usually dying in them." Her fingers tensed, digging into me a little. I stroked her forearm gently and it seemed to surprise her enough to relax again.

"Maybe now that you shared her story, your dreams will change. You never know."

"I guess not." She smiled a little. "You're a weirdo."

I laughed hard at the non-insult insult. "At least we agree on that."

"Alice?"

"Hmm?"

"Thanks." She offered me a soft smile and, although it

made it to her eyes, lifting the corners of them, sadness still tainted them with a darkness I would never understand but now, at least I knew why.

***

If I order pizza, will you eat it? I texted Stella a few days later. We'd shared a few messages in between our work shifts, but her three-day stint covering someone else's job kept our connections brief.

Will there be wine? she replied.

It can be arranged...and I even cleaned up. A little.

Deal.

"Did you bleach the bathroom?" Marc walked into the living room, his hair dripping wet, with a toothbrush hanging out of his mouth.

"Yes. Don't make a mess!" I pointed at him, then waved him off toward the bathroom.

"Did you change your sheets, too?" He scurried away from me, laughing as I slapped his naked shoulder. "Ow!"

"Shut up and yes."

"Ohhh, your pretty doctor is coming over, isn't she?"

"Are you going to Gavin's or what?" I huffed at him and pointed at the toilet seat that was not as clean as I left it half an hour ago. "Clean that. Why do men pee on seats?"

"Because it jiggles!"

"Gross!" I slammed the door in his laughing face.

Stella arrived a few hours later, exactly ten minutes after the pizza arrived, which in my book was perfect timing. Wet hair tickled the shoulders of her freshly laundered set of scrubs but she shivered a little as she hurried inside. "It's so cold."

"Because your hair is wet. You could've showered here. I cleaned the man-gook out of the drain."

She laughed, allowing me to take her coat and hang it on the hook beside the door. "Thanks. No idea how you live with a guy."

"Please. I have no idea how he lives with me. Pizza is

already here." I waved her inside and she obliged.

"I'm starving. I have no idea if I ate today."

"No wonder doctors are so healthy."

We sat together on the sofa while Stella plated us slices and I poured the wine. I handed her a glass and she slid a dish to me.

Over the next few weeks, this became a comfortable habit. Every few days, we'd get together for a meal and drinks while just talking. I'd avoided work, save for finishing up a few reports and poking around the notes Jackson and Porter had on the Wildrose vandalism case. By the third week, Stella invited me to her house for dinner that she'd cooked and I brought over a bottle of her favorite red. If anything, she'd become a fast friend, but it didn't stop me from melting every time she looked at me, or stealing a glance at her curves when she wasn't looking.

By the time we sat down to a dinner of roasted veggies coupled with a delectable pasta dish made with sausage and peppers, we were already a glass in. I poured out our second glasses and watched as she smiled around the forkful of her most recent bite. She nodded her thanks and I sat back, crossing my legs as I dug into the rest of my dinner.

"This is amazing," I told her. "In case I haven't mentioned it."

"You did and thank you. I don't cook much for other people except when I'm bringing something to my dad."

"How is he?"

"Good. Crowned poker champ by his buddies. He never liked poker before. I think it gives him a forum to preach about neuroscience to a willing audience."

"Neuroscience?" My brows flicked upward when my mind's eye envisioned elderly sophisticated neuroscientists playing poker.

"Yeah." She smiled fondly as she thought of him. "Of all the things Alzheimer's stole from him, it never touched his sciences and most of the time he knows me immediately. Only once did he say how old I look."

"You're not old," I said, chuckling softly.

"To him I am. He expects me to be twenty but when I show up almost thirty-seven, it shocks him. He gets over it. He still has most of his wits about him. Taking care of his basic needs was always the hardest," she told me. "I'd get calls from the police that he was wandering down the road half naked in the snow, pretending to lecture an invisible class on something." She shook her head. "That's when I knew I couldn't take care of him by myself."

"I'm sorry you had to make that decision alone. Is he very elderly?"

"Eighties, so not very. How old are your parents?"

"Younger. Sixties, but young sixties. You'd never know it. My dad's a veteran who lost his right leg in Afghanistan. He works at the V.A. now. My other brother, Ryan, is also a veteran of the same war. Mom always stayed at home with us while Dad was deployed but she volunteers at a lot of places," I said, smirking as I vomited some random family facts to her.

"They sound like an interesting bunch."

"You have no idea. They're absolute chaos. My house growing up was never quiet. And if you think about my invitation to come for Christmas dinner, you'd get to meet this wild and wacky crew."

"I'll think about it," she said, setting her fork down against her empty plate.

"That's what you said about Thanksgiving and ended up hiding here all alone." I cocked a brow at her and nudged her with my foot under the table. She laughed a little.

"Well, to be fair, I didn't know you as well then." Her fingers met my arm in a gentle swat.

"Think about it for real then."

"I will."

We cleaned up our mess together, and I loaded the dishwasher while she took care of the large pot in the sink.

When we were done, our routine then was to take our wine to the living room. It was second nature at this point, as was choosing a movie to end the evening. Since the day she told me about Clarissa, I'd let her lead and didn't force anything on her. Her insurmountable grief needed time and, though my feelings for her hadn't changed other than growing exponentially, we didn't talk about our relationship. And I didn't ask her how she felt about me either.

Half way through the drama-filled psychological thriller, I caught her looking at me instead of the screen. She stood suddenly, nodding to the kitchen. "Need ice. Want some?"

"I'm good, thanks." I watched as she rose from her spot beside me on the sofa, then turned my attention back to the movie. Clinking of ice against glass echoed in the background.

Stella returned to sit beside me, a little bit closer than before, and I fought the urge to glance at her when something tickled the back of my neck. For a moment, I stayed still until the sensation of fingers through my hair grew clearer. Shivers raced down my spine, turning my skin to gooseflesh in a heartbeat. I let her do it, not drawing attention to the gentle caresses until her fingernails grazed the sensitive part of my neck. The shivers turned to shudders, setting off an ache in my core that had only been a mild want until then. Cautiously, I looked at her, and she smiled. This time, the gesture met her eyes and she ran the knuckle of her index finger over my cheek.

"Hey," I whispered. Her chuckle made me smile.

"Hello." Her return was just as quiet.

Gentle fingers tucked my hair behind my ear and I leaned into her touch as delicately as possible, until my lips met the inside of her wrist in a clandestine kiss. It didn't scare her away yet, and I let myself enjoy it for the time being. When her palm flattened against my cheek, I met her gaze again until she caressed my hair from root to tip.

My bottom lip found its way between my teeth and I shuddered. "Like that?" she asked, her tone barely audible.

"Yes," I confessed, gnawing my lip to keep a cap on my reactions. Her hand tumbled down my body, tickling my neck to the place where my blouse buttoned over my breasts. I watched as her eyes followed along with her tentative touches until she flattened her palm against my stomach.

Only then did any harsher movement erupt from her. She moved toward me, her arm sliding across my middle until she rested against me with her head falling to my shoulder. Without hesitating, I wrapped my arm around her, and nuzzled her forehead with my chin.

As if nothing happened, we returned to watching the movie. Or not watching the movie, in my case, as I listened to each soft intake of breath and the exhale that followed as her body rose and fell against mine. I let my hand fall to rest on her forearm and, although I feared her recoil, she didn't at all.

We stayed that way for the rest of the movie until the credits rolled to darkness and we were left with only the light from the smoldering fire in the hearth. Stella leaned back to look at me and we smiled at the same time. When she broke away, the cold left in her place made me want to pout, but I didn't have a chance to. Fragrant perfume lingered in the space between us until she moved closer, her knee edging against my hip as she cupped my face in her hands. I stroked her arms, allowing her to do whatever the fuck she wanted at this point. And what followed was well worth the wait.

Like last time, she initiated the ease into a kiss that left my lips burning against hers. Sweetness from the wine lingered on her breath as I reached up to stroke her cheek. She leaned me backward until I'd fallen against the cushions of the sofa, with her knee between my legs. Part of me ached so badly to touch her in other places but I didn't, sticking strictly to above the neck. I ran my fingers through her hair as my insides burned like embers sparked from flint and tinder that belonged only to her.

When she finally pulled back, her gaze lingered on mine as she stroked both of my cheeks with her thumbs. She smiled, though a single tear fell from her and landed on my chin. "Tell me what you want, Stella. And...I'll try." I reached up, brushing away the remaining dampness on her face.

"What I want…" She laughed a little, still touching my face and hair as more tears tumbled away.

"Just tell me." I stroked her arms gently.

"I fucking want to see you naked. Completely *naked* in front of me. And it destroys me that I want that so badly." She spat out her words and dropped her forehead against mine. I pulled her into a hug which she didn't rile against, returning the gesture with a firm resolve.

"That's very forward of you," I teased, against her ear. "I'm not sure I can handle such an intense request." Her laugh, genuine but soft, had me chuckling when she leaned back to look at me again. "Is that really what you want?"

She nodded. "To kiss you and see you naked."

I broke away from her and stood up as she melted back against the sofa, almost flinching as if expecting me to leave. Instead, I unbuttoned my blouse and let it fall off my shoulders in a fluttering heap at my feet. Her eyes lingered on my chest as her fingers dug into the sofa beside her. My bra landed beside my shirt and there it was, her bottom lip between her teeth at the same time that she tucked her hair behind her ears. It made me smile and egged me on to continue. I reached behind my back and pulled my side arm out from the back of my pants, then set it and the holster on the table. She laughed softly and I wagged my brows at her as I released the button of my jeans. "Still want the same things?" I asked, hesitating a little. But her nod told me there wasn't a need. I tucked my thumbs into the waist of my pants, hooking my panties as well as I tugged them down and stepped out of them, leaving only my socks.

Stella looked at me as if seeing me for the first time, or seeing anything for the first time. With shortened breaths, wider eyes, and want twisting her features, I moved closer to her and she held her hands out to me. My fingers laced with hers as she guided me to straddle her lap. Her fingers squeezed mine as her gaze flickered all over my torso to start.

"How many scars do you have?" she asked, quietly.

"Not sure. Going to count them?" I laughed and she squeezed my hands tighter.

"No." Her legs under me relaxed a bit as her eyes wandered from my neck down to my nether region then back up again. "Tattoos?"

"One." I bent my leg up to show her the Venus tattoo on my ankle. "Typical lesbian ink. You?"

"None for me." Again, her fingers squeezed mine as if afraid to fall off the edge of something. "You're beautiful, Alice."

"You're just saying that because you like naked girls." I rolled my eyes dramatically and she laughed, leaning forward to nudge my forehead with hers.

"I do. And I like you."

"I like you, too." I sighed softly, though I became acutely aware of how this position aroused me, and that there was a strong possibility she'd notice soon enough. Her lips brushed mine again, and we shared several small kisses until she finally let go of my hands to cup my face again. I stroked her hair, tucking it behind her ears and, when she made to move her hands downward, she stopped at my shoulders. "You can," I whispered. "If you want to."

She nodded but it only brought more tears to her glimmering eyes. Instead of allowing her to lead, this time I pulled her into a hug. After a moment's hesitation, she wrapped her arms around me and cried openly while I rubbed her back. Her fingers dug into me and, she melted with me, in a heap of pain and despair.

***

Stella's alarm woke us up the next morning and she rolled over to turn it off. My body ached, not from an uncomfortable bed or position, but from the desires I'd spent the evening suppressing. She turned over, sliding her hand over my naked stomach between the sheets. Her body pressed against me, warm and soft from sleep.

"Morning," she said, her voice a groggy mess as she rested her chin on my arm.

"Five in the morning?" I groaned softly as her hand slid lower when she stretched. "Doctor hours suck. And good morning."

Stella laughed softly, her breath puffing against my neck. I wrapped my arm around her and she settled against me, both of us growing quiet. As we watched the sun slowly rise from behind the cityscape, I toyed with tendrils of her hair while thinking about the past twenty-four hours. I'd never been in a relationship like this, or whatever this ambiguous thing was that had me naked in a woman's bed, without having had sex.

"What are you thinking about?" she asked me and I looked back at her.

"Did you live here with Clarissa?" The question left me before I could stop myself.

Stella shook her head, though her body didn't tense. "No. We had a house just outside the city together."

"Still have it?"

"No." She smirked and caressed my stomach faintly. "After she died, I left it and everything in it. My dad sold it for me and…" A shrug lifted her shoulders. "That's it."

"Stella, you don't have a single picture of her in this whole apartment. She was the love of your life."

Her eyes trained on mine, but she didn't speak for a while until she said, "It's easier this way."

"Avoiding it?"

"Is this a normal conversation to be having with you

while you're naked in my bed?" she asked, her voice cracking a little.

"For people who care about each other to have?" I nodded, reaching over and stroking her cheek. "Yeah. Have you ever talked about it before?"

"Only to you."

Again, silence fell and we just held each other for awhile. It was the alarm on my phone that interrupted our reverie an hour later.

"Today is evil," I said, and Stella chuckled softly as I swiped the alarm off, letting my arm flop back onto the bed. "We should get up."

"I'm already late," she said, moving slowly and pulling the blankets back. She let her hand wander down the center of my body, stopping barely an inch above my clit.

"Dangerous territory." I sucked in my breath, gnawing the shit out of my lip.

"What?" She glanced down and started once she realized where she was. "Sorry." Her brows flicked upward while she looked down at me. "That laceration healed horribly. It's still purple."

"Where?" I leaned up on my elbows as she poked around the spot she'd bandaged several weeks ago. "Oh. I'll deal. One more for the collection."

"Stop that. Don't collect scars." She held her hand to me and I took it before she pulled me into a hug.

"I'll collect stamps in my next life." I returned her embrace and swatted her knee. "Off to work with you."

Stella and I took an Uber together downtown. I exited with her at the hospital, catching her elbow before we parted. "You good?" I asked and she nodded, though the look on her face told me otherwise.

"Call me later?"

"Of course," I said, and she hugged me again suddenly. I rubbed her back and she melted against me for a second before breaking away.

"Bye, Allie."

I smiled when she used to my nickname. "Bye."

***

Pleasure coursed through me, curling my toes as I moaned into my pillow, nearly biting at it. My orgasm peaked, pushing me over the edge as I tried really hard not to make a sound. I imagined her hand, slipping lower, caressing me in just the right—

"It's been *two* days since you've talked to me." Marc's voice bellowed from outside my bedroom door, startling me as he knocked on it loudly. I dropped the toy that I'd been playing with and it hit the floor with a loud thunk, bouncing around across the wood loud enough to wake the dead. The door flung open and I yanked the blanket over me.

"Marc!"

"What was that?"

"Nothing. Get out!"

He stared at the vibrator on the floor, then looked at me. "Gross."

"Marc!" I laughed away my embarrassment, covering my face as I flopped into the pillows. "I hate you. Go away."

"Shut that thing off." He cracked up, snatching it off the floor then threatening me with it. "Open up, Allie."

"Marc!" I beat him with a pillow and he finally dropped it on the bed. It took me half a second to snatch it up and turn it off. "Asshole. You could wait for a confirmation to enter after a knock."

"Are you naked from the waist down?" He grabbed the blanket and pretended to tug it away.

"Stop that!" I kicked at him, but he kept on laughing.

"Okay okay." He grinned as he pounced on the bed beside me. "Did I interrupt your big *O*, Allie?"

"No." I huffed, tucking the covers around my middle. "You interrupted my second one."

"Kinky." He snickered and I punched his arm. "Doctor Hotpants got your pussy all bent out of shape?"

"I spent the night in her bed, completely naked while she lay next to me totally clothed. Do you know what that did to me?"

"Made you a horny bastard?"

"Yes." I whined and pulled the blanket over my head. His laughter continued on and my urge to beat him up grew.

"Where is said hot doctor?"

"Still at work."

"Allie, you've been so quiet. For weeks now. What's going on?" Marc rested his head on his hand as he watched me. "Is it Doctor Corwin?"

"Partly her, partly work. I hate my job, Marc. I hate what it's become. But I really like Stella." A sigh left me as I covered my face. "And I know she likes me, but she's afraid."

"Why?"

I debated on whether or not to tell him about Clarissa, deciding on taking a less detailed route. "A long time ago, her fiancée was killed in a car accident. She loved her a lot and I think she's scared of letting someone in."

"Well...she sounds like you then." Marc shrugged, sighing heavily. "Not trusting anyone because of how they might hurt you. Not that different. What are you going to do about work?"

"I don't know. I can't even think about it right now. What are they doing about Butler?"

"He's still in jail. Trial starts next week, but..." Again, another shrug. "Who knows, really. Trials can go either way. His fancy attorney versus her legal aid one. His good word versus her bad reputation. It doesn't look good, Allie, which is why I.A. warned you about his possible return."

"I know. But Marc, I've been really considering leaving. I could do something else. Work for the youth center or something. Security. I don't know." I groaned, covering my face with my hands. "Honestly, that pales in comparison to my thoughts about Stella though. She's so afraid."

"Well, make her unafraid. Show her you're worth taking a risk for." He leaned over and yanked my arms away. "More importantly, show her she's worth your risk, too."

***

Stella's work shift seemed endless so instead of waiting patiently, I picked up two cups of coffee from Allegro, and showed up at the hospital at ten o'clock at night.

"Is Stel—Doctor Corwin around?" I asked the same red-headed nurse as last time.

"Hi, Detective. She's right over there, but with a patient." The nurse pointed to a curtain-drawn bed. "She'll be done soon."

"Great. I'll wait." I hopped up to sit on the countertop and the nurse laughed when I sipped my coffee. My brow cocked in her direction. "What?"

"Nothing. But something tells me you're the reason she's been smiling this week." With a tap of the charts on the counter, she spun away from me with a cheeky grin.

I waited less than ten minutes while listening to Stella's cautious doctor voice talk to someone about a wrist fracture. The curtain hid her from my view, but I imagined her controlled expression, clinical smile. Even in that light, she was amazing.

Finally, she came into view, holding a paper chart and scribbling something down as she walked toward the nurses' station. Like the typical nerd that she probably was, she didn't look up while she wrote. "Call up to the O.R., please. She's going to need surgery on that compound fracture," she said.

"And what, exactly is an O.R., Doctor Corwin?" A grin melted over my lips when I said it, but the way she started cooled it some.

"Alice." She dropped the chart and pen with a clatter on the counter. "Are you okay?" With wide eyes, her hands fell to my knees.

"Easy there, Stell. I just brought you coffee." I lifted the second cup from the counter and offered it to her. "I'm fine." She took the cup and set it down at my hip as her lips pressed together to a thin line. "Hey." I gripped her hair after caressing it and she nodded faintly.

"I know. I know you're okay." She placed her hand over mine and offered me a smile. "Thank you for the coffee. I'm about to pass out."

"Busy night?"

"It was earlier, but sometimes slow makes me more tired." The coffee found its way to her lips and she took a deep pull. "Mmm. Latte."

I laughed softly, swinging my legs a little to brush my feet against her knees. "Just how you like."

"I like a few things." She smiled at me from over the cup, swaying a little as she leaned her stomach against my legs.

"Yeah?"

"*Ahem*." Someone cleared their throat and Stella jumped. We both turned to see a gaggle of nurses watching us. "Doctor Corwin, we'll need you to sign off on these charts before the end of your shift." The redhead, whose name I could read from her badge now that I paid attention, smiled wickedly.

"Um...yeah. I'll, uh, take them to my office until we have another arrival," she said, holding out her arms for the stack. "Thanks, Kylie."

"Uh huh." She smiled, turning away from us, but the others faded in a slew of murmurs.

"I think we're distracting them from their job, Doctor," I said, muttering as Stella stepped away from me. She picked up her coffee, then nodded for me to follow her.

"I could use your help in my office, Detective Lange."

"Well, good thing I showed up then."

Once tucked away in her way-too-neat-to-be-real office, she set the files down and settled into the chair behind her desk, taking yet another long draw on her latte. I flopped down in one of the chairs opposite the desk, and propped my feet up, crossing my legs at the ankles.

"So, Doctor Corwin, do all of your colleagues know about your lesbianism? Or was their ridiculous ogling a part of a covert operation to unhinge my confident exterior?" I teased, leaning my cup on my knee.

Stella laughed, her eyes twinkling when she looked at me. "They know. Most of them knew Clarissa."

"And so their teasing of the two of us means…what?"

"It means...they know of your lesbianism, too," she said, her face serious until her lip twitched.

I laughed hard and lifted my cup to salute her. "Cheers to that." We both sipped at the same time. "Sorry I scared you when I showed up."

"It's okay. History tells me that when you're here, you're hurt."

"I'll have to show up randomly more often," I promised.

"I'd like that." Quiet fell around us for a moment until she spoke again. "I also liked when you stayed over the other night."

"Me too." I dropped my feet and set my coffee on the desk. "Come here, Stella."

"Why?" She didn't fight it despite her question, and rose to join me. I took her hand and guided her to sit in my lap. When she did, her body tensed a little and, almost immediately, her glassy eyes told me of the tears that would follow.

"No reason." I kept a hold of her hand. "Have dinner with me tomorrow night?"

"At mine?"

"No." I dragged my thumb over her knuckles. "At a restaurant."

That did it. Every inch of her tensed and her mouth fell open with surprise. I squeezed her hand, and she shook her head a little. "Like...a date?"

"Or just dinner. Whatever you want it to be, Stell."

"Tomorrow?" Dimness faded from her gaze when she smiled a little bit nervously.

I chuckled. "Yeah. Just dinner. I'll pick you up and we'll go to dinner. What do you think?"

"Okay." She nodded, and I watched as her eyes shimmered again. I held my arms to her and, slowly, she leaned in to hug me. We'd gotten a handle on hugging so far and hair touching. That was better than running away and crying at least.

"Good. What time do you get off tonight?"

She tucked her hair behind her ears and I tried to hide my smile at seeing her little anxious habit resurface. "Midnight."

"Yuck."

"I know. But then I'm done for the week. Three twelve-hour shifts works out well sometimes."

"It does," I said, and toyed with her hands in her lap. "So then, I'll see you for dinner tomorrow. I'll pick you up at seven."

"Okay," she said, gnawing her bottom lip a little.

"*Okay*," I mimicked which finally got her to chuckle.

CHAPTER EIGHT

"Where have you been?" Jordan asked me when I showed up mid-day at Wildrose to check on their progress. "Literally, you vanished like a ninja." She paused, folded her arms, then cocked a brow. "There's a girl, isn't there?"

"A little." I shoved her as I helped unwrap the new glasses. We lined them up carefully on the bar counter.

"It's that doctor, isn't it?" She squeaked out her question

"A little. Quit pressuring me!"

"Allie!" Jordan grabbed my shoulders. "How's the sex?"

I laughed, pushing her off. "Stop it. There's been no sex. It's super new and we're taking it really slow."

"Allie...you don't know the definition of slow."

"In this situation I do."

"What situation is that?" Hands fell to her hips and she wagged her brows at me.

"It's just new. Knock off the interrogation, would you?" I nudged her with my elbow and she laughed.

"Your roots are showing." Switching tactics from questioning to playfully insulting was Jordan's specialty. "Come by for a touch up soon."

"Yeah yeah." I scowled at her and she snickered,

leaning over to bite my shoulder.

I shrugged her off, laughing. "What would your girlfriend think?"

"I think she would enjoy the fact that both you and I are dating doctors. Two unlikely match ups."

"Very funny." My glare only made her laugh more. "Also very true. Especially when you've slept with a good eighty-percent of the lesbians in Seattle and I tend to pick uncommitted ones."

"Correction, Allie. You pick uncommitted women who also tend to be *bisexual*." With her finger in the air like a self-righteous asshole, I shoved her hard enough to make her stumble. Jordan's contagious laughter, as obnoxious as the rest of her, had me chuckling when she went for me. I dodged her grab only to swat her shoulder.

"Jerk."

"I don't sleep with every lesbian…" she commented, her reaction delayed.

"Eighty-percent is enough. You even slept with Eve knowing she was a one-night wonder," I said.

"I slept with Eve *because* she was a one-night wonder, Allie. Get it right. We one-nighted it a few times. Friends with benefits and all." She shrugged and we returned to unpacking the next set of glasses.

"That never works out and you know it. And you were the one with leftover feelings that time, not her."

"Well, I've got Ainsley now. And she's different…"

"Way different because you're in love with her." I glanced at her and watched as a smile curved her smart mouth. "The same way Eve is in love with Ciara."

"I do love Ainsley," she admitted.

"I know. Have you said it to her?"

"We've said it now." Her movements slowed as she unpacked a glass. "I wouldn't ever cheat on her, Allie."

"Because you're in love with her. If you truly love someone, you don't cheat. That's how I feel about it anyway."

"Before Ainsley, I might've questioned that, but now…" She shook her head. "I understand it."

"Kari didn't love me like that. She loved what I had to offer," I said, smirking as I leaned my hip against the counter.

"Solid job, a place to live, some money." Jordan glanced around us. "You should own this bar, Allie."

"Well, I don't. Kari runs it well on her own. Down payment be damned."

"Is your name still on the deed?" She pushed herself to sit on the bar counter, the pink strands in her hair bouncing a little when she swung her legs.

"Sort of." I ran my fingers through my hair and sighed. "The property is mine, not the bar."

Jordan held her hands up suddenly. "Wait...you own the property? This is your building?"

"Yeah, why?"

"Allie." The floor creaked when she jumped down, her winter boots colliding with the hardwood. "Who knows this?"

"No one. Kari? You? The city?"

"Allie!" She grabbed my shoulders now, shaking me once. "You're the damn cop here. Some asshole puts you in the hospital then a building you own gets vandalized."

"Yeah, but nobody knew that…"

"Allie!"

"Quit shouting my name!" I pushed her off of me and whipped out my phone. "It's been years, Jordan. I didn't even think…"

"I know. Report it already. What if this is about you?"

"It can't be…"

"But what if it is?"

When the line opened, Porter's voice asked, "What up, Al?"

"Listen, about the vandalism case…"

***

"How, Allie, *how* did you not think about the fact the

building was yours?" Marc reprimanded me as I sat in the conference room at work.

"Me? You didn't think of it either."

"It's yours, you dope." He chuckled but stopped when Porter entered with Walsh and Jackson.

"Do we think this is connected?" Marc asked them right away.

"We're not sure," Walsh answered. "Goldman, while it is unusual—"

"Don't say it's a coincidence, Walsh." Marc held up his hands. "Butler pushed her first and threw her so hard that he split her head open. Who treats a colleague like that? And now, the one piece of property in this entire city with Alice's name on it gets vandalized with homophobic slurs."

"I'm still in the room, you know," I piped up, frowning at them.

"Butler's in jail. That'd mean he'd have hired someone to do it." Porter chimed in, dropping the case file on the table.

"Hey. All of you, stop." Jackson knocked on the tabletop and glanced between us. "None of you are allowed on this case. I.A. is investigating this. Our hands are off. Got it?"

"What are we supposed to do then? For weeks we've been fucking around in here doing what?" I shoved my chair away from the table and stood. "Not to mention that you've canceled all my speaking engagements, Jackson."

"I'm sorry about that, Lange, but we've been taken down to bare minimum both by the accusations against Butler and the vandalization of your property. And this thin slate will continue until the charges against him are assured and we catch who went after your goods, Lange," Jackson finished, finally sitting at the table with everyone else.

"Somehow, Jackson, the two are connected." Marc stood with me. "And eventually, that will be really clear to all of you." He glanced at me then nodded to the door.

"Let's go, Allie."

"Don't make rash decisions, Lange," Walsh warned, calling after me. "Stay away from this."

I flipped him off and headed out with Marc to his car.

On the ride home, neither of us said anything until we were back in the apartment. Immediately, I tossed off my jacket, and my shoes followed. "I have to pick up Stella in an hour."

"Allie, don't you want to talk about this?" Marc followed me into my room while I undressed.

"Honestly, Marc. I don't. All I want to do is spend a night with a beautiful woman who I care about very much. In case you haven't noticed. In case anyone hasn't noticed that my priorities have shifted." Every inch of clothing hit the floor as I stomped into the bathroom, turning on the shower. Marc followed me right in.

"I did notice, Allie. I know you like her a lot. Don't grump at me for trying to care about *you*." He sat down on the toilet. "And please tell me you're going to shave those legs."

I laughed as I punched him in the shoulder before getting into the tub. "Shut up and yes, I am."

"Not to mention the other things." He gestured wildly and I closed the curtain. "Stubble is unbecoming."

"Again, shut up. How's Gavin?" While we talked, I lathered up and took care of whatever I needed to. Marc and I weren't modest around each other at this point in our roommateship.

"He's really good, actually. Are you going to Stella's after dinner?"

"Probably. Is he coming here?"

"He's been here almost every night. You haven't noticed?" He chuckled and I heard the sink turn on followed by the medicine cabinet opening.

"I haven't. Maybe I'm used to him already."

"He's used to you, too. So he doesn't annoy you?"

"Nope." I propped my leg up on the side of the tub to

shave. "That's a good thing. I usually hate your fuck boys. But he's different."

"He is."

"Do you love him, Marc?" I smiled when I asked since he couldn't see me.

"Yeah…" he answered after a moment of quiet.

"Good. Let yourself fall for him. He's good for you." I ducked under the shower head and let the hot water run over me.

"Thanks, Allie."

"For what?" My question came on the tails of a sputter.

"Being my family."

"Yeah, well, thanks right back at you because you're mine, too."

An hour later, with the aggravation of the day washed down the drain, Stella and I sat together in the quiet covered patio of my favorite Mexican restaurant. A fire roared in the huge hearth on one end, warming the open space and offering a romantic glaze to every inch of the place. Stone floors, thick wooden tables, and cozy high-backed chairs made the environment a perfect first date choice.

Stella, in her black jeans and heels, coupled with a sleek dark purple sweater, stunned me in her casual presence. I did everything I could not to stare at her too much in fear of scaring her away. My attire hadn't changed much, partially because most of what I owned belonged to my work-appropriate wardrobe of button-down shirts, blouses, and black slacks. Heeled boots and my trusty weapon tucked in at my waist, and I was...exactly the same as usual. Except less hairy, and happier.

We started dinner with salsa and tortilla chips, followed by fajitas for me and enchiladas for her. Like usual, we shared our dishes with each other, neither of us had to ask to do so.

"This is a nice place, Allie. Thank you for taking me," she said, then sipped her fruity Sangria.

"It's one of my favorite places. I'm glad to be here with one of my favorite people," I told her, lifting my margarita in a playful toast to her.

"You have other favorite people?" Her chuckle made me smile.

"Just one."

"Not your family?"

"God no. They're crazy." I laughed now and she covered her mouth, as if hoping not to spit out her drink.

"How's work been?" she asked afterward. "You seem to be working less."

"Work has been pretty sucky and I am. Though it gives me extra time to visit you randomly for your breaks."

"You're my favorite coffee matron, I must say."

"Ah, you just love lattes, Stell." I grinned at her, then pointed at my dish. "Last bite of chicken. Want?"

"I do and yes." She stabbed it with her fork and wagged her brows when she ate it. "Thanks."

"Welcome." No one made me smile like Stella did, and that's saying something.

The waiter returned for our empty plates and we ordered cappuccinos. With the fire blazing a few feet from us, and an almost-snow rain falling outside the patio, the warm drinks coupled with the atmosphere and company something settled inside me. It blocked out my unpleasant thoughts and allowed me to lower my guard.

"This is nice," Stella said, her voice soft as she gazed at me. The firelight twinkling in her eyes.

"It is." I leaned back in my seat, cupping the warm mug in my palms. "Would you want to do it again?"

"I would, Alice."

"With me?" My lip twitched when I fought the tempting smile.

"Only with you." Part of me expected her to smile, but the seriousness that fell over her had me staring.

"Alice?" A male voice from my left called out. I turned in time to see the familiar face.

"Jake, hey," I said, standing up to accept the hug he offered. "Good to see you." In the dim light, his flashy purple shirt was almost hard to miss.

"You, too. And who's this?" He let go of me, and his dark eyes fell on Stella. She stood, her charming, professional smile returning in barely a blink.

"Stella Corwin," she said, shaking his hand. "Nice to meet you."

"Jake runs the youth runaway shelter for LGBT kids. And the LGBT center downtown," I told her, clapping him on the shoulder.

"Well, that's admirable," Stella said, nodding to him.

"Thanks." He offered her a bright grin then looked to me. "Where've you been, Al? It's been weeks."

"Our whole unit isn't operating normally right now," I said, vaguely.

"Well, the kids are asking for you. Just come down on your own then." He shrugged. "Unofficially. We're having a Christmas party next Saturday before actual Christmas. They'd be happy to see you. We all would." He smiled softly and squeezed my shoulder again. "I'll let you get back to your dinner. Good to see you, Alice, and nice meeting you, Stella."

"You, too." Stella shook his hand when offered.

"Bye."

"Later, Jake."

Stella and I settled back into our seats, her eyes trained on me. "You work at the shelter?"

"I used to go every week to talk to the kids about their rights, emancipation, hate crimes, and things like that." I shrugged then finished off my coffee.

"I didn't know you did that." Stella leaned her elbows on the table. "What else don't I know about you, Detective Lange?"

I laughed, shaking my head then mimicking her posture, our hands now almost touching in the center of the table. "I'm not sure. Ask me a question."

"Anything?" Her brows lifted as she thought about it.

"Sure."

"What's your favorite food in the world?"

"Safe question. Chocolate ice cream." I cocked a brow at her and she caressed my thumb with the side of her index finger. "Next."

"How come you haven't been working much?" There it was, what she really wanted to ask.

"I told you what happened with Butler and what he did to me," I began. She nodded for me to continue. "My friend's bar was vandalized, you know, Wildrose."

"I heard about it on the news, yes. Bias crime?"

"Yeah, but they won't let us on it. I.A. is all over everything and they have another unit doing our job until the shit with Butler's trial is over."

"And…" She linked her finger with mine.

"And?" My brow furrowed, but I allowed her to hold onto me.

"There's something you're leaving out, Allie."

"That Kari used to be my girlfriend and I still own the property where her bar is at?" I smirked at the stupidity of it. Her eyes widened with surprise. "Yeah. I forgot about the last bit, too."

"I don't understand...your property?"

"Kari and I were together for two years. Before I learned she cheated on me, I bought the lot with the building where she could run the bar and we could live upstairs. And gave her the down payment for the bar." I laughed a little as unexpected emotions tightened my throat. "She was cheating on me with a guy for six months, and then a girl after that. I walked out and abandoned everything. Moved in with Marc and stayed."

"Hey." She unfurled my hands and held both of them. "Maybe we shouldn't talk about this here."

"Yeah." I nodded and she squeezed my hands.

After a mild war of who would pay, that I won because I asked her to dinner in the first place, Stella and I walked back to her apartment, light snow falling around us. The first block, we walked with our hands in our pockets, until she held her elbow out to me. I slipped my arm around hers and she seemed to settle.

"Did you give her all your money?" she asked, quietly.

"Everything I had back then, but that was almost ten years ago. Eventually, we became friends again, sort of."

"Doesn't sound like a good friend to me," she said, her heels clicking on the pavement as we walked at a stroll. "But what do I know about friendship anyway."

"There are levels of it. Kari and Melinda taught me not to let too many too close. Marc is my only best friend, and Jordan is too but I don't tell her everything. And...well, you're edging your way past Marc every day."

"You're my only friend," she said, keeping her gaze on the busy street ahead of us. "Now anyway."

"What about the people you work with?"

"Work friends are convenience friends. They aren't lifelong. If you leave, they dissipate. If your shift changes and theirs doesn't, you don't share meals anymore."

"I get that." I squeezed her arm gently and she looked at me.

"I have another question…"

"Okay."

"Does the police department think that your property being defaced means you've been targeted by the man who assaulted you?"

"I'm not sure. But it's the only property I have on record and if Butler wanted to get back at me, it's an easy target."

She nodded, her grip on me tightening a fraction until we arrived at the front of her apartment building. We turned to face each other. "Come up for a bit?" she asked.

"Are you inviting me up to your apartment after our first date? Isn't that a little forward of you, Doctor Corwin?"

"Yes." She nodded, though her expression fell to a

remote seriousness again.

"Then I'll come up on one condition…" I fought the half-smile that threatened to reveal itself.

"What?" Her brows flicked upward.

"That you'll really consider coming to my family's house for Christmas. Like really consider it. And, if it matters to you, I'll go with you to visit your dad beforehand."

Her lips pressed together in a thin line as her eyes flickered over my shoulder. "I'll really consider it."

"Deal."

Stella hurried us through the halls in between waving at random people who greeted her. When we made it to her apartment, we both slipped out of our shoes, as usual, before entering her carpeted living room, and Stella swept into the kitchen. "Red or white?"

"Hmm. Have any rosé?" I dropped down on the sofa and tucked my feet up beside me.

"I do. Because you brought it last week." I heard the cork pop and the swift pour that followed, before she carried two glasses to the couch. "For you, my queen."

"Yay." I accepted the glass she offered and sipped it. "Mmm. Thank you."

"Welcome," she said, taking a seat beside me and mimicking my posture. "Allie…"

"Hmm?" I leaned the glass on my knee and met her gaze.

"I'd be lying if I said that I wasn't worried about Butler targeting you." She reached across the back of the sofa to rest her palm on my shoulder. I tilted my head to brush my lips over her hand.

"I know, Stell. I do."

I watched as she set her glass on the coffee table. "Come here."

"Where?" I asked, setting mine down, too.

"Here." She shifted her position to lie back on the sofa, then held her hands to me. I watched her as she beckoned me, wiggling her fingers and laughing softly. "It's okay."

"You're sure?" I crawled over her, until she pulled me into a hug as her answer. My body relaxed into hers and I lay down on top of her, my hips between her knees. Our embrace lasted longer than usual until I leaned back to look at her.

"Thank you for dinner," she said, the shimmer returning to her sapphire gaze.

"You said that already." I smiled as I poked her chin. "Twice."

Her chuckle bounced both of us a bit. "I mean it. It's the first time I've been out with a woman since…"

"I know." I let my hand fall to the space between her breasts for lack of a better place to put it in this position. Her hips shifted under me and her knees squeezed me faintly. Tears brimmed her eyes and she reached up to stroke my hair, twirling a strand around her finger. "Where did you go with Clarissa on your first date?"

"Um…" Her bottom lip quivered and she sniffled. "There was this barbeque place outside of Seattle, not far from where we lived." She laughed a bit. "Clarissa used to eat ribs like a messy, gross man. I loved watching her." Damp cheeks shimmered in the dim light as she sniffled. "I loved watching her in general."

"Was she pretty?" I used my thumb to wipe them away and watched as she leaned into my touch.

"So pretty." A content expression fell over her, smoothing her features and turning her lips up in a soft smile. She watched the ceiling for a moment before looking back to me. "Like you."

"Hardly." I laughed softly, and dabbed at her cheeks again. "Maybe someday you'll show me a picture."

"Maybe someday."

I scooted up some so that I could hold myself up over her, watching her with my head tilted as I contemplated her beautiful face. Would she hate it if I kissed her right then? She smiled at me as I lowered myself down to place a soft kiss on the space between her eyes. A rattley breath left her and she sighed deeply. Moving my way down the bridge of her nose was the easy part. My lips hovered a breath above hers and, with caution, I closed the space between us.

Beneath me, her body writhed faintly as she placed one hand on my cheek and the other gripped a fist full of my hair. It didn't seem like she hated it at all. Stella pulled me to her more forcefully than I expected, and I relaxed my arms enough to lie on top of her again. Our lips tangled until I braved the waters that'd sent her fleeing the first time. My tongue poked her lips and this time, instead of running, she met me with a tango of her own.

My body ached, my insides thrashed, and this time it was me pulling back before I took it too far. As my hands trembled, I fought not to grab hold of her tits.

"Stella…" Her name came out on heavy pants. "Tell me what you want."

"This. You. And this." She grabbed me back into the kiss, her hands tangled in my hair. I lost myself in her, gripping her side in effort to keep hold of myself. Her mouth explored mine, tongue swirling vigorously between my lips. A soft moan left me, lingering between us until I ended our connection again.

"Are you sure?" I cupped her face between my hands. "Because, Stella, if you keep doing this, I'm not sure I can stop."

"I'm sure." Nails tickled my scalp as she grabbed my hair again. "I want you naked."

"I want you naked, too," I confessed, capturing her in a kiss at the same time that she shifted beneath me until her knee pressed between my legs. A cry left me when her knee connected with my middle. "Stella."

A laugh left in a rush as she stroked my cheeks. "You're very cute."

"I am not."

"You are when I surprise you." She pecked me on the lips sweetly. "Bedroom?"

I nodded, nuzzling her with my chin before taking her hand and guiding her up to stand with me. With both of her hands in mine, and a coy smile on her lips, I walked her backward into her room.

When the back of my knees hit the bed, I watched as she took her bottom lip between her teeth. She dropped her hands and watched me, like she did the last time she asked to see me naked. I began unbuttoning my blouse, letting it fall away as she gripped the waist of my pants. Her finger flicked the fastening free, and she tugged the zipper down as her knuckles grazed the spot above my mound. My whole body quaked and it made her smile.

"Like that?" she asked, to which I nodded.

"I do." When my bra fell away, I reached for her, tugging her into a kiss as I shoved the hem of her sweater up. She pulled it off her head and I reached around her to release her bra. She shrugged it away and, the moment our naked torsos collided, a shudder struck her so hard that she braced herself by holding onto my hips.

With as much caution as I could muster, I tickled up her sides until my hands cupped her breasts. Goosebumps coated her flesh and she ended our kiss, her forehead pressed against mine. Hot breath between us told me that she wanted this, on some level, though her fear and hesitation was ever present. No warning came before she shoved my pants down, pushing my panties with them until I was naked in front of her. There was an edge to her movement that resembled anger, and I released her breasts to wrap my arms around her torso. She hugged me, our breasts pressed together as she kissed my shoulder. Every time her flesh grazed mine, arousal burned between my legs and I wasn't sure how long I could lie in stasis.

"Talk to me," I implored, rubbing her back as she buried her face against my neck.

"Lie down," was all she said after a quiet moment.

We broke away from each other and I crawled up on the bed to lie on my back. Her jeans hung off her hips, revealing a taut stomach and the perfect curves that angled toward her hidden core. My body quivered when she knelt beside me, gazing down at me like she hadn't ever seen anything like me before. Illuminated only by the glow flooding the room from the city lights, she was the most beautiful thing I'd ever seen. Perfectly round breasts, perky with hardened nipples, a smooth, contoured abdomen, and sharp hips that begged to be touched, all set fire to my insides. Dampness spiraled in my most private places and I gnawed on my lip in hope of not embarrassing myself.

Stella's eyes wandered over every inch of me, her left hand following with them. She touched my shoulders first, then moved down my body almost as if examining me. The look on her face, a narrowed brow and pursed lips, spoke of an intensity I'd never seen before in this situation, but it was her sapphire eyes that gave away her true intention. Pain and curiosity mingled with the tears I knew she'd fight until she couldn't anymore.

By the time her hands met my thighs, a single tear fell from her cheek and landed on my stomach. "You're so beautiful," she whispered. "So beautiful, Alice."

"But I make you cry. I cause you pain, Stella." My throat tightened as I watched her, arguing against my own emotions.

"No, Allie." She shook her head, sniffling a little. "My own pain causes me pain. Not you." Through all of it, she never stopped touching me and, when her fingers danced over my lower abdomen, my whole body tensed under the sensation. She inched closer, her fingers barely grazing the top of my mound and I sucked in my breath, holding it as my body ached for more, ached for her. "Can I touch you?"

"Yes," I croaked, nodding hard but trying not to be too desperate about it. "Can I touch you?"

"Yes, but I'm afraid," she admitted, her eyes flickering to mine.

"Tell me what you're afraid of…"

"Not yet," was all she said before she slid her hand down the center of my body, over my clit and parting my folds in an exploratory caress.

My mouth dropped open and my hips betrayed me, lifting toward her hand. She knew what she was doing, there wasn't any doubt about that. Stella leaned over me, her lips an inch from mine as she cupped my pussy almost possessively. I forced myself into silence while she explored me but when she gently rubbed my clit, I let out a squeaky gasp.

Stella's smile, warm and playful, replaced her tears as she leaned down and kissed me. Only then did her grip on me strengthen and her skilled fingers worked me in a way no one had in years. Pleasure raced through me, radiating from my pussy down to my toes and fingertips. Desperation captured me, threatening to make me come faster than I wanted to. I reached up, holding her to me as my tongue explored her mouth with a hunger I couldn't control anymore.

She met me there, nudging my legs apart and crawling on top of me but her fingers on my folds never stopped. I cried out the moment she slipped inside me, ending our kiss as my back arched to meet her there. I tore at the blanket beneath me. Stella's heavy chuckle against my neck preceded the kisses she planted along my clavicle.

"Stell, I—"

Her movements grew faster as if her body and mind finally unlocked. Lips wrapped around my nipple and she slid a second finger inside me, thrusting deeply then pulling back in a slow draw as her thumb worked my clit. Moans escaped me as I held on to her, one hand in her hair while the other brought my fingernails to her back. She slipped and slid in and out of me, my wetness a surprise that brought both delicious lust and pleasure that erupted so deeply, I did everything I could not to scream.

My toes curled and I lost myself to her, all of me a crying mess of writhing bliss at her fingertips. As I came, she worked me through it, lowering herself on top of me and hugging me to her as my body began to relax. I gasped for breath, wrapping both of my arms around her as I trembled and quaked from the strength of my climax.

With care, she exited me, and hugged me tightly to her, burying her face in my hair. She shook just as much as I did. Emotions rushed me and I found myself sniffling, closing my eyes and squeezing her tighter than I intended to while stroking her hair. In time, her body relaxed on top of me though her lips never left my neck. Soft puffs of breath on my skin set off another round of goosebumps while we held each other.

Stella didn't move, didn't say anything, but the way she held me, touched me every so often, told me she needed to be as she was—in control and cautious at the same time.

Eventually, her quick breaths settled to rhythmic ones and I held her well into the night while she returned the gesture.

CHAPTER NINE

Stella's alarm didn't go off the next morning, and I assumed that meant she didn't have work. While she slept, I texted Jackson and called out sick, not caring about his response. The morning light flooded her bedroom, and when the sun beat down on the bed through the biggest window, Stella stirred beside me. Before she even opened her eyes, her hand slid across my middle, the way it had the first time I fell asleep naked beside her.

"Hi," she said, before opening her eyes.

"Hi, pretty." I leaned over and kissed her gently. She smiled through it, peeking her eyes open to look at me.

"No work today?" she asked, her voice a little raspy.

"Called out." I stretched a little, turning on my side to face her.

"Good." She wriggled closer to me and hugged me with much less restraint than she had previously. I brushed my lips over her shoulder and she nibbled my neck. "Feel okay?"

"Yeah. Really good, but I think that's your fault." I leaned back to meet her gaze again, tucking her hair behind her ear while I watched her.

"I'm glad it's my fault." She caressed my stomach and a sudden whimsical smile melted over her lips.

I laughed softly. "What?"

"You were so wet." That smile turned into a grin and I nearly cracked up.

"Stella! What'd you expect after making me lay there for twenty minutes, completely naked, while you touched every inch of me? And with your perfectly perky tits in my face, mind you." I swatted her rear a few times over her saggy jeans and she laughed.

"Allie." She laughed so hard that her cheeks turned bright red.

"Not funny." I poked her nose, grinning right through it. "I bet your panties weren't exactly dry either, you evil witch doctor."

"That's my secret," she said, smiling as she traced a single finger over my lips.

I nibbled her finger first then dug my heel into the bed and rolled her onto her back. Her eyes widened with surprise but she continued laughing as I held myself above her. "Oh yeah?"

"Yes." She grinned at me, grabbing my hair and tugging gently.

"Just you wait." I kissed her chin, moving my way down her chest and, at the same time, pushing her pants and panties off her legs. When my lips reached her belly button, her laughter stopped and her fingers tensed in my hair. I looked up at her, my face barely an inch from her bare pussy. "Talk to me, Stell."

"I'm okay…"

"If *okay* means you look about ready to hurl." I lowered myself to the bed between her legs, and rested my chin on her stomach. I held my hands to her and she laced her fingers with mine.

"I'm afraid," she said, her eyes shimmering with fear.

"I know, Stell. What are you afraid of?"

"I just am." She squeezed my hands gently.

"Want me to stop?" I kissed her belly and she shook her head. "Are you sure?"

"I don't want you to stop," she said then held her breath for a second.

"Okay." Hesitantly, I brushed my lips over her lower stomach, then kissed my way down to the top of her mound. The warmth of her made my heart pound, setting my core on fire again. I watched her, my eyes never leaving hers as I flicked my tongue once over her clit to gage her reaction.

Stella's mouth dropped open, but a single tear streamed down her cheek. The death grip she had on my hands told me she was still unsure despite her words. Knowing this, I kept my attention gentle and let my tongue part her glistening folds with caution. The cry that left her, one tangled with both pain and pleasure, worried me. Her hands shook so hard and her feet writhed against my hips. I repeated the gesture, focusing now on her clit as I allowed my tongue to swirl around it.

Her toes dug into my calves and her fingernails pressed into my palms. I stopped, fearing that I wasn't truly giving her what she wanted until she lifted herself to my mouth. There wasn't mistaking that move at all. Again, I kept to her clit as my insides warred somewhere between complete delight and terrible fear that this wasn't the right course of action. I lashed my tongue over her sweet, hard clit a few more times and suddenly, she tensed when she sucked in her breath. Her face reddened and she nearly screamed as she tore at my hands, her feet pressing into the mattress beside me.

Slippery nectar seeped from her, coating my lips as I enjoyed her soft folds, lapping at her through her orgasm. My pussy quaked, sending shivers up my spine. When she collapsed back on the bed, she trembled and the cries that left her were no longer of pleasure.

"Allie," she said, sobbing out my name as I crawled quickly up to her. She grabbed me in a hug and wrapped her arms and legs around me as she nearly screamed against my shoulder.

"I'm sorry, Stell. I'm sorry." Had I done the wrong thing in continuing? It sure as fucking hell felt like it.

I held her while she cried, latched onto me as her body wracked with sobs. Though she never once stopped petting my hair. "You're okay," I whispered against her ear and she nodded. Tears streamed my cheeks as well as hers. "You're okay."

***

I woke up alone, in Stella's bed, with the sun no longer glaring through the window. It was still daylight though; I couldn't have been out too long.

When I made to slide out of bed, I found her sitting on the floor with a wooden box between her knees. She wore my white blouse but nothing more. I watched over her from my silent perch above and she didn't seem to notice me yet. A quiet sniffle told me that she cried again, or still, I couldn't tell. Stella cried a lot and it worried me. My presence in her life brought her so much anguish. She placed her hand in the center of the box, stroking it fondly.

"Open it," I whispered against her cheek before I kissed it.

A soft laugh escaped her as she reached back to caress my face. "I'm afraid."

"I know, Stell." I slid from the bed then, and moved to sit behind her. I wrapped my arms around her and moved my legs to cradle hers. "I'll hold you so you can."

She melted back against me, nuzzling my chin with her nose before looking back to the mahogany box. Her breath left her in a rattling exhale as she carefully lifted the cover.

Inside, two beautiful diamond rings lay beside each other on top of a stack of photos and a flash drive. With a trembling hand, she lifted the photos and held one up of a beautiful blonde woman, laughing in the candid shot, her hand held out as if trying to grab the camera. Happiness, pure happiness in that shot.

Stella moved through the photos, pausing briefly on

each. Two beautiful women hugging each other beside a Christmas tree, a brunette and a blonde so perfect, so joyful, that they belonged on the cover of a romance novel. Clarissa sprawled out on a lounge chair at the beach, wearing a skimpy purple bikini and offering the photographer a cocky grin while looking at her from over a pair of sunglasses. The two of them in a few selfies while riding on a train. Stella's distress faded away, leaving her with a gentle smile as we looked on together. Occasionally, a tear trickled down her cheek, and mine as well while I rested my chin on her shoulder. At the next photo, she laughed softly as a naked Clarissa tried to cover herself with a pillow. There were a few like that.

When we reached the end of the pile, she set the photos down and picked up the rings. One of them, perfect in its own right, the other, slightly battered and scarred with what looked like dried blood. She showed them to me, in the palm of her hand, and I kissed her temple.

"It's nice to finally meet Clarissa," I told her, because it was, in a way, and because in meeting Clarissa, I got to know more of Stella.

"My dream changed," she said, setting the rings back in the box.

"Did it?" I kissed her shoulder and she turned a little so we could see each other. I thumbed away the wetness from her cheeks.

"She smiled at me, in the dream, instead of dying and bloody." She took my hand in hers and squeezed. Her smile, though still laden with sadness, was without its usual despair.

"I'm glad, Stell. I'm glad your sleep wasn't tortured." I kissed her gently, and her return was a firm, warm one.

When we parted, she made to cover the box again but I stopped her. "She doesn't belong in a box. Which is your favorite?"

"The Christmas tree," she said, separating it from the

others.

"Here." I took it from her then reached over her to prop it against the lamp on her nightstand. "Leave it there for now."

"Okay," she said, turning around to hug me after sliding the box back under the bed. I wrapped my arms around her and kissed her shoulder.

"Do you work tonight?"

"Covering a shift at seven," she said, sighing softly against my neck. Her lips brushed the tender flesh.

"How about I make you breakfast today and we spend the rest of it on your sofa watching horrible movies?"

She chuckled, leaning back to hold my face between her palms. "Why are you so amazing?"

"Because you are." I stroked her arms, smiling at the ease of her affection now. "C'mon. Let's go."

Our plans played out just as intended, but on the drive to the hospital, Stella fell quiet. The closer we got, the tighter she held on to her purse, and when I pulled up to the staff entrance, her knuckles whitened. At first I thought it was the darkness of December's nights, but then the thought of the repeated pattern came to light.

"Stella…" She glanced at me, her face frozen and clinical. "I'll see you in the morning."

"Okay." Every inch of her held tightly to her emotions and I knew that whatever I did next would matter more than anything else at this point.

Instead of idling, I shifted the car to drive and pulled into a parking space a few yards away. Stella immediately unlocked and her brow furrowed. "What are you doing?"

"Dropping you off," I said, releasing my seatbelt and opening the car door. "Remember who drove you? You're already late. Come on."

"Alice...what?"

I didn't give her a chance to panic before I walked around the car to meet her. She stood from the passenger seat, her bag over her shoulder. I held my elbow to her the same way she did to me after dinner, and offered her a soft smile. She took my arm and leaned her head on my shoulder as we walked toward the hospital entrance.

"Are you okay walking in like this? I mean, holding on to each other?" I asked her once our feet hit the pristine floors of the emergency room.

"Yes." She turned and hugged me immediately. The smile she brought me not only made it to my eyes, but my heart. I kissed her cheek and when she leaned back, her smile, pure and light as ever, sent tingles of joy through my body.

"I *will* see you in the morning, Stella." I reached up and stroked her cheek. "Trust that."

Her nod, coupled with pursed lips, looked more like determination than fear this time. In the semi-busy emergency room, people shifted around us and the nosey nurses at the desk looked on. "Are you going home?"

"Yes."

"Text me when you get there?"

"I will." A wicked grin tugged my mouth, lifting my cheeks more than I intended. "Are you going to kiss me in front of this work audience of yours?"

She glanced over her shoulder in their direction and most of them jerked away, pretending to look busy. Stella chuckled and returned her attention to me. "Was there ever any doubt?" she asked, then closed the distance between us. Her lips against mine, hot and confident, had us both smiling when we parted. "Bye."

"Bye." I fanned myself when I released her and the last thing I heard as I walked off was the sound of her laughter.

***

"Gross! Man sex on the sofa." I hollered out my presence as Gavin and Marc made out on the sofa. They both laughed when they broke away from each other to look at me. "Is there jizz in the bathroom, too?"

"Nah. Bedroom." Gavin grinned and I about gagged.

"Yuck."

"Where you been, Allie?" Marc leaned up to kiss my cheek as I bent over the back of the sofa to smooch each of theirs. "Did you steal my car? Oh wait. I know. Finger-deep in a hot doctor."

"And don't you forget it." I swatted him upside the head. He grabbed me by the arm and yanked me over the sofa to tumble between both of them. "Hey! Why do all the men in my life pull me over the back of sofas?"

Gavin laughed, shaking his head as Marc hugged me. "Allie, we need to talk."

"Utoh...are you pregnant?" I looked at Gavin and he grinned.

"Oh yeah. Ready to pop." He patted his gut and I snickered.

"Not about that." Marc stuck his finger under my chin so that I'd look at him. "We need to talk because you haven't talked to me or anyone. You called out of work today, you've ignored phone calls from your family so much that they're calling me, and Jordan has started texting too. What's going on?" He wrapped his arm around my neck and sighed heavily. "Gavin agrees with me."

"It's complicated to explain." I smacked his arm then looked to Gavin. "Do you?"

"Sure, why not?" The prettiest boy in the world winked at me and I just laughed.

"Cute."

"Tell us about Stella," Marc implored. "Since she's the one you've been with." He cocked a questioning brow at me.

"It's complicated," I repeated my mantra and, although my thoughts were steadfast, they didn't find their way to my lips.

"What's so complicated about it, Allie?"

"Stella...isn't like any other woman I've dated. She's…" I stared at my feet as I propped them on the coffee table.

"Complicated?" offered Gavin with a gentle smile.

"Yeah." I chuckled, folding my hands over my stomach. "She's got significant baggage that she's working through."

"For what reason?" asked Marc.

"I don't know. Sometimes it seems like it's for me. But it's really for her."

"Alice." When Gavin said my name, I looked at him. "Do you love her?"

"Is it possible to love someone after only about two months of knowing them?" I asked, meeting his gaze.

Gavin's smile, purer than most, brought with it an intrinsic comfort. He had an innocence to him that created an endearing, genuine quality. "Of course."

"What's the answer then, Allie?" Marc rubbed my arm gently.

"Yeah. I do." I covered my face with my hands and sighed.

"Does she love you?" asked Gavin.

"I don't know." I dropped my hands and stared up at the ceiling. "She's still afraid, but less so. And she kissed me in front of all of her coworkers just an hour ago."

"That's saying something." Marc patted my arm again. "Are you going to see this through?"

"Yeah." A smile parted my lips when I met his gaze. "I am."

"Well, while your girlfriend is at work for the next twelve hours, how about you return the calls of every important person in your life?" He shoved me from the sofa, forcing a squeak from me followed by a laugh. "And take a shower. And stay in your room."

"Marc!"

Did Stella love me? I thought about Gavin's question while I showered, and changed into the clean pair of jeans and T-shirt that followed. I did love her, even if she was still in love with Clarissa. But how could I deny that, the more of her grief she worked through, the closer we became? Was it just a function of her feeling for Clarissa or was it me? Part of me didn't believe it was me at all.

That same part, the one that often led with the inability to trust, screamed warnings at me. Told me to not feel too much. To enjoy the sex and move on.

But I couldn't.

When I saw how she lived, alone with no significant people in her life save for work commitments and an ailing father. When I thought about the way she looked at me, and how we laughed together, and how comfortable I felt with her, it changed things. But nothing changed them as much as today, when I saw her fear of me driving away after dropping her off. Her worry for me, and that kiss in public.

I had to believe that she had deeper feelings for me, too. For now, loving someone was the easier part. Allowing myself to fall in love, that was another story...

For the next few hours, I called my brothers and parents, then talked with Jordan about attending dinner at her house on Sunday.

"Bring her," she said. "Invite her, Allie. If you care for her, just do it."

"I'll see if she wants to."

"Allie, you've been known to get caught up in pussy before, but what's got you—"

"Jordan, please."

"I just don't understand why you've disappeared."

"I'm right here, Jordan." I fought to keep the sigh from my voice. "But right now, I'm choosing to be with Stella. And that's not the only thing. Work hasn't been pleasant and I'm questioning my job. Plus the vandalized club. It's a lot."

"I know, Allie. And you tend to shut down. It's how you are." She paused for a moment. "I guess I'm just used to you shutting down *with* me."

"And sleeping on your couch while you cook for me." A smile crossed my lips and I listened to her chuckle.

"What are friends for?"

"Thanks for checking on me."

"I'll always check...on you." Her voice lifted at the end.

"Is Ainsley nibbling in naughty places, Jordie?" I laughed at her, holding the phone to my shoulder while I pulled on a pair of sneakers.

"Hmm…yes. Bye!"

"Don't ever change. Bye."

***

I purposely waited until it was well after midnight to appear in Stella's emergency room with two hot lattes. Snow covered my shoulders and I dusted it off as I hopped up to sit on the desk at the nurses' station. Again. While another doctor, who I recognized after all my visits, tended to a patient, and several other nurses bustled around, I addressed the one nurse that usually busted my chops.

"Hello, gingery nurse." I smirked at her when she started, then laughed when she looked up at me.

"Kylie." She pointed to her name tag. "How many times have you been here now, Detective Lange?"

"Oh...a few. Where's Doctor Corwin?"

"Hmm… Jog my memory. Is she the brunette who was kissing some faux blonde-ish woman in the foyer before?" Nurse Kylie tapped her lip, lifting her gaze to the ceiling. Her colleagues behind her chuckled, but only a few pretended to hide it.

"Perhaps. Was said brunette hot and leggy?"

"I think so." She turned to the others. "What do you guys think?" One of the male nurses pointed over her shoulder while he snickered. Kylie turned just as Stella emerged from around the corner of the long hallway. Immediately, she pretended to jump back into her work but I just laughed at her.

"Hot and leggy has arrived," another nurse muttered. Stella cocked a brow at him, her hands in the pockets of her lab coat until she saw me. Her whole face lit up with the smile she tried to temper.

"Hot and leggy?" she asked, her gaze locked on mine.

"We were just talking about the barista who fixed these." I could not stop grinning as I handed her the cup. She took it and leaned against my knees.

"Oh really? The barista?" And there went her bottom lip between her teeth. It made me laugh and I drew a circle on the back of her hand that she let fall to my knee.

"Best barista I've ever had," I said. Laughter erupted from the peanut gallery behind me and I watched as Stella waved them off.

"Come on. Let's take a walk." She stepped back and I hopped down to walk with her through the hall, leaving a playful murmur behind us.

"They're funny," I commented.

"And nosey. They've been on me for weeks about you."

"And just what are they on you about?"

She glanced at me, smiling after sipping her drink. "Information. I didn't expect to see you tonight again."

"It's the morning. I told you I'd see you in the morning."

She stopped walking and turned to face me. "You did. Didn't you?"

"I did." I moved to her and wrapped her in a gentle hug, both of us cautious of the hot liquid in our hands. "Especially after how I left you."

"I'm sorry about that," she said, holding my hand after ending our embrace.

"For caring about me? Because that's what it felt like…"

She squeezed my hand and we turned to walk further down the hall together, neither of us speaking for some time until she asked, "Do you work tomorrow?"

"Yeah. Probably shouldn't call out again. Even though I want nothing more than to call out forever." The admission left me on a mild sigh.

"Are you that unhappy with your work?" She glanced at me and urged me to sit with her on the bench in the vacant hall. Hospitals always creeped me out at night. For some reason, it made me feel like the dead watched us. But I would never say that aloud.

"I am."

"I can't say that I'm sad about it. Working a dangerous job, getting shot. *Twice.* Battered and stalked by a colleague—"

"He didn't stalk—"

"Possibly vandalizing a property that even you forgot that you own? That takes some research." She cocked a brow at me as she paused to sip her coffee. "And a bias crime, to boot."

"Your point, Doctor Corwin?" I smirked at her and she chuckled.

"That I'm in support of you hating your job," she said, simply.

"Thank you." I laughed and she squeezed my hand again. "Has it been busy here?"

"On and off. I'm not the only doctor on so that helps."

"Do you like your job?"

"Very much, for the most part. The helping people part."

"Yeah. I like that part of mine, too." A deep exhale left me as our fingers laced together. I hadn't really talked too much about my feelings regarding work lately, but it was a start. "Are you on the same shift tomorrow?"

"I'm covering again, but then I'm off for a few days while Morris takes my shifts." She brought my hand to her lips and kissed the back of it.

"Three twelve-hour shifts, four days off? I like that schedule."

"Want to go to med school?" She laughed and I turned fully to her, planting a kiss on her chuckling lips. She released my hand to cup my cheek, pressing me backward until my shoulders hit the wall beside us. My insides burned, screaming for more of her as our kiss spiraled into something deeper. Her tongue explored my mouth until a screaming shrill tore us apart.

"Shit." I flinched as she looked down at one of the three pagers clipped to her pants.

"Incoming. I need to head back." She stood up, tugging me with her. "How about dinner at my place Friday? I'm off but you can come after work."

"Sounds good to me." The invitation warmed the already overheated parts of me as I ached to indulge in her. Parting, after sharing our first night together, was hard enough without all of the unspoken words I hadn't yet said to her.

"I'm glad." She bumped into me with her shoulder on purpose and I laughed softly until we entered the emergency room.

People raced everywhere, tossing on coveralls and grabbing all sorts of medical equipment.

"Stay here a minute." Stella immediately let go of my arm and dashed toward the workers gathered by the entrance. I didn't want to fight my way through the chaos so I stayed to the side by the reception area and watched.

An ambulance, with screaming sirens, pulled into the bay just outside the door and EMTs joined the fray. A few moments later, the group rushed in with a gurney that carried a blood-covered person who was much smaller than the table itself.

"What've we got?" Stella asked, now clad in latex gloves and a top covering her lab coat, but missing the lower portion of it.

"Female, ten, gunshot wound to the chest. Respiratory distress," a brawny male EMT said, pushing the gurney while another pressed air into the patient with a balloon thing over her mouth.

"Drive-by, at least two entry wounds," said an EMT as she moved away from the scene.

Stella began shouting out ridiculous commands to the nurses and technicians around her. Only a few terms did I recognize; *stat*, *O-neg*, and *intubate*. None of it sounded good. But I watched as a confident, commanding Stella took over the entire room. She pointed, grabbed, juggled tools, and at one point, climbed up onto the gurney with the girl and seemed to bounce up and down on her chest while performing compressions.

I hadn't noticed until then that I gripped the center of my jacket in a fist so tight that my fingers ached. My heart pounded in my ears and, when Stella hopped from the bed, I watched as she grabbed a scalpel. Monitors screamed warnings. Sneakers squeaked on the bloody tiles, and a woman ran into the hospital screaming, "My baby! My baby!" Her knees hit the floor in a loud crack but two nurses, or technicians, raced to her aid. A uniformed police officer, who I recognized from the beat, knelt down on the floor with the woman as they all tried to soothe her.

"Move away," Stella demanded, drawing my attention back to the treatment room, and everyone stepped back. One nurse grabbed some sort of tube from a cabinet and I watched as Stella shoved bloody gauze from the kid's chest, then sliced into it near her ribs. I cringed at the sight of the blood pouring out of her. Stella then inserted the tube and fluid eventually funneled through it. She paused, and watched as the girl's chest inflated, before she handed something off to the nurse and moved on. "We need to get her to the O.R."

"I've paged ahead," someone answered her.

The monitors continued to shout for attention but they weren't screaming as loud as before. Stella, now elbow-deep in blood, continued to work on the girl though the fury in her movements wasn't as strong. I couldn't see what she was doing but it didn't mean that the adrenaline pumping in my veins decreased at all. Bandages covered the wound where the tube hung out of the girl's chest and finally, her olive skin and braided hair came in to view. The second I saw her face, with her eyes closed and wires hanging all over her, my breath caught in my throat as the pressure of emotions built behind my eyes. Like when I'm on the job, I pushed those feelings aside and focused on the task at hand. Except I didn't have a task. I only had a Stella, and so I focused on her. A beautiful, amazing, heroic Stella.

I watched as she pulled off her coveralls and the team of nurses and techs wheeled the girl from the treatment room down the hall. Stella looked at me, her eyes as wild as her untamed hair. Once her gloves were off, she pulled it back into a ponytail. Free of her confines, she jogged over to me and pecked me on the lips. "Got to get that bullet out. I'll call you after my shift."

"You're a fucking hero, Stell." I squeezed her hand, which was hot and nearly shaking from endorphins.

"Like you." She grinned at me then hurried off after the group to the operating room. To save a life.

CHAPTER TEN

"We're charging him," said Ramos as soon as we all sat down at the conference room table. Again. "With vandalizing your property, and the bias crime for targeting you. This doesn't look good for the rape case either."

"How'd you connect him to Wildrose?" I asked, glancing between Ramos and Walsh. Jackson sat quietly, his hands folded in front of him.

"Security camera and facial recognition software pegged one of the guys who participated. We confronted him and he rolled on Butler hiring him and a buddy to do it. And he left a few boot prints at the scene which matched a pair he owned," explained Ramos.

"So Butler, my former partner and someone I trusted, is now targeting me. How did he even know that I owned that property?" Anger spiraled around in my gut, tightening my fists, but I kept my cool for the most part.

"Easy property lookup," Walsh added.

"Can any of you explain how an aggressive and violent sociopath ended up on the Bias Crimes Unit, and, in the course of a few weeks, committed two bias crimes of his own? That's some bullshit if you ask me. And don't go blaming it on drugs or some other crap. I'm the only woman on this team. Mind you, I'm the only *gay* woman on this team. I might've mouthed off to him, but no amount of verbal taunt equates to physical violence let alone picking me up and throwing me like I wasn't anything more than a bag of shit." The more I spoke, the angrier I grew.

"Lange, we understand your frustration. With these new charges, Butler won't be returning and we're re-establishing the team with you, Goldman, and Porter. You're all free to return to your normal roles now," Ramos finished, but her words soothed me none.

A laugh escaped me as I gripped the edge of the table. With a sudden clarity, I shook my head and stood, pushing my chair back a few inches. "Honestly, I don't care."

"Lange, just calm yourself down here a damn minute." Walsh stood up when I did.

"No, Walsh. I...I just don't care anymore." Again, I laughed as every emotion, every bit of anger, frustration, and sense of doneness roared to an apex. "I just don't care."

"What are you saying here, Lange?" Jackson asked, his voice tamer than Walsh's.

"I don't care." I pulled my badge from around my neck and tossed it on the table.

No one tried to stop me when I turned away and, when my heels pounded the obsidian floor of the hallway, only then did tears stream down my face.

***

"You just walked out?" Marc asked, his eyes wide and saucer-like. "Just like that?"

"Yeah." I sniffled and wiped my eyes on my scarf. "And I don't feel bad about it."

"Then why are you crying, Allie?"

"I'm overwhelmed and relieved." I laughed a little. "And going to be homeless soon, just so you know."

"C'mon, that won't happen." He rubbed my back as I folded myself against my knees, burying my face in my hands. "Have you told Stella?"

"No. She's still at work."

"You should tell her."

"I will when she's off her shift. She stops kids from eminent death. This isn't worth interrupting her," I said, drying my face on my jeans.

"Come here." Marc grabbed me and gently pulled me toward him. A rush of something hit me and I braced myself against his chest.

"Don't. Please don't."

"What?" He stared at me, concern crinkling his brow. "What's wrong?"

"Don't lift me. Don't touch me, okay?" I shot up to stand, my hands shaking a bit. "I'm sorry, Marc."

"Allie, what's the matter?" He rose with me, holding his hands out in front of him.

"Nothing. I'm fine." I shook my head and backed away from him. "I'm gonna shower and just…"

"Okay...I'll just...I'll just stay out here, okay?"

"Yeah." I took a swipe at my nose before turning away from him. "Okay."

My bed, a mess of sheets and the clean laundry I'd tossed on it while finding an outfit this morning, wrapped itself around me. I let it swallow me and hid my face in the pillows.

What had I done? For months, maybe longer, all I wanted was to be free of my job. I chose bias crimes. I chose to become a cop. But what had changed? What had made me despise something I thought I used to love?

Was it seeing the faces of the hurt and injured every day? The women raped, just for being women. Or men being beaten just for being gay? I couldn't blame Marc for staying closeted about himself. What he risked by being out was far worse than what I did. Kids kicked out of their homes. Immigrants taken advantage of. Refugees gathered in concentration camp-like projects. I saw so much and, unlike Stella, I didn't help them in the same way.

I couldn't.

City lights illuminated my room, flashing red, green, and white under the thrall of Christmas decorations. I had no idea how much time passed since I collapsed on the bed, and the warmth of it told me I'd slept for some time though my thoughts weren't any less intense. I closed my eyes, and hoped to slip back under the spell of unconsciousness.

The door to my room opened but I didn't move. I knew Marc would check on me eventually, usually with food or coffee at least. But when the bed sank at my hip, it wasn't with the heaviness that usually accompanied my best friend. Gentle fingers brushed the hair from my face, tangled with the familiar fragrance of the sweetest kind. I opened my eyes to see Stella, still in scrubs, looking down at me with a worried expression.

"Your room is a *mess*," she said, her voice barely above a whisper.

I laughed, and the gravelly sound startled me a bit. "See why your place is better?"

"It's like a teenager lives here," she continued to tease me, a smile tugging the corner of her mouth.

"What time is it?"

"Two in the morning," she said, her hand falling to my stomach when I rolled over. "You didn't answer my texts, but then Marc finally called me and told me you were asleep and upset beforehand."

"I left my phone in the living room. I'm sorry. I didn't mean to worry you. Aren't you supposed to be at work?"

"Dinner break." She rubbed her hand in slow circles around my belly and the soothing gesture had me turning my eyes to the ceiling. "I've never seen you upset before."

"I know. I'm sorry."

"That's the second time you've apologized, Allie, and I don't know why," she said, nodding to the pillows. "Scoot over." I obeyed and shifted so that she could lie down beside me. With her head propped on her hand, she draped her arm over my middle. "What happened?"

"I quit my job today. Sort of." A sob caught in my throat. "Stell, seeing you in that emergency room last night was incredible. You're amazing. You're a superhero right out of a comic book. The way you move, think, act. I'm in awe of you. You saved that little girl's life."

"Allie—"

"Don't deny it. You save people. Probably a lot more than you don't save. For awhile now, I feel like all I do is push paper and meet quotas for community outreach. It's not really helping people. Not in the way I want to anyway. Talking to people who've been victimized about how to report their crimes which most of them don't do anyway because they're scared. Scared of the clapback or going to court or getting deported." I paused to catch my breath and fight the third round of tears. "I don't want to anymore."

"You don't have to do anything that makes you unhappy, Allie. But let me tell you something…" She pulled me closer to her and ran her fingers through my hair at the same time. "I didn't save that little girl. She died on the operating room table."

"But...she was doing better." That only made me cry more and I reached up to touch her face. Her soft smile carried with her as she turned her head to kiss the palm of my hand.

"Sometimes it just happens that way. We do the best we can when we can. But sometimes, hearts stop beating when bullet fragments break them. And there's nothing else we can do. It's part of the work," she told me, then kissed my palm a few more times. "Sometimes I save people. Sometimes I don't." A sharp intake of breath followed as if whatever she said next would cause her great pain. "Even Clarissa."

I nodded, holding her gaze as her eyes shimmered in the dim, flashing lights. "The world took away your most perfect love. It's not very fair."

"The world isn't a fair place. My dad always told me that. He still does sometimes."

"Thank you for coming to see me," I said, pulling her into a hug. Her embrace, perfect and loving, warmed even the most frigid parts of me.

"Thank you for coming to see me, too."

"What?" I laughed a little as we leaned back to look at each other again. "I didn't."

"Not today, but plenty of other times when I needed you to."

"I didn't know you needed it. I just thought—"

"You just thought of me. That's enough." She ran her finger over my bottom lip. "Marc told me something that bothered him. He said you told him not to touch you. Is that true?"

"Yeah," I admitted, leaning my head against her shoulder.

"He said you never told him that before. What's different?"

"I don't want to talk about that right now. Not when you have to leave or when I'm already upset."

"Okay. I'll respect that," she said and I nodded.

"How long until you have to leave?"

"Half an hour or so."

"Just lay with me?"

"That's the plan." She settled into the bed more comfortably and guided my head to her shoulder. It'd been a very long time since I'd let anyone hold me in such a way, but I didn't hate it. "Though, I bet we could pick up this room in that time, too."

I laughed hard, pinching her arm. "No way. Leave it alone."

"But Allie, come on. There are clothes *everywhere*."

"The problem isn't with the clothes. I'm afraid of what's under them."

"*Touché*. Snuggling it is."

"Yay."

Stella left before her break ended and I found the energy to emerge from the bedroom. Marc dozed on the sofa so I snatched my phone off the table and saw the two missed text messages from Stella. The first was her typical greeting and asking me how my day was, but the second asked me if I was okay. One missed call followed but the second showed it'd been answered. I slipped the phone into my back pocket and sat down beside Marc. He stirred, opening his eyes to look up at me.

"You okay?" he asked.

"Yeah."

"Need a big gay snuggle?" He held his arms up to me and I chuckled.

"A little." I lay down next to him and he big-spooned me, both of us growing quiet as the news flashed across the television screen. Marc changed it to some stupid comedy show then dropped his arm over my middle again. "Where's Gavin?"

"Work."

"What does he do again?"

"Attorney, goon. Remember?" He poked my stomach and I squirmed.

"I forgot…"

"So your doctor lady came rushing over here," he said. I couldn't see him, but I could hear the smile in his voice. "She's something."

"She's incredible."

"And you're smitten."

"Trying not to be too *smitten*."

"Why, Allie?" He tugged my shoulder back until I looked at him.

"Because, Marc. Look at my track record. And she's still getting over her dead fiancée. She cried the entire time we had sex the first time, and I wasn't far behind. And, we've only slept together once." I told him most of the things I hadn't confessed to him before.

"That's...pretty complicated. But wait, you, Alice *Rabbit*

Lange, only had sex with Doctor Hotpants *once*? And you've been dating—"

"Hanging out—"

"*Dating* for over a month?"

"Yes. Those facts are correct, Marcus *Jerkoff* Goldman." I punched him in the shoulder and he laughed.

"No wonder I caught you masturbating. Your poor neglected tiny penis." He patted the top of my head and I laughed hard, tossing a punch at his shoulder.

"Shut up and leave my tiny penis out of it." I grabbed a pillow and attempted to smother him. Marc's muffled chuckles had me cracking up. He shoved me from the couch and I landed on the carpet with a grunt. "Jerk."

"Shut up and watch the movie."

"Then order food."

"Hmm. Good idea."

***

I arrived at Stella's, a bottle of red wine in hand, and knocked on the door to her apartment. I waited only a moment until it swung open and she appeared. With her hair swept back, and clad in a casual pair of blue jeans and a T-shirt, the brightest thing about her was her smile. She greeted me more readily now, with less tentativeness and more affection than she had in the beginning of our friendship or relationship.

"Sorry, I'm late," I said when she kissed my cheek.

"I'm prepared for your chronic lateness and willing to accept your offering." She held her hands out and I laughed as I plopped the bottle of wine in them.

"For my sins, my penance."

"You're forgiven," she said, chuckling after. "Dinner's almost ready."

I slipped out of my jacket and left my soggy boots by the front door. "I thought we were ordering in."

"Nah. Figured you'd enjoy something different."

As I made my way down the hall, the delicious aroma of herbs and something meaty wafted my way. "Smells great."

"Anything you don't eat or that you're allergic to? I realized I never asked," she said as she brought the corkscrew to the dining room table. Two place settings, with neatly folded napkins and shiny silverware, sat adjacent to each other. Stella set the bottle down and I watched as she uncorked it like a professional wine connoisseur.

"I eat everything and no allergies to food," I said and moved the two wine glasses closer to her.

"Any other allergies?"

"Penicillin, but I doubt you're pretreating dinner with that, Doc." I laughed softly as she poured the wine.

She chuckled and set the bottle down on the table. "Sorry. Can't take the doctor out of me sometimes."

"I wouldn't want you to." I picked up my glass and held it to hers, letting them gently clink together. "Cheers."

She mimicked the gesture with a smile. "What are we toasting?"

"Hmm." I licked my lips after a sip of the sweet red. "Your beautiful eyes."

"Really?" She laughed, shaking her head at me. "If you get to toast my eyes, I get to toast your smile."

"Deal." Again, we clinked glasses and indulged in our beverages together.

"I made salmon and roasted veggies. That sound okay?"

"It sounds amazing. Can I help with anything?"

"You brought the wine. Now I'm happy." She swept into the kitchen and, for a moment, I took the opportunity to check out her rear. In her relaxed fit jeans, it hid the sharper components of her hips, but they hung low enough to reveal the gentle curve below her navel. It made my mouth water way more than the thought of dinner.

Stella returned to the table a few minutes later with two plated dishes, and set one at each spot. We tucked in together, and our comfortable routine fell into place. The salmon melted in my mouth at the very first bite and I couldn't help smiling. "This is great," I told her. "No one has cooked for me like this in a really long time."

"I'm happy to and I'm glad you like it." She smiled after sliding her fork from her lips. "Tell me about what happened today with work?"

"Walsh called me and gave me time off to think about my decision. I told him I was sure, but he said I had two weeks paid vacation, at the very least, to think about it," I said, my gaze meeting hers. "Will you still see me if I'm unemployed and homeless in six months?"

She swatted my arm then continued. "Are you completely sure about it?"

"I feel sure for now. I'll give it the two weeks and see, but when they told me that they'd connected the vandalism to Butler officially..." I paused, shaking my head a little. "That was kind of it for me. I'm not happy there and add that to it…" I shrugged. "I'll find something else. Law enforcement wasn't what I expected on any level."

"You've been in it ten years?"

"About that, yeah. Right after college."

"Did you always want to be a cop?"

"I wanted to be a lawyer, initially, but that's too much school. My dad and brother were both deployed at the time. I didn't want to worry about loans and tests and finding a job as an attorney. Mom needed me at home, especially after dad got hurt."

"His leg, right?"

"I.E.D. in Afghanistan. Ended his career. My brother came home with PTSD and it ruined his marriage for awhile. It was messy," I told her, half our plates nearly gone at that point. "But it worked out for everyone. Did you always want to be a doctor?"

"I did, but I liked emergency medicine best and trauma surgery. I figured I could do both, somewhat, in the E.R. My dad is a neuroscientist, or was. Alzheimer's has taken away some of his ability to take care of himself, but he can tell you all about the brain and its function. I used to think

I wanted to be a neurologist and a neurosurgeon but..." She shook her head. "No way. That's too delicate for me."

"Like getting your hands dirty, do you?" I cocked a brow at her and she laughed.

"I do." She nudged a piece of broccoli around her dish as a gentle hush fell between us for a heartbeat or two. "I really like spending time with you, Allie. You're the first person whose company I've enjoyed in years."

"Right back at you. Honestly, I've never spent time like this with another woman. Not in this way where there's quality time and talking, along with everything else." A smile melted over my lips before I even spoke my next phrase. "I could talk to you forever. About anything."

"I know the feeling. I haven't talked to anyone about my life since Clarissa died. You're the first person I've talked to about it in general..." She set her fork down, with only a few bites left on her plate.

"Did you talk to Clarissa the way you talk to me?" Our gazes met and she hesitated for a second before answering with a faint nod.

"Yes. But she's the only one."

"You don't deserve to be locked away from the world, Stella. It's much better with you in it. At least my world is," I confessed, leaning back in my chair now to look at her. "We have a knack for turning things serious. Don't we?"

"We do, but I don't hate it."

"Me either."

After we finished the rest of our dinner, we carried our wine into the living room and took up perch in our usual spaces. Unlike last time, however, we sat much closer to each other, our knees almost touching. In the quiet comfort of Stella's living room, with the cozy sofa and a fire crackling in the hearth, all the bad things in the world seemed so far away.

"Jordan's having a get together at her house on Saturday night. I usually go alone, but would you want to come with me? It's just dinner with a bunch of lesbians who like to talk about sex and pretty hair. No doubt someone will get a haircut," I said, broaching the subject with caution.

"How many people?" She tucked her hair behind her ears, but didn't refuse me right away. I loved that her nervous quirk became immediately obvious to me.

"Usually seven. I'm the one who makes things odd, so eight if you came. Ainsley will be there."

"Hmm. Is it important to you?"

"Not particularly." I let out a soft chuckle. "Only if you want to come. No pressure."

"How about a tentative yes for now?"

"I'll take it."

Stella smiled, scooting a little closer and laying her hand on top of mine on the back of the couch. Her fingers snuck under the sleeve of my sweater to stroke my wrist. I let my other hand fall between us to rest on her knee.

"You're still a little upset from yesterday," she said, softly. "I can tell."

"How?" I met her gaze and she offered me a soft smile.

"Moving slowly and appearing as if you'll cry at any moment. And not looking at me as much as you were over dinner."

All I could do was nod to that declaration. "I'm sorry."

"And apologizing for what again?" She reached forward and stroked my cheek. "Now it's your turn to tell me what you want, Allie. Because you know what I want already."

"To see me naked?" I laughed, leaning into her touch.

"Always." She chuckled and just the sound of it lifted my worries away.

"To be fair, I always want to see you naked, too. That's never a question or doubt." I offered her a grin and she snickered, moving forward then and catching me in a kiss that nearly took my breath away. I let her lower me backward onto the sofa, one hand on my hip as she guided my legs around her. My fingers in her hair sent it tumbling over us in a sweet-smelling canopy as we explored each others' mouths with vigor.

Any concerns about life dripped away from me and I lost myself in the beautiful woman above me. This time, neither of us were tentative about our movements or wants. I grabbed gentle handfuls of her breasts, massaging them through her shirt as she immediately released the button of my jeans, pushing my sweater up to expose my navel. When I released her breasts to grab the hem of her shirt, she ended our kiss to allow me to pull it off her and toss it away. She held herself above me, the sensual muscles of her biceps flexing under her weight. I met her gaze as heavy breaths left the both of us, then reached around her with one hand and popped open her bra. It fell down her arms and she threw it on the floor. My mouth accompanied my hands on her breasts, and I took one of her nipples into my mouth.

Stella's eyes closed and she arched under my affection, as lust and desire burned between my legs. I'd been waiting days for this, to have her again. With less pain and fear than our first time together, Stella seemed to ache for the same. She leaned back, kneeling between my knees then helped me out of my sweater and bra at a hurried pace. She lowered me into the cushions again to catch me in a hungry kiss. A soft moan escaped me the moment her hands gripped my breasts. There wasn't anything hesitant about her tonight and I loved every minute of it.

Fingers tickled down my stomach, reaching the waist of my panties. She slid her hand down them, caressing my lower stomach gently until she landed on the top of my mound. A single stroke of my clit had me shuddering until she cupped me in the palm of her hand. Heat rushed my cheeks when I felt my own wetness against her, and my gasp ended our kiss. Heavy breaths left her, mingling with mine in the space between us. She watched me, her gaze locked on mine as she worked my pussy with confident strokes. My body lifted toward her and she leaned down to nibble my bottom lip.

"You're beautiful," she told me. "So beautiful, Allie."

My heart skipped a beat as I rocked against her, shaky hands making for her breasts again. But she slipped out of my grasp and removed her hand from my panties at the same time. I nearly cried when she disconnected, but when she tugged my bottoms off, I braced myself from appearing too wanton. Still kneeling between my legs, she looked down at me like she had last time, except now the brighter light allowed her to see more of me.

Firm hands massaged my thighs, her thumbs caressing my folds as her gaze lingered on my core. I gripped the cushions of the sofa, gasping again when her thumbs met my clit at the same time. "You're going to kill me, you know."

"Good thing I'm a doctor," she said, chuckling as she leaned down to kiss my stomach below my navel. "I've been waiting a long time to do this."

"My God." My hands fell into her hair, and I nearly whimpered, but I bit my tongue to prevent it. "Why wait?"

"Good question." More kisses followed until her lips hovered above my clit. I watched as she parted my folds, touching me with gentility meant for thin glass. At times, her exploration of my pussy seemed fear-based, tangled with a curiosity that I remembered only from my first time with a girl. But Stella wasn't a virgin and I reaped the benefits.

At first, gentle swirls of her tongue over my clit had me moaning, my back arching to meet her, until she moved down to lap at my folds. A cry escaped me and I tore at the cushions under my hips. I watched as a smile accompanied her movements, her gaze locked on mine a moment before she took me without any reserve.

My body screamed under her treatment, writhing and building quickly toward the release I craved. She slipped inside me, her tongue diving deep and hungrily as she rubbed my clit rapidly from side to side. When she switched to sucking my clit and sliding a single finger inside me, I nearly screamed when my pleasure peaked, exploding into an orgasm so strong that every muscle in my body seized with enjoyment. Cries left me, tangling with moans as she worked me through it, until I collapsed in a trembling mess under her.

Attention left my sensitive clit, but she continued to massage my pussy as she crawled back up my body. I grabbed on to her, pulling her into a hug so fiercely that I worried I'd freak her out. But I didn't. She wrapped me up in a secure embrace, kissing along my neck and shoulder. I buried my face in her hair, but my shaking only intensified with the emotions that rose without control.

"It's okay," she whispered, the same way I had to her our first time. She kissed the space below my ear as she held me.

Why did we do this with each other? Why did sex mean crying? All the pain and fear that I'd kept shoved down deeply inside me over the last few days made it to the surface, disrupting my afterglow, but not stopping my pussy from throbbing against her thigh. I hadn't noticed when she'd removed her pants, but the skin-to-skin contact soothed me. I rocked my hips against her and she shifted her position so that I could feel her core, hot and soaked, against my leg as well.

I released her, leaning back to cup her face and capture her in a heated kiss as we began grinding together, our centers colliding in a centrifugal dance. Stella's overheated body and confident movements encouraged me to meet her with the same voracity. We bucked against each other while I sucked her bottom lip then moved on to her neck. For the first time, we moved in unison, and that passion, that fire, tangoed with lust, desire, while sweat coated our skin.

Her moans in my ear, as she raked her teeth over my shoulder, had me biting my lip in fear of making a sound that disrupted her enjoyment. My nails scratched along her spine at the same time that she reached between us, cupping my pussy in hurried fashion. I returned the gesture, grabbing her in the same way as our grinding turned to thrusting, as we both loved and fucked each other.

So badly I wanted to feel her come against me, to see the mark I left on her flesh by sucking her skin, tagging her as mine. Wetness rushed my palm, at the same time that fire built in my belly. Stella cried out, arching her back as she pressed two fingers deep inside me. I returned the favor and she clenched my fingers as she came, her face contorted in beautiful, tragic ecstasy. I bucked against her, joining her when a second climax threatened to break me apart at the center. My mouth watered, catching my breath at the same time that she captured my mouth.

We rocked together, kissing and holding our way through the gentle downfall like the cascade of ash following a volcanic eruption. It sprinkled us with sensation, comfort, and happiness and I allowed myself to fall under the swell.

Our kiss ended and Stella collapsed on top of me, her head on the sofa beside mine as we panted together, our legs tangled in a sweet heap of flesh and sex. Neither of us spoke for a long time, until our breathing returned to normal and the coolness of the air around us reminded me of our nakedness. She rolled to the side, though her pussy still pressed against my thigh in a manner I never wanted her to leave, and pulled the knitted blanket from the back of the sofa. It draped over us and we shifted so that we could hold each other better.

I kissed each of her closed eyelids and she smiled, her fingers tickling up and down my side in a delicate caress. Goosebumps coated my flesh while I let her keep me melted, in a puddle pooled only for her with her fingers leaving ripples in my soul.

By the time the fire smoldered to embers, at least an hour or two later, I rolled in and out of lucid sleep until Stella shifted beside me.

"Stay over?" she asked softly, her lips a breath from mine.

"Yes." I closed the gap between us and kissed her gently while stroking the chilly flesh of her shoulders. "You're cold."

"A little. Let's go in the bedroom."

"Okay."

We stood together, holding hands while Stella led me into the room after snatching her phone from the hall table. She pulled back the comforter and top sheet, and gestured for me to precede her. I crawled into the cool comfort of her bed, pulling the covers over me while watching her. Dim light filtered into the room from the cityscape similar to my apartment, but not nearly as intense. Stella climbed into bed beside me, the screen on her phone illuminating her pretty face.

"I just need to check the service app for work," she said, tapping a few things while I watched her.

"What's that do?"

"Gives me updates on any of my patients if needed, messages, or if doctor coverage is needed. I'm not on call, but I check it to make sure shit isn't hitting the fan," she explained, while I brushed my lips over her shoulder. She draped her leg over mine and stroked my calf with her toes.

"No shit on the fan?"

"Nope." She smiled, turning to me but still holding the phone up with the screen light on us. When the app closed, a shutter sounded and I flinched, recoiling a little when my knees bent in reaction.

"Don't take my picture."

"What? I'm not." She lowered the phone to the bed, and turned to me, her brow furrowed. "Allie?"

"I just don't like it." My words came out much more pressured than I intended.

"Okay, good to know. You don't like any pictures at all?" She turned on her side now so that we were facing each other, our lower halves pressed together when I relaxed my legs again.

"No, it's okay. Just not when I don't expect it."

"All right." She reached forward and ran her fingers through my hair, tugging gently when the length of it stretched past my chin between us. Her smile evoked my own and I dragged my thumb over her bottom lip.

"You're so pretty," I told her. "And your lips get really red after sex." I laughed softly and she tugged my hair again.

"That's news to me." She chuckled. "But until you came into my life, it'd been five years since I'd had an orgasm. Maybe my lips are making up for it." She kissed my thumb then pretended to bite it.

"Wait...five years without sex or without an orgasm?"

"Both."

"I would die without an orgasm for five years."

"You wouldn't die. It's physically impossible. Doctors know these things." She laughed softly and I swatted her arm.

"I'd be the first medical marvel to drop dead from lack of coming. You can pronounce me and Ainsley can cut me open." I laughed at the expression on her face and the way her belly jumped against mine as she cracked up.

"Are you a serial masturbator, Allie?"

"Guilty as charged." My cheeks heated under my laughter and the topic. "That first night, when you asked me to get naked for you, I went home and committed at least three crimes."

"Alice!" Hysterics ensued and I about died from it. I loved seeing her so happy and unreserved in both our sex and conversation. "You're too much. I love it."

"It's the truth," I said once we calmed down, and she leaned in to kiss me, both of us still chuckling.

"Good." She scooted closer and we wrapped each other in a hug.

"I can't believe five years."

"Five years since everything, Allie. Until you." Seriousness fell around us again in its usual way and she nuzzled me gently while I squeezed her.

"Well, at the very least, I hope it's been worth it."

"More than you know."

CHAPTER ELEVEN

"I'm so happy you came, Stella." Jordan, with her pink and blue streaks mixed in with her usual black, gushed to Stella as we stood in her kitchen, pouring our second glasses of wine.

"It's been lovely meeting Alice's friends," she said, her hip pressed against mine while I listened to the chattering voices of everyone. Ainsley talked Kari's ear off while Grace and Cin picked out a few appetizers from the various plates set around the island counter.

Jordan's apartment, above the Mermaid Salon, wasn't extraordinarily large, but her kitchen was to die for. Marble tile, black furnishings, and silver everything else made it the sleekest room I'd ever stepped foot in. The dining room off the big kitchen and the living room that followed wasn't the same. Vibrant colors accented the sleepy grays, just like Jordan herself.

"Stella, come here and look at this a moment," Ainsley called out, waving her to Kari. Stella glanced at me but broke away with caution, and made her way to Ainsley. In her tight black jeans, and long tunic sweater, I couldn't pull my eyes away from the way she moved. Her boots, a moderate heel, clicked on the hard tiles.

Jordan dragged my attention back to her by squeezing my wrist. "I'm sorry I forgot to warn you about inviting Kari. After everything, I felt—"

"Don't worry about it. I understand why you did. She's still my friend. Not necessarily a close one, but a friend," I said.

"It's not awkward?"

"It's been years since we ended it. I'm fine, Jordie."

"You know what else is *fine*?" She glanced over to Stella then back to me. "Your doctor is fucking gorgeous."

"Shh." I swatted her arm to keep her quiet. "Don't scare her off. She's not a huge social event person."

"Don't tell me that. Ainsley's the scary one. What the hell are they doing? Are they taking out the stitches in her arm?"

I laughed as I watched Ainsley pull out a first aid kit. "I think so."

"We're both dating doctors. Crazy ones, mind you. Most docs can't be bothered with *working* outside of *work*."

"Stella's different. She really cares about people."

"Ainsley's just awkward."

"And you love it."

"I do." She smiled, wagging her brows while she sipped her wine. "So...Marc told me you're jobless."

"Sort of. I semi-quit. I still have time to decide."

"Are you sure you're ready to turn in your badge, Alice? It's meant a lot to you."

"Has it? Doesn't feel like it. Got any job openings in your gay underwater hair place?"

"Hmm… janitor is free. And hair sweeper-upper."

I laughed and shoved her shoulder. "I'll take it."

After some time, the seven of us brought the snacks into the living room along with our wine. Small conversations wove in and out among the women, but Stella grew quieter in the large group. She took a seat on the sofa, setting her glass down on the end table. When I sat beside her, I slid my hand into her lap.

Grace joined us, taking a seat across from us on the coffee table. "I approve of your girlfriend, Allie," she said, grinning as she glanced at Stella then looked back to me.

"Thanks?" I laughed at her, nudging her ankle with my foot. "I don't need your approval. Take a hike."

"Yeah, yeah." She winked at Stella, turned on her Doc Marten-covered heel, then ran her fingers through her short spiky pink hair before heading back to Cin. I looked to Stella who wore a half-smile on her semi-frozen doctor-face. "You good?"

"She's interesting. I'm okay. Does she often *approve* of your entanglements?" She cocked a brow at me.

"I didn't sleep with her." I chuckled and Stella laughed at me. "Kari's the only one in this room that I've slept with other than you."

"Uh huh…"

"I mean it." I swatted her leg and she snickered. "You know, Grace called you my girlfriend before I did."

"I know," she said. Again, that seriousness fell on us. "Am I?"

"Do you want to be?"

She nodded, leaning forward to nudge my forehead with hers. "Yes. What've I been to you before now?"

"Stella. What've I been to you?"

"Allie." She smiled then kissed me gently.

The evening carried on generally uneventfully, filled with talk of who was now sleeping with who and the Wildrose drama, to how everyone was doing at work. Eventually, Eve and her girlfriend, Ciara, showed up. Eve, with her auburn bob and constant awkwardness bordering on calamity, with Ciara, the epitome of grace and sex appeal, drew the attention of everyone when they arrived. And I pointed out to Stella the connection that Ainsley had to Eve, and how Eve introduced her to Jordan.

"Just exactly how much *co-mingling* has occurred in your friends group, Allie?" Stella laughed softly after asking.

"Depends on who you're asking about."

"Tell me about *The Chart* of present." She linked her arm with mine while we watched everyone greet the new arrivals.

"Well…" I laughed, leaning my head on her shoulder. "Who should I start with?"

"You." She bumped my forehead with her chin.

"Easy. Kari only. Next question."

"So if you're the conservative one, who has the most connections on the lesbian chart here?"

I laughed harder now at her almost-diplomatic way of asking who was the sluttiest. "That'd be Eve, no doubt."

"Are you talking about me, Lange?" Eve narrowed her eyes at me as she made her way over to kiss my cheek. She did a double-take when she saw Stella, and her gaze lingered on her as if trying to place her.

"I am and this is my...girlfriend, Stella C—"

"Corwin. Doctor Corwin. From the hospital, I remember." Eve shook her hand then leaned against the arm of the sofa. Her service weapon poked out from the spot at her hip, though her sweater only covered some of it. It reminded me that mine remained tucked behind my back, but without the accompanying badge. "Good to see you. I had no idea you were dating," she said, returning her gaze to me.

Neither did we, I wanted to say but went with, "We're pretty new."

"So what gossip were you sharing about me?" Eve smirked, glancing at Ciara who still chatted animatedly with Cin and Grace.

"Just telling Stella how everyone knows each other," I said, sidestepping the truth.

"Uh huh. And?"

"We work together." I laughed because I couldn't hold onto it anymore. Stella chuckled beside me. "Eve works in homicide—wait, sex crimes now."

"I do and word on the beat is that you're thinking of resigning?" she asked, as if she'd been waiting to for ages.

"Yeah. But it's not worth getting in to right now."

"When Walsh wanted to transfer me to sex crimes, I quit. Walked right out." She gestured toward the door. "But they bullied me back and I unquit."

"Do you like sex crimes better?"

"No, but it's more active and I get to shoot more people."

Stella's eyes widened and the two of us laughed.

"She's kidding," I said, squeezing her hand.

"Partially. It's more active in hunting down suspects and helping vics. Bias crimes is the least active in that sense."

"It depends. It's least active for me because I do a lot of outreach. It was more active for Butler and Marc until Butler lost his shit."

"I heard…"

Awkward silence. Which was Eve's specialty.

"It's fine," I said, breaking the pause.

"So, are you telling Stella about how much of a slut I am?" she jested.

"You mean how you have the most connections on the chart?" I stuck my finger in the air and pretended to draw. "Eve to Jordan, Jordan to Ainsley. Eve to Ainsley—

"That doesn't count. We didn't sleep together—"

"Eve to Grace, Grace to Cin, Cin to Kari, Kari to Alice. Eve to Ciara. Eve to Kari, Kari to Alice. Alice to... *literally* no one else, you giant whorebag." I cracked up as Eve began shoving my shoulder, knocking me into Stella who laughed just as hard.

"Oh my God, you two," Stella said.

"Shut up, Lange." Eve smirked. "If it wasn't for me, no one would be friends."

"How come the two of you never got together?" Stella asked, rather bravely.

"She's awkward as all hell." I pointed at Eve. "No joke. Total nightmare."

Eve pointed right back at me. "She doesn't trust anyone

at all. Like no one."

I had no answer to that at all.

"Evie, what are you doing to Alice?" Ciara sauntered up behind Eve and ran her fingers through her hair. Ciara's stark red hair stood out against the dark dress she wore. Stella's eyes widened when she approached. "Good to see you, Alice."

"You two. Ciara, this is my girlfriend Stella." I gestured between them and they shook hands cordially.

"Nice to meet you," Stella said.

"You, too." Ciara smiled then gave Eve's hair a tug.

"Hey." Eve elbowed her gently. "I'm not doing anything to her. She's calling me a slut."

"Well...you are." Ciara grinned and we all laughed when Eve grabbed her roughly around the middle. "*Ouch*, with that damn gun already." She rubbed her hip and Eve laughed.

"I'm starving. Feed me." Eve pouted at Ciara who tugged her hair again.

"Fine. Let's go eat and wine you up." They stood together and, as usual, Eve nearly tripped over her stilettos.

"They're cute," Stella said, returning to holding my elbow. The rest of the women in the room chatted so intensely that is sounded like twenty people joined us.

"They are. Been together two years. Eve's longest relationship ever. She's really in love with Ciara, and Ciara with her. It's nice to see," I said, resting my hand on top of hers. "Doing okay in this crowd?"

She nodded. "They're very entertaining. When you're here alone, who do you talk to the most?"

"A little of everyone. I'm on the quieter side sometimes."

Stella grew quiet for a moment then asked, "Do you really not trust anyone?"

Hesitation caught me for a moment, and I met her gaze. "It's been hard to. Kari cheated on me for the last six months of our two-year relationship. Some of them knew and didn't tell me. How could I trust them after that?"

"How'd you find out?"

"Jordan told me when she learned of it."

"Did you love Kari?"

"As a person, sure. Was I in love with her?" I shook my head. "No."

"Ainsley fawns over Jordan." She nodded in their direction where Jordan sat across from Grace while Ainsley stood behind her, playing with her hair. The three of them talked together, but I couldn't hear what they were saying.

"Jordan's not far behind. She loves Ainsley. And Jordan is just as bad as Eve about sleeping with everyone. Eve's a one-nighter though. Jordan's the short-term relationship type."

"Lesbians," Stella said, smirking a bit. "And then they stay friends."

I laughed, nodding along with it. "Yep."

"Do you trust me, Allie?" she asked out of nowhere.

"I do, but I'd be lying if I said that it didn't scare me…" I glanced away from her then met her gaze again when she squeezed my hand.

"I'm highly monogamous, if that soothes you any," she said, reaching up to stroke my cheek.

"It does." I leaned into her touch and she smiled.

Ainsley joined us a bit later and I listened as she engaged Stella in an animated conversation about Alzheimer's brains post-mortem. Stella shared some information about her father and it made me happy to know that she spoke to someone readily other than me. While we all indulged on Jordan's enormous spread of foods and alcohol, dishes began piling up on the tables around us and forks clinked against dinnerware.

Kari approached us, smiling gently as she called my name. "Allie, can I talk to you a minute in private?"

"Um…" I glanced to Stella who slipped her arm from

mine in an approving gesture. "Yeah. Okay," I agreed, standing to join her. She led me away from the group to the quieter area near Jordan's bedroom. "What's going on?"

"I know we're here to have fun, but I got this." She pulled a bunch of papers from her purse and handed them to me. "From the insurance company."

"Oh. Right…" I took them and glanced over some of the figures they offered for reimbursement. "Does it cover everything?"

"Yeah and a little more…"

"Okay." I looked back to her, holding the papers between us. "What do I need to do?"

"Just sign that after you read it. It's your building and stuff…"

"Could've fooled me," I said, snatching a pen and signing off on the bottom of the document. Kari shifted her weight uncomfortably and, when I leaned down on the table, I noted that she still wore her usual combat boots and skinny jeans combination.

"Allie, I know I don't pay rent or anything, for the apartment or bar—"

"Look, Kari, I really don't care—"

"I can buy it from you, if you wanted. I mean, it's been ten years and up until now I haven't really needed to bother you with anything about it…" She folded her arms over her middle and, when I faced her, her subdued posture remained as she watched me, tentative eyes tucked between her dark curls.

"Do you really want to buy it?"

"Yeah. I mean, the appraiser had to come out after all the damage and he gave me a number for the value of it."

"With or without mortgaging it?" I asked, crossing my arms over my middle as I glanced down the hall toward where Stella still spoke with ease to Ainsley and Jordan.

"Without...the insurance money helped."

"Okay. If we just do a private transaction like at the

bank or something. I don't want to do lawyers and mortgages and get tied up with stuff for weeks," I told her as relief flooded me at the thought of being free of that attachment.

"Really?" Her eyes widened and she dropped her arms as her excitement built.

"Yeah. I don't care. It'll be easier." I shrugged, barely getting a chance to react when she rushed me in a hug. I started, returning it half-heartedly.

"Allie! This is amazing. I never thought you'd say yes!" She nearly squealed, squeezing me so tight, and lifting me slightly. I wriggled out of her grip.

"Don't lift me like that. You know I hate it and it's not a big deal, really." I held my hand up between us, keeping her at a distance as my heart pounded.

"Sorry, I got overwhelmed. You'll really sell it to me?"

"It's your bar, Kari. Yeah. It's fine." I reached behind my back, allowing my fingers to graze the gun that lingered in the waist of my jeans. "Call me after you get things set up. I'll meet you to sign whatever."

"You're amazing. Thank you."

"Like I said, it's your bar." I nodded to her and handed her back the papers from the table. We didn't say anything else as I stepped around her and headed back toward the group. I found Stella and Ainsley by the dining room table where Ainsley showed her something on her phone.

Stella looked up at me, smiling at first then her expression dimmed. She turned from Ainsley and held her hands to me. "What's wrong?"

"Nothing. I'm fine," I said, gripping her hand tightly.

"You look about ready to faint, Alice," Ainsley pointed out. "Or have a panic attack."

"I'm fine." Though I felt the anxiety shift to anger as I glanced at Kari. Why did she have to lift me like that?

A bang sounded, followed by the crunching crash of something below my feet. It reverberated enough through the building that I felt the tremor under my boots.

Everyone quieted and I looked to Jordan, my own emotions squashed away immediately. "Is someone supposed to be in the salon?"

"No," she said, hurrying toward the door, but I rushed to grab her by the arm.

"Stop." My gaze met Eve's and she was beside us right away. "We'll check. You stay here. Where are your keys?"

"Here." Jordan handed me her keys after lifting them from the table. "Alarm code is four-seven-three-one."

"Call the cops," Grace said, moving to Jordan's side at the same time Stella stepped closer to me. "If the alarm didn't go off."

"We are the cops, Grace," said Eve, smirking as she pulled her weapon from its holster.

"Call more cops then," Grace pressed, her lips pursed.

"Go ahead." I nodded to Jordan then glanced to Stella. "Stay here."

"Alice—"

"Just stay here. Okay?"

Stella's face froze and I watched as her hands curled into fists the same way they had on the night I dropped her off at work. Breaking away from her was incredibly difficult, but Eve and I hurried out the door together.

Once outside, I drew my weapon and looked to Eve. "I'll lead," I said.

"No, I'll lead, Lange. You've surrendered your badge. We need this clean if it's targeted," she said, which told me she knew pretty much everything about what went on with Butler.

"Fine. Okay." I gestured for her to move first and we hurried down the wooden staircase on the side of the building.

We made our way to the side door of the salon, taking the alley around back. Darkness wasn't our friend, but Eve's cautious, nearly silent steps led the way. She nodded toward the thick metal door and I slipped the key in the lock. It clicked and she nodded for me to step aside. I gripped the handle, pulled it open, and she swung inside with her weapon drawn.

Inside the dark salon, only the glow of the neon lights from the sign out front brought any sort of visibility to the scene. Bright blue and pink, occasionally flickering, dampened my senses. I flanked Eve and poked the code into the blinking alarm panel. Eve glanced at me as we made it to the front part of the salon. She nodded right and I moved in that direction, weapon in the lead, as she shifted left.

Save for the hum of some electronic equipment, no sound met my ears until something crunched under Eve's feet. She looked down then to the front door that had a giant crack in it with a hole in the center. Glass littered the floor near it. We paused for a moment, then checked the rest of the salon before flicking on the lights.

"Clear," I called out. "No one's here."

"No one but a broken door," she said, holstering her weapon to take a walk through. "See what broke it?"

"I don't. Maybe they took it with them."

"No brick with a creepy note wrapped around it?"

"Nope. And I doubt it's a coincidence that a gay-owned salon was vandalized after a gay bar was just weeks ago. And both of them have ties to me." I leaned against the salon chair, frowning at the glass on the floor.

"I wouldn't say it's connected yet. This is Seattle after all," she said, pulling out her phone. "I'm going to tell them we're good."

Sirens wailed in the distance and Eve unlocked the front door to allow the uniforms entry when they arrived. By the time they got there, the rest of the women from our party joined us. Jordan, Ainsley, Ciara, and Eve stayed outside with the grunts to file the report.

Stella moved to my side immediately, and when she extended her arms, I made no attempt to hide my eagerness to accept her hug. She held me, her lips pressed against my neck and I squeezed her tightly. Her return was just as strong and, when she moved aside toward one of the chairs, my foot lifted from the ground and sent a jolt of anxiety up my center.

"Don't lift me," I told her, releasing her and taking a step back, my hands on her shoulders.

"Allie, I'm not lifting you. That's the second time I've heard you say that tonight. What's the matter?"

"Can we go? I want to go." My gaze fixed on her sleek black heels as I fought the anger and emotion that tightened my throat.

"Of course," she said, her voice soft. "Can you look at me please?" She ran her fingers through my hair, and I did so. Her eyes darted over my face then she took my hand, leading me toward the side door.

She pulled out her phone and ordered the Uber for us while we waited by the corner of the shop. Jordan came over and hugged both of us. "They're going to file the report."

"We're going to head home, Jordan, if there isn't anything else you need from us," Stella said, compensating for me for the first time ever. "Thank you for inviting us."

"We're good, but thank you for coming. Allie?" Jordan squeezed my shoulder and her eyes searched my face just like Stella's. "They don't think it's connected."

"It's fine. I'll talk to you tomorrow."

"You're upset," she said, glancing between Stella and me.

"I'm just—I just want to go, okay?

"Yeah," she said, grabbing handfuls of my hair as she pulled me toward her, her forehead pressed against mine. "I'll call you later."

"I'm sorry," I told her.

"Did you break my door?" She smirked, tugging my hair before letting go. "Didn't think so."

The Uber pulled up a second later.

"Bye, Jordie," I said as we broke away from her.

"G'night, Al." She glanced to Stella and the two shared

a brief moment before we piled into the car.

***

"You know, up until this point, you haven't reminded me of Clarissa," Stella said as she sat next to me on the sofa, handing me a hot mug of tea. "But right now you do."

"How?" I asked her, accepting her caretaking at the moment. "Thanks."

"She had this brightness about her all the time, until something hurt her deeply. It dimmed the light in her eyes and she wouldn't look at me. Just like you're doing right now," she told me, and I looked up to meet her gaze again. "I know this situation with your ex-partner at work has hurt you deeply. And I know that you haven't talked about it with me which makes me think that you haven't talked about it at all."

"I'm sorry, Stell. I suck at life when I'm angry," I said, sipping the tea then holding it in my lap.

"The anger is covering something else, Allie. I can feel it and see it in you. Whatever it is made you freak out when you thought I was taking your picture, and then I heard you shout at Kari about lifting you, then you stopped me from doing it even though I wasn't," she pointed out, her hand falling to my knee. "And the other night Marc told me you didn't want him touching you. I'm a doctor, Allie, I know what this level of fear response means and it worries me that you're not talking about it."

"You didn't talk about Clarissa," I said, not really knowing my point.

"I didn't. To anyone but you. If I hadn't talked about her, then I don't think we'd be where we are together. And I'm glad I told you, I'm glad to have you in my life because of it."

That did it and the tears I'd been holding on to tumbled silently down my cheeks. "I'm glad to have you, too."

"Talk to me, Alice, because whatever is bothering you, is getting more intense every day. It started when Butler picked you up and tossed you, didn't it?"

"Yeah." I laughed a little at the admission, taking a swipe at my eyes before setting the mug on the coffee table. "Reminded me that I'm a sack of shit that men can toss around and take advantage of. I'd almost forgotten about that."

"Not all men."

"Not all." I sighed, leaning my head on my hand while propping my elbow on the back of the sofa. Stella's fingers tangled with mine and she held my hand in her lap. "I mean, I don't remember any of it, but I had to watch it."

"What do you mean?"

I shook my head. "Sorry. When I was in college, sophomore year, these guys who I thought were my friends, they put roofies in my drink. So much that I passed out for almost a whole day, I think. I don't even remember passing out, but what I know is that the two of them recorded themselves having sex with me. They put the video on the internet, and I saw it. The only thing I remember is the sensation of being lifted up. But watching them do that to me…"

"Easy," she said, moving closer to me and only then did I realize that I was sobbing so hard my chest heaved, but I couldn't stop the words from falling out of my mouth.

"It wasn't violent or anything, but half the school saw that video. The guys got expelled, charged with rape and whatever else, but it didn't matter. That video, you can't take that shit back once it's out there. I had to down pills to not get pregnant, and deal with all of my friends knowing. My girlfriend broke up with me. My parents never found out. I was an adult. And it was around the same time my dad got his leg blown off and my brother was deployed again. I came back to Washington and didn't tell anyone except Marc and eventually Jordan." I wiped my face on my sleeve and sniffled. "And became a cop to help other people to protect themselves."

When I met Stella's gaze again, tears pooled in her

sapphire eyes, and she leaned forward to hug me. I melted against her and, the moment the warmth of her engulfed me, I cried for real.

All the emotions that I'd kept locked up since the incident with Butler flowed freely after everything. I was a fool to think that it didn't bother me in the same way, and reminded me of what happened to me when I was barely nineteen.

"I'm sorry that happened to you, Alice." Stella kissed my cheek, keeping her lips against it while we embraced. "You deserve so much more than what people have given you."

"You deserve more than just pain and isolation," I told her, my cries slowing to quiet sobs again. I held on to her forearm so tight that a welt lingered on her skin when I let go.

"We both deserve more," she said, resting her forehead against mine.

"Can I stay here tonight?" I closed my eyes, breathing in her breath and the gentle fragrance of her perfume.

"You can stay here every night. Waking up beside you is one of my favorite things," she whispered and it made me smile.

***

I told Stella, I texted Marc early in the morning while she slept beside me. *I'm sorry I've not been myself.*

It's OK, Al. Glad u told her

Me too.

Double date soon?

Def.

Stella's warm hand snaked across my stomach, her T-shirt bunching up around my middle. I set my phone down and turned on my side to face her. She offered me a soft, groggy smile. "Hi."

"Hello," I said, smiling as I stroked her hair.

"Did you sleep?"

"A little."

"Come here." She held her arms to me and I scooted closer so she could pull me into a hug. I snuggled into her embrace and, for once in my life, I let someone console me.

"I'm selling the property to Kari," I told her. "For a decent amount."

"Is that what she wanted to talk about?"

"Yeah."

"You look very tired, Allie." Stella stroked my face, a soft smile lingering on her mouth. I leaned in to kiss her gently, stroking the soft curve of her neck.

"I'm a little tired," I told her. "But I don't want to sleep. What's the date?"

"Twenty-fourth."

"Is it really Christmas Eve?" I rolled on to my back and covered my face. "Do you work today or tomorrow?"

"I don't, but I was thinking of seeing my dad this afternoon…" She rolled on to her stomach, propping herself up on her elbows to look at me when I dropped my hands. "Since we're seeing your family tomorrow." She smiled at me, flicking her brows upward when I leaned up a bit.

"You decided to come?" Excitement jumped in my gut.

"I did. I survived Jordan's with you. Can't be much scarier than watching my girlfriend pull out a gun and run into danger," she said, her gaze lingering on mine.

"I'm sorry about telling you to stay put." I sat up now, leaning against the pillows and headboard. Stella rested her chin on my knee while looking up at me.

"Sometimes I forget you're a cop…"

"Sometimes I forget that you're a doctor until you touch me with your firm, deliberate hands that know exactly how to handle a human body, Stell." I ran my fingers through her hair, smiling while I took in the sight of her pretty face and the way her hair fell over her shoulders. She kissed my knee, then rubbed her hands up and down my sweatpants-covered leg. "What are you thinking about?"

"A few things."

"Tell me."

"I'm thinking that I'm worried about you being a cop. I'm angry about what happened to you and that you were alone in it," she admitted, sitting up now so that we were facing each other. I scooted closer so that I could wrap my arm around her bent knee.

"What else?" I watched as she glanced to the photo still perched on the nightstand.

"Today's Clarissa's birthday." With the final confession, her eyes darkened under her furrowed brow. "I've spent this day alone for five years. So much has changed, Alice. Part of me feels bad about everything."

"I didn't know that." I took her hands in mine and held them. "What do you feel bad about it?"

"Every year, I spent alone, sad, and locked away. Visiting Dad is a constant reminder sometimes." She sniffled, but her tears weren't uncontrolled like they used to be. I didn't connect how her father acted as a reminder but I just listened. "And now, today, and every day for the past few months, I'm happy. I woke up this morning happy to be beside you. Not obsessed with the date or day or its meaning. You were my first thought. You *are* my first thought. Not Clarissa anymore."

"What's that like for you? Knowing that?" I rubbed my thumbs over her knuckles. Tears continued to tumble down her cheeks but she laughed a little.

"Liberating, but sad. Half of me is so happy. The other half feels like I should be sad and devastated still. It's all I knew for so long."

"There are other ways to keep Clarissa in your life, Stella, than paralyzing grief. You had the greatest loss in the world and it takes time." I tugged her toward me, pulling her between my legs where she cuddled up against my chest. I wrapped my arms around her, and squeezed her with my legs. "What would she want for you?"

"We talked about it." She sniffled again, her tears fading. "A few times. I know she'd want me to be happy as I'd want her to be."

"Then be happy, Stella." I leaned my head against hers, sighing softly when she caressed my thigh.

We stayed together like that for a long time until her phone chirped. She grabbed it from the table and hit the silent button. "I should shower and get dressed."

"How do you feel about me joining you to see your dad?"

She watched me for a moment before answering, "He has Alzheimer's so sometimes he says things—"

"I can handle it."

"Then I'd like you to come."

"Good." I kissed her softly, and slid from the bed, tugging her with me on the way to the bathroom.

CHAPTER TWELVE

"Heterogeneity of subcortical brain development, Stella. That's the name of it." Doctor Corwin, the senior citizen version, ambled about the living room. The most jarring part of meeting Stella's father was his age. My parents, in their early sixties, seemed so young compared to the eighty-year-old former neuroscientist in front of me. His neatly combed gray hair matched the rest of his paleness, leaving him appearing slightly washed out. In neatly pressed green slacks and a yellow shirt, the pink socks he wore stood out like neon lights. "Increases in white matter and ventricular volume—"

"Dad? Come here a moment. I'm trying to introduce you to someone," Stella repeated a third time until her father finally stopped pacing and made his way to her. One of the walls in his apartment had dozens of pictures stuck to it and labels with names and notes. Stella's mother, Lena, as the writing beneath it revealed, looked just like her, except with lighter eyes. They shared dark hair, and a stunning smile. On the bottom of the card, in Stella's handwriting, it reminded him that Lena died years ago. Clarissa's picture was not on the wall with the rest of the family.

"Stella, basal ganglia is important," Doctor Corwin Senior said, looking from her to me.

"I know, Daddy. It's very important." She offered him a soft smile as she squeezed his hands. "Dad, this is Alice." Stella held his elbow and mine as she introduced us to each other.

"Clarissa, are you making cupcakes for my baby girl?" Doctor Corwin asked, his shaky blue eyes staring into mine. I watched as his bottom lip shook with the same tremors that had his hands bouncing.

"Dad, this is *Alice*," Stella repeated, though I watched the stress tighten her features.

"It's nice to meet you, Doctor Corwin." I shook his hand and watched as his face lifted into a bright smile.

"Abe, call me Abe." His whole face lit up suddenly and he shook my hand. His warm, firm but trembling, grip made me smile.

"Nice to meet you, *Abe*."

His smile faded as he stared at me, then looked back to Stella. "Princess, I have rounds now."

"Come on, Daddy." Stella urged her father back to the sofa in the small living room. He sat with her without complaint and I joined them.

"My princess is a beautiful bride," his voice wavered, his eyes on her. "Your mother will be happy."

"I know, Daddy." Stella's eyes shimmered and she glanced at me, her lips pursed as she tried to hold on to her emotions. Was she always this upset when she saw him? "We brought you something."

Abe grew quiet, watching her somewhat blankly for a moment. Stella reached into her bag and pulled out a thick textbook of sorts. She placed it in his lap. His watery eyes dropped from her face to the book. With a shaky hand, he opened the cover, then lifted it. The title, *Ion Channels for Excitable Membranes* told me absolutely nothing about the actual content of the book.

"Clarissa, pass me my glasses there," he said, pointing at

me.

Stella turned her face away from us for a moment. I found his glasses on the small end table and handed them to him. He put them on a little crookedly, so I crouched in front of him. Pearly eyes lingered on mine as I adjusted his glasses for him.

"How's that?"

"Good." He patted me on the head as if I was a little kid, then immediately began to read.

Stella stood up, moving behind him toward the kitchenette. She leaned against the wall, her head tilted back. I'd recognized her fight and snuck away from him to join her.

"It's okay," I whispered, rubbing her arm.

"I didn't think he would think you were her," she said, hiccupping after. "I didn't think he'd call you her name. I'm sorry."

"Stella, I understand. He's sick."

"He still thinks she's alive and that Mom is alive sometimes." Her voice lifted a pitch and she fought a sob. "Sometimes he's more coherent."

"It's all right." I pulled her to me, rougher than usual, and hugged her tight. "I'm sorry you have to face this."

At first, she just leaned against me, but then she let herself go and cried quietly on my shoulder. I rubbed her back, keeping my own emotions in check as I soothed my girlfriend, because she was *mine*. No matter what, Stella couldn't be turned out to float alone in the world anymore, surrounded by death and drowning in her own pain. I wouldn't allow it. Even if I could bring her the smallest of comforts, I would.

Abe sat there reading, completely ignoring us for a solid hour before his aide returned. We bid him farewell, Stella kissing his forehead before crouching in front of him. She lowered the book and finally, he looked at her.

"Princess, what's upset you?" His gnarly fingers stroking her cheek.

"I'm fine, Daddy. I'll be by tomorrow for Christmas, okay?"

"Christmas." He scoffed, his demeanor shifting slightly. "You know I don't care for holidays built around the exaltation of fictional messiahs."

Stella paused, her eyes widening but it was me who laughed.

Abe looked up at me and grinned. "She knows." He pointed at me, then looked back to Stella. "And you know, too."

"He's better after he reads," the aide whispered to me and I nodded my understanding.

"Science, Daddy, yes." Stella smiled softly. "I'll come see you anyway."

"Okay, Princess. At least bring me cookies." He kissed her cheek. "The kind your mother used to make."

"Really?" Stella leaned back, standing up to full height as she looked at him.

"The little peanut butter ones," Abe said, picking up his book again.

"Okay." Stella chuckled. "Love you, Dad."

"Love you, too, Princess." He waved at us as we moved toward the door. Just as we stepped into the hallway, he called out, "Bye, Alice."

My eyes widened and I leaned back inside to say, "See ya, Abe."

Stella closed the door and paused in the hallway. The minute the lock clicked, she started crying, covering her mouth in the way she usually does when she fears making a sound.

"It's okay, Stell. It's okay." I rubbed her arms and she met my gaze. I watched as she warred with herself, muscles tensing as if she fought moving forward and fleeing.

"I can't do this. I *can't*, Alice."

"You're already doing it." Emotions choked my throat, squeezing it as I watched her crumbling the way she had the first time she kissed me. It scared me, boiling my worries to the surface. Every inch of her shook as she fought the sobs that kept catching her.

"I need to go," she spat, swiping at her face as she wrenched herself from my grip and stormed off down the hall.

"Stella!" I hurried after her, our boots slamming the pavement when we made it out to the busy streets.

Christmas decorations covered every lamppost, and big fat bows hung in nearly every doorway. Shoppers and tourists filled the streets and, although it was still bright out, all of the tiny holiday lights twinkled around us. I caught up to her, nearly knocking a woman over when I crashed into her giant crunchy department store bags.

"Sorry! Stell...Stella. *Stop.*" I grabbed her by the arm and she spun around so quickly, I flinched as if expecting a blow. "Stop."

"I can't do this, Alice. I can't." She sobbed, tears streaming down her cheeks as she both pushed and pulled at me simultaneously.

"Stella. Take a deep breath with me." I moved her backward, walking her off the sidewalk into the alleyway next to Starbucks. "Breathe."

"Alice, I can't." Her nails dug into my jacket, pinching at my skin beneath. "I'm *afraid.*"

"Of what, Stell? You've said that before, but of what?" I cupped her face and leaned myself against her. For some reason, this restraining gesture calmed her down slightly. "Tell me."

"Alice." She met my gaze then gripped my wrists, coughing as she tried to speak. I rubbed my thumbs over her soft skin and eventually, she said, "Everyone I love dies." Her words left her tear-dampened lips. "*Everyone.* First Clarissa, who I loved more than anything in this world," she said, slowly and full of sobs in between. "Then my mom, not long after. And then Dad. And I'm not sure what's worse, Alice, losing someone to death or losing them like my father. So I can't."

"Stella." A sob chopped up my voice but I didn't let go of her. "Please don't say that."

"I can't." She cried, tears streaming her face. "I'm *afraid* to love you, Alice. I'm *afraid* to care about you too much because if I do, you'll be gone." She closed her eyes. "You'll be gone and I'll be alone again. Because I'll lose you, too. And I can't lose you. I can't."

"Don't say that. Please don't." I couldn't help her calm down anymore because now I was a mess, too. "I'm right here in front of you, Stella. Look at me." I grabbed a handful of her hair as she obliged. "I'm right here."

"Any minute a criminal could take you out while you're at work." She cried, touching me so delicately that I wondered if she envisioned me a corpse. "Or a drunk driver in a truck when your car is a tiny sedan. Or a disease that eats your brain to the point of extinction, leaving only your body behind like a zombie. A fucking wraith left of what I loved *so* much."

"Stella…" I closed my eyes when she dropped her forehead against mine. Finally, she stopped fighting and her crying cooled to sniffles. Our hot breath puffed between us, hers warm against my lips. In my whole life, my heart never crumbled so completely before. Never pounded so hard in my ears. Even when I walked away from the rubble that was Kari, and Lara before that, that pain didn't compare to this.

"I'm sorry," she whispered, brushing her lips against mine. "Please don't leave me…"

"Stella," I implored, opening my eyes to look at her. "I don't even own a car. Or have a job."

She laughed softly, though it only made her cry more. "Allie…"

I kissed her, right there in the alleyway, with tears peppering our lips. Her return, although disrupted by quiet sobs, mirrored mine in its emotion. When we parted, I hugged her so tight, both of us hiding against each other's shoulder.

***

"Is Stella coming today?" Marc asked as I fussed with my hair in the bathroom. He stood beside me, looking at himself in the mirror from over my shoulder and attempting to smooth out one stray hair on his head.

"I don't know. Actually, I don't know anything. We may or may not have broken up last night. I don't even know that." My words burst from me in harsher tones than I intended. "And my roots are fucking horrible." I slammed the brush in the sink and ducked under his arm as I stormed out of the bathroom.

"What do you mean you might've broken up?" He came after me, grabbing me by the elbow, but he released me right away as if I was made of hot steel.

"I just don't know, okay? Stella got *so* upset after we visited her dad. He called me Clarissa a few times." I sighed, turning to him now as he urged me to sit on the bed with him. "Told me that she's afraid to love me or care about me because I'll be taken from her, too. Like her mom, like Clarissa, or like her father."

"She's just scared, Allie. The same way you are."

"I'm not scared." I frowned at him, then stood up to grab a pair of heeled boots from the closet. I pulled them on over my thick socks, zipping them up my calves while listening to him.

"You are. You're just as scared of relationships as she is. Because she'll leave you, or cheat on you and then leave you. Every relationship you've had in the past decade has been you ending it early because you refused to trust them," he said, throwing all the truth in my face that made me want to throw a fist right back in his. "Have you talked to her since you left yesterday?"

"No. And I don't care about any of it," I spat, standing up and yanking a scarf out of the closet. "Let's just go and get this Christmas bullshit over with."

Marc stood up, blocking my exit from the room. "Alice,

look at me."

"No. Why the hell does everyone tell me to constantly look at them? Just *move*."

"Nope." He folded his arms and stood there like an oafish brick wall. "Look at me."

"You're an asshole." I glanced up at him and he dropped his hands to my shoulders.

"Right now I am. You do care about it or else you wouldn't be upset." He squeezed me gently; a gesture which only elicited a swell of emotion from my chest. "By not talking to each other, you're doing exactly what each of you fears...leaving each other. You can't trust her because she's afraid to commit, and you fear she'll leave you for someone else. She can't trust you because she fears you'll die and therefore, leave her too. Wake up, Allie."

"It's not the same," I said, as tears trickled down my cheeks. Again. No one in my life had ever made me cry as much as Stella did.

"It's *exactly* the same! You stubborn shit. It's the *same*." He shook me a little and I wiped at my eyes. "Do you love her, Al?"

"It's not the same."

"Do you *love* her?" he shouted at me and shook me again. I shoved his arms off, but he put them right back to rest on my shoulders.

"Yes! Okay, I fucking love her." This time, I broke away from him and pushed past him to escape my room. My insides twisted, churning with the agony of my confession. I clenched my fists and fought the urge to lash out at Marc.

"And you're going to let her go, just like that?" He snapped his fingers in my face. "Because, Allie, don't do it. She might not be able to work through her grief right now and do it herself, but you can look past yours. I know you can because you've done it already. You visited her at work. You texted her asking her to coffee. You initiated the first date. And she responded to all of it."

"Yeah but—"

"But nothing." He pointed at the front door. "Now is not the time to give up. You told me last night that yesterday was Clarissa's birthday, plus seeing her father and having to relive everything again in front of you—in front of anyone—is something she's never had to deal with before. I might sound like I'm totally on her side right now, don't get me wrong, I am, but I'm on her side because being on her side is being on *yours*." He took a deep breath, pausing his tirade. "What I'm saying is...don't give up, Alice. Don't stay down that fucking rabbit hole when the clear path is right above you. You'll regret it and end up hurting way more than you do now."

Quiet tumbled around inside me as I considered his words. My heart pounded in tune with the soft sobs that had me quaking. "Marc…"

"Get out of the hole, Alice…"

"What if you're wrong?"

"What if I'm not?" Silence fell between us as he handed me a tissue. "Call her."

"What if she doesn't answer?" I took it and wiped my face. "Thanks."

"Then go find her."

"Can I borrow your car?"

He nodded. "Gavin and I will Uber to your parents. Go get the girl.

CHAPTER THIRTEEN

"I think four cookies is enough for now, Abe," said his chipper health aide as she wrestled the tin of peanut butter cookies from him.

"Give 'em here, you bossy nincompoop!" He growled, his gnarled grip holding on to the edge of the container.

Stella hadn't answered my calls, nor was she home when I made it to her apartment, and picked the lock just to be sure she wasn't hiding inside. I watched as her father warred with his health aide, whose name turned out to be Lory, until she finally got the tin away. He scowled at her, almost pouting when he sat back in his reclining chair, and kicked up the footrest with such a force that the springs *boinged.*

"Abe," I said, trying not to chuckle at the fight in the fiery old man. He looked at me, his brows narrowed but the pursed lips, those belonged to his daughter. "Who brought you cookies today?"

"*My* daughter. They're *my* cookies," he said, continuing to frown.

"What would she think if she knew you ate all of them at once?" I pulled my hand from behind my back and offered him the cookie that I hadn't eaten.

"She'd be proud." He snatched it, grinning up at me as he tucked it into the breast pocket of his shirt.

"I'll see you again soon, okay? I've got to go find her," I told him.

He grew quiet when the aide handed him the same book he had yesterday. She offered me a kind smile and I nodded. Abe stroked the cover, his fingernail scratching at the lettering.

"Thanks for letting me in," I told the aide and she nodded.

"Wish I could be of more help," she said.

"You take good care of him. That's what matters."

"He matters." She patted his shoulder and Abe looked up at me, his pale blue eyes shimmering.

"Don't look too hard, young lady." He wagged a finger at me, scolding me for what I couldn't fathom. "Princess is in her castle."

"I checked there, but thank you," I told him, slipping my hands into the pockets of my jeans and heading for the door. "Take care, Abe."

"Not that one!" he shouted just as I gripped the doorknob. I started, turning back to see him pound his hand on the arm of the chair. "Doctor castles, Clarissa."

My brow furrowed and I glanced to Lory who shrugged. "Behave yourself, Abe. Maybe Lory will give you another cookie."

"Bye," she said, chuckling as she waved.

"Bye," Abe mimicked, though his eyes narrowed in my direction as I pulled the door open to the long hall.

"Bye, Doctor Corwin," I said, and just before the door clicked shut he called out, "Bye, Alice."

Any luck? Marc's text greeted me when I checked my phone after starting up the car. Snow fell in light puffy balls, barely sticking to the windshield.

No but she did bring her dad cookies. All okay there?

Ur Mom has Gavin in an apron. Luv it.

Lol…

Where to next?

Unless you know what a doctor castle is, no idea.

Doctor castle? lol Hospital? His response brought me pause as I considered it.

Her father said she was at a doctor castle.

Maybe went 2 work. Check!!!

Why didn't I think of that?

Pussy-drunk?

Marc!

Get out of the hole, Rabbit.

Very funny.

My heart raced as I carried two hot lattes into the emergency department of UW Medical on Christmas day. The snow turned to a chilly rain then back to snow again while I drove through the busy streets of holiday travelers. It took me an extra fifteen minutes just to get to the hospital after stopping for coffee.

Despite it being a holiday, the E.R. was particularly busy, and there seemed to be more staff than usual. I didn't see Stella, but two other doctors that I recognized tended to patients, while nurses and technicians went about their job duties. Kylie, as usual, stood behind the nurses' station, and she smiled at me when I hopped up to sit on the countertop.

"Merry Christmas," she said, nodding to a latte. "Is that for me?"

"You wish. Maybe if you tell me where my girlfriend is, I'll forfeit one." I held it in front of her nose and she laughed.

"*Girlfriend?* You mean the *hot and leggy* brunette with the sad eyes and broken spirit who isn't even supposed to work today but came in anyway to spend the entire morning in her office reading charts?"

I nodded, my heart skipping a beat. "That'd be the one."

"She hasn't left her office in an hour." Kylie held out her hand, grinning, and I plopped my drink in it.

"If she's not there, I get it back."

She waved me off while taking a sip and moved to the back counter when the phone started ringing. I slid from my post and carried the remaining coffee down the hall. My boots squeaked obnoxiously so I slowed my pace as I made it to Stella's office. Before knocking, I took a deep breath. *What if she really didn't want me? What if I shouldn't have listened to Marc?*

I knocked softly on the door as dubious thoughts continued to assault my psyche. *Maybe she'll slam the door in my face. What if I made her feel worse about everything?*

The door opened and, just like Kylie described, Stella appeared with her expression drawn. Her sapphire eyes, darkened by emotion, burned into mine. In a pair of blue scrubs, with no lab coat, she stared at me, as a single tear slid down her cheek. I handed her the coffee, and it seemed like she accepted it out of sheer surprise.

"I had to break into your apartment illegally, watch your father wrestle a tin of peanut butter cookies from his aide until he sent me on a mission to decode a *doctor castle*, and then had to bribe a nurse with my coffee just for information in order to find you. Truth is, I should've checked here first," I told her, entering her office without invitation and closing the door behind me. "So hi."

"Hi," she said, a small chuckle leaving her as she set the cup down on her desk. She was already crying and I hadn't even begun to say any of the things that would make both of us weep.

"I know you're not really working today and if the two seats at my mother's dinner table aren't filled by three in the afternoon, I'll never hear the end of it. Do you realize that?"

She nodded, sniffling as she finally took a few steps closer to me. I could barely hold on to the humor I'd brought as my armed guard into this situation. I reached a hand out to her and she took it, her fingers icy cold. "I'm sorry."

"So am I, Stella. I'm sorry that the world has taught you to be afraid of letting people in. And I'm sorry it has taken away the people you've loved. But I'm not going to let any of that scare me off just to spare you from a hypothetical future pain, unless you truly and honestly don't care about me and you're really breaking up with me." I squeezed her hand and pulled her closer to me. Her free hand fell to my waist as she sniffled, her gaze never leaving mine. "When we haven't even gotten started yet."

"I care about you," she said, biting her bottom lip as I stroked my knuckles down her cheek.

"I know."

"I care too much about you." She closed her eyes, leaning into my touch so that her lips brushed my fingers.

"No such thing as too much, Stell. I know at least that much about life."

"I'm so afraid of losing you, Alice. I'm so afraid." She cried quietly as I hugged her, rubbing her back as she held onto me. I thought of Marc's words of encouragement, and channeled the feelings of balance and determination that spurred from them.

"And I'm afraid that you'll hurt me by lying or stepping out on me." I took a swipe at my cheeks as I leaned back, both of us holding on to each other. "The way I look at it, Stell, is we get over it and try, or we don't. But you have to make that decision, too."

She nodded, pursing her tear-stained lips. "Try. I want to try."

"Are you sure? Because yesterday you woke up sure and by dinner time you ran away from me."

"I'm sorry. I'm sure." She grabbed me into a firm hug, and this time it was me clinging to her rather than the other way around. "I'm sure, Alice. I'm so sorry for doing that."

"I know." I sniffled as I held on to her.

Eventually, we both calmed down enough to make it to the car together. I drove while Stella nursed the lukewarm coffee I'd brought her.

"I'm so tired," she said. "I should stop home and change."

"We're really informal and my parents' house is chaos. No one will care you're in scrubs," I told her. "And besides, it's a little impressive."

"All the more reason to change," she said, smirking at me as I stroked her hair while waiting at a red light. "Did you steal Marc's car in your great heist to find me?"

"A little." I chuckled and she grabbed my hand, kissing it after. "Your dad called me Alice again when I left."

"He has good days and bad ones. But I'm glad he did."

"Me too." We drove on for awhile more in the heavy traffic until her apartment came into view in the distance. "Do you want to change for real?"

She shook her head. "As long as you're okay with it."

"Stella, if you showed up dressed like a rubber chicken, I'd be okay with it."

"I feel bad. I didn't bring anything; no food or gifts."

"Do you see me packing food or gifts?" I gestured to the empty back seat. She stared at me, her brow furrowing when I laughed. "What?"

"No gifts for any of your family?"

"Nope. We have a rule about no gifts."

"Really? Why?"

"Because we just end up giving each other stuff we don't need. Dad is an ornery bastard sometimes, Mom doesn't like anything, and my brothers don't buy anything for anyone because they're jerks. So it evens out if we all agree to not," I told her. "I warned you that my family is chaos, right?"

"You did." She laughed a little bit, dropping her head back against the seat.

"Take a nap, babe. We've still got at least a forty minute drive," I said as I turned the heat up when she pulled her coat tighter.

"You called me *babe*," she said, setting her cup in the

console between us.

"It slipped."

"I don't mind." She smiled softly, her eyes closing without much of a fight. At the next red light, I reached into the back and pulled my jacket off the seat. I spread it out over her and she snuggled into it in her half-sleep.

It took nearly an hour, maybe more, to make it through to my parents' house outside of the city. I pulled into the driveway and parked the car behind my brother's truck. Stella remained asleep and after removing my seatbelt, I turned to stroke her cheek. "Stella," I implored at a whisper. "We're here."

She stirred, stretching her legs before opening her eyes to look at me. She searched my expression, smiling a little after as I tucked a stray bit of hair behind her ear. "How long was I out?"

"About an hour. A lot of traffic. Feel okay?"

"Will you stay over tonight?" she asked, handing me back my coat as she sat up.

"If you want me to, I will." I nodded and she leaned over the center of the seat to kiss me gently. Melting into her was the only thing I wanted to do but instead, we had to face my family for the first time. When she leaned back, I asked, "So are you ready for a barrage of questions, a lot of shouting, and tons of food?"

She nodded, chuckling softly as she sat up fully and pulled the visor down to fuss with her hair in the mirror. "Do I look a mess?"

"You look perfect."

"To you maybe. How do I look to the rest of the world not looking at me with beer goggles?" A soft pout curved her mouth and I leaned forward to kiss it.

"Just as beautiful. Come on." I nudged her and we exited the car together.

By the walkway, I held my hand to her and she took it without hesitation. "Oh, and don't mind my mom who occasionally thinks being gay is a phase. She's completely blind to the fact that fifty-percent of her guests today are of the gay persuasion."

"Noted." Stella laughed hard as we climbed the steps to the brick-faced house of my youth. I opened the door and, sure enough, before anyone noticed we were there, shouting greeted us.

"Come on! Fucking losers!" my father shouted at the television.

"Goddammit!" Ryan's voice followed.

"Will you two keep it down in there! We have company!" cried my mother. "Gavin dear, you're doing a lovely job on those potatoes."

"If you're really on the market for a new one, don't get a hybrid, not worth it yet," Evan said to Marc as they sat together at the dining room table. "Go full throttle."

"Not sure I'm an off-roading kind of guy," Marc answered, and leaned forward when Evan showed him something on his phone.

"Have a look at these," he said.

Stella's wide-eyed expression had me grinning as I led her into the house. Honey-colored floors and Christmas *everything* brightened the usually darker rooms. The giant tree by the unlit fireplace stood proud beside a mantle full of stockings.

"You think this is bad? My niece and nephew aren't even here today. Then it's ten times worse," I muttered and she squeezed my hand. We took off our coats and I hung them on the hooks in the hall.

"Rabbit!" Evan announced suddenly. "About time." He shot up from his chair and hurried over to both of us. "Mom! Rabbit's here!"

"Jesus, Ev, yell much?" I hugged him briefly because he moved on to Stella in a heartbeat.

He completely ignored me. "Good to see you, Stella. Come on, I'll introduce you."

"Oh...well, okay." Stella laughed as Evan nearly dragged her into the living room. I followed them, leaning over the back of the sofa and hugging my dad around the neck.

"Hi, Daddy," I said, smooching his cheek.

"Hi, baby girl." He patted my arms then looked up when Evan dragged Stella into the room. He stepped in front of the television and Ryan nearly growled.

"Move it, bro."

"In a minute. This is our brother Ryan and our dad, Paulie." He gestured to them and I laughed as Stella stood there awkwardly. "Stella's Rabbit's girlf—er—fri—*person*." Evan's eyes bugged out of his head as he looked at me.

"Girl person?" Ryan stood up, scowling at Evan as he turned to shake Stella's hand. "That's new. Is that a unique platonic term or something?" Ryan's brow crinkled as he met her gaze.

"No." Stella laughed hard, her cheeks bright red as she shook his hand. "Girlfriend is the more common term. Nice to meet you."

Evan appeared simply relieved at the confirmation and flopped in the armchair.

Ryan's expression fell a little while still holding Stella's hand. His eyes wandered over her from head to toe. "You're a doctor?"

"Girlfriend, huh." Dad grabbed me by the shirt and pulled me over the back of the sofa like he usually does. I landed on the cushions with a *flumph*, my head on the pillow in his lap.

"*Ack*. Yes. Girlfriend." I looked up at him and his grumpy face twitched around his mouth as if threatening a smile. I patted his hand then looked back to Stella and my brother.

"I am," she said, her expression melting to the still, clinical glaze that, at times, seemed impenetrable. I swung my feet around and sat up properly.

"At UW Medical?" Ryan continued to query.

"Yes." Stella nodded. Her faint smile barely cracked her poker face. I watched as my brother broke away to pace in an awkward side-to-side movement, his hands lifting above his head. When I stood up, he stopped and looked from me back to Stella.

"I know her," he said, but Stella remained silent.

"You do?" I asked him, my brow furrowing when he ran his hands through his neatly combed hair.

"Yeah."

"You know my brother?" I asked Stella, but she just kept her gaze on Ryan. The way she looked at him, so gently and with care that encouraged him to answer instead.

"Yeah, she knows me." He finally stopped moving and his dark brown eyes shimmered under the glow of the Christmas lights. "She saved my life twice."

"What do you mean?" I asked. The room around us grew suddenly quiet. Both Evan and my dad looked on with interest. Stella said nothing and it only made me more worried. "Stell?"

Her gaze lingered on Ryan, though her hand fell to the small of my back when I moved closer. "You have to tell her. I can't," she said to him.

"A long time ago. Six years?" He glanced at me then back to her. "The first time I O.D.'ed by accident. Then the second time when I tried on purpose."

"Shit, Ry. I had no idea that she was your doctor," I said, giving his arm a squeeze.

"She saved my life." Only then did he smile, and the misty-eyed expression faded. "And sent me to rehab."

Stella chuckled, her posture relaxing now that Ryan told the story. "You look good, Ryan."

"I've got two kids now. Twins." He pulled out his phone right away and showed her. I glanced to my dad who wore a slightly baffled expression, then Evan who looked just the same.

"They're beautiful. What are their names?" Stella's genuine smile sent tingling warmth up my middle.

"Tabitha and Nathaniel. That's their mom there." He pointed at his phone. "We're divorced but good friends."

"It's good to see that you're doing well, Ryan. I can honestly say that I didn't expect to see you here," Stella said when he pocketed the phone.

"Six, almost seven years changes things. You helped me turn my shit around when you yelled at me that time." He laughed a little. "I'll never forget it."

"Good." She grinned and gave his shoulder a squeeze. "What are you doing with your life now other than raising beautiful kids?"

"I'm a probation officer working with fucked up kids." His proud grin radiated right through him. "Yelling at them to get their lives turned around."

"That's amazing." Stella's laughter brought a smile to my face.

"What's going on in here? Why's the TV off—*oh*." Mom stopped short, her ruffled apron flopping against her lap. "Doctor Corwin."

"Well, Rabbit, your girlfriend's more popular than Mom's papier-mâché snowman centerpiece on the dinner table," Evan said. Both Ryan and my father laughed as well as Marc and Gavin from the peanut gallery behind us.

"Thanks for having me to dinner, Mrs. Lange." Stella's professional, friendly face remained steadfast as my mother embraced her.

"Of course, dear. And call me Sara." She smiled, her gaze lingering longer than it should until she glanced to Ryan.

"We already got past the fact that she saved my life, Ma," he said. "We're good. No need to be awkward or bring it up twelve times."

"Mind your manners, boy." Dad picked up his prosthetic leg, which I now noted to not actually be attached to him, and smacked Ryan in the foot with it.

"Hey!"

"Dad!"

"Paul!"

"Oh my God." I covered my face and about died.

"I love this family!" Gavin announced in between hysterics that mixed with Marc's.

"Told ya," he said.

When I lowered my hands, I looked at Stella who was laughing quietly, her blue eyes wide and bright with amusement.

"For heaven's sake, let's go eat." Mom waved her hands around wildly. "All of you. In the dining room. And Paul, put your leg on."

"You quit picking on my leg already," Dad said, but he did what he needed to do and was up on his feet in no time. On his way past, he clapped me on the shoulder.

When everyone left the living room, I turned to Stella who continued to grin. "Are you regretting this yet?"

"Not yet."

"I can't believe you know my brother."

"Quite well. We've had numerous run-ins. It surprised me."

"Did I ever meet you way back when?" I nodded toward the dining room and we headed over together.

"I would've remembered you, Allie, for sure."

Dinner wasn't the worst event in my life. I'd managed to steer Mom away from any prying questions directed toward Stella with Ryan's help. Normally, he was the less talkative brother, but today, his eagerness to share and talk with us spoke of his pride in how far he'd come since his leaving the Army, and his vestment in recovery.

It took Mom all day to make a hearty meal of turkey, ham, mashed potatoes, and half-a-dozen other side dishes, but it took us only twenty minutes to eat it. In typical Lange fashion, the guys edged their way back in front of whatever sports game was on while Mom, Stella, and I began cleaning up. Marc and Gavin helped, of course, because they weren't lazy bastards like the Lange men. But they, too, faded off when the clean up shifted into dessert prep.

"How come I haven't heard more about you, Stella?"

Mom took the first opportunity to ask when the three of us sat alone at the table, waiting for the coffee to brew. Four different kinds of pies lined the center of the table.

"You'll have to ask Alice about that," she said cordially, and both of them glanced at me.

"Because you're nosey, Ma. And half the time you think my lesbianism is a phase," I said, flat out.

"Oh, Alice. I'm perfectly aware that you've been gay all your life." She waved me off.

"Ma, two months ago you told me to marry Marc, because we'd both get over being gay." I huffed, crossing my arms over my chest.

"Well, it would perhaps be better than the horrible women you've brought home in the past decade." She set her napkin on the table and stood. "Coffee's done." How she knew that, I hadn't a clue.

"So wait, you're only acknowledging my gayness because you like Stella?"

"Yes." Mom's expression lifted and she turned on her heel, heading off to the kitchen.

When I turned back to Stella, she was laughing so hard behind her hand that I nearly knocked her off her chair.

"That's *so* not funny," I said, scowling at her.

"You're right. It's hilarious. You're not nearly as funny as your family. Did you know that?"

"Stell!" I laughed at her, shoving her shoulder. "Someone needs to be sane around here."

She cocked a brow and it only made us laugh more. Eventually, a genuine smile replaced her silliness and she leaned over, nudging my forehead with hers. "I like your family."

"No doubt they like you, too. What with the life-saving and lesbian-confirming awesomeness, how could they not?"

"Know what else?"

I shook my head.

"I really like you, too," she said, pecking me on the lips.

"Good thing." I smiled as heat rushed my cheeks.

"Why?"

"Because I really like you."

***

"You look better now than you did this morning," I said as Stella climbed into bed beside me. Both of us wore one of her T-shirts because, again, I wasn't prepared to spend the night.

"I feel better. Your family is a lot of fun."

"In small doses maybe. Growing up was like a circus. But it was generally fun until a third of them decided to go off to war."

"I can understand that. Everyone calls you Rabbit." She tucked the blanket around her middle as she leaned up against the headboard. "It's really cute."

"Are you gonna start, too?" I smirked, scooting closer to her so that I could face her.

"Nah. You'll always be Allie to me."

"Did you have a nickname growing up?"

She shook her head. "Not really. Dad called me princess but my mom called me her little star. *Stella* means Star in Italian."

"Does it?" The thought of it made me smile.

"Yeah," she said, laughing softly. "I used to sign my name with a little star at the end when I was a kid."

"I like it. By the way, I have something for you..." I reached under the blanket and pulled out a box wrapped in red paper. It wasn't the most fancily wrapped package but the pretty white bow helped.

"What's this?" She took it, her brows lifting with the question. "I thought you didn't do—"

"It's not a big deal. And that rule is just for my crazy blood relatives. Significant others don't fall into the same equation."

"Okay then," she said, holding up a finger to me as she reached over and pulled open the drawer to the nightstand. When she sat back up, a small box wrapped in metallic blue paper sat in the palm of her hand. "Also not a big deal."

"Atheists give Christmas gifts?" I accepted it, laughing a little bit at our idiocy.

"Significant others who celebrate Christmas don't fall into that equation either."

"You go first," I said, pointing at the box in her lap.

"No way. You go."

"Nope. I gave it first so you go first."

"Double nope. You're in my bed, so I make the rules." A small grin curved her lips and I laughed.

"Oh really? You make the rules in this bed do you?" I crawled forward until my nose was an inch from hers.

"Mhmm. I do." She nodded, biting her bottom lip in the way that made my insides scream with delight.

"Fine. You win but payback isn't far behind." I kissed her quickly then rolled back to sit. With caution, I unwrapped the little box then pulled the lid off. Inside, attached to a keychain in the shape of a silver star, dangled a single key. I looked up to her and before I could ask, she explained.

"I know you have a difficult time trusting people." She paused, biting her lip once before releasing it. "So this is a key to my apartment. I have nothing to hide from you, Allie. My life is open to you, and so is this place." She gestured around us. "And this bed."

I gripped the key in the palm of my hand, holding on to it and the gesture at the same time. All I could do was nod, fearing the uprising of emotion that threatened me. Finally, I leaned over to hug her. She kissed my cheek, rubbing my back at the same time. "Thank you," I whispered, nuzzling my lips against her neck.

"It's funny how you said that you had to pick my lock this morning," she said, chuckling when she leaned back. "Could've given this to you last night like I intended."

"Hindsight is twenty-twenty." I laughed softly, stroking her cheek as I fought a sniffle. "Your turn." I held on to the keychain like it was the anchor to my everything.

She looked down at the gift, her hands frozen on either side of it.

"What's wrong?" I asked, scooting so that my crossed knees touched hers. She looked up at me while caressing the edge of the package.

"I haven't opened a gift in a long time. My dad isn't in any condition to give gifts, and there isn't anyone else, really…"

"There's me now," I told her, reaching forward and placing my hands on hers.

"You have such a lovely, big family, Allie..."

"I can't believe you saved my brother's life." I took her hands in mine, running my thumbs over her knuckles. "Twice."

"Did you know how sick he was?" she asked, squeezing my hands as I brought them to my lips and kissed them.

"Not at first. When he came back from Iraq, he was moody and we fought a lot. Mom kept it from us because after Marisol kicked him out, he lived with our parents. He left rehab like three times, but only after he had the psych admission did he finally get it together."

"That was me." She smirked, now she stroked the palms of my hands with her index fingers. "Forced him into a seventy-two-hour hold then convinced the psychiatrist to admit him. I shouldn't be telling you this."

"He told us you helped him. I'm sure he'd tell the rest if he had a chance now. Did you know, before that, he punched me in the face so hard that he knocked my tooth out?" I pointed to a molar in the top left side of my mouth. "That's an implant."

Her eyes nearly bugged out of her head. "Really?"

"Yeah. His suicide attempt was a few hours later. He felt so bad about hurting me. Evan had to tackle him. He went for my gun, or what he thought was my gun. I didn't have it tucked in the back of my pants like usual. I don't usually when I go there. It upsets my dad," I said.

"Jesus, Allie."

"It was all in the matter of a few months."

"I know. That's why I remember him. I saw him a lot, and your mother too, toward the end. Ryan alone nearly a dozen times when he was brought in for evals or suspected overdoses. I'm really glad he's doing well."

"He's committed to sobriety, his kids, and work. Therapy helped his traumatized brain. Dad wasn't much better. He's usually friendlier though when sports aren't on."

"He's in pain though, too. His leg is bothering him," she said.

"How can you tell?"

"He kept taking it off or adjusting it. Tell him he needs it refitted and a different sock for the socket."

"Me tell him?" I laughed at the suggestion. "He'll get mad and put me in a headlock. You'll have to tell him, Doc."

"I really shouldn't…"

"You also really shouldn't be sleeping with me since you were my treating physician, but who cares," I said and she laughed at that.

"Barely."

"Uh huh. Wait, enough distraction." I waved my hands between us. "Open your gift."

"Is it a sex toy?" She cocked a brow at me. "You seem like someone who would gift a sex toy."

I laughed hard. "Why? Do you need one?"

"Why would I need one when I've got you?" She smiled, though her cheeks tinged pink. I loved when she played back with me. So much of our time over the last few months had been uber serious. Laughter left me in hearty waves.

"Do you really not have any?"

"Nope." She poked my nose. "Don't tease me, naughty girl."

I made to bite her finger and she squeaked. "Will you

open that already?"

"Okay okay."

I watched as she peeled back the paper cautiously as if expecting something to jump out and bite her. When half of it fell away, immediately her lips pursed to a line and her eyes glistened with mistiness. She lifted the framed photo collage from the wrappings and stared at it, her eyes darting over every picture.

"She doesn't belong in a box," I repeated what I told her the first time she pulled the hidden stash of Clarissa pictures out from under her bed. In secret, I swiped them, had them copied, and assembled them all in a sleek black frame to match her apartment decor.

Tears rolled from her cheeks, tumbling onto the edge of the frame. She sniffled, continuing to stare at it. Clarissa wasn't alone in all of the pictures. I'd found some with the two of them as well. Stella sobbed and I scooted over to wrap my arm around her, the star keychain held tightly in my fist. We leaned into the pillows and looked at the photos together.

"What's this?" she asked, her voice barely audible, as she took hold of the tiny knob at the center of the base.

"Pull it open."

She did and inside, empty velvet pillows filled the tiny drawer. "When you're ready, you can put your rings in there."

"Alice." She turned suddenly, and hugged me so tightly that it nearly took my breath away. Her fingers dug into my shoulders, and only then did I allow my own emotions to bubble to the surface. A mix of sadness for Stella, but happiness for the way she connected with me so easily now.

"It's okay," I said, kissing her cheek as I sniffled. She nodded against my shoulder as I rubbed her back.

It took her some time to calm, and she leaned against me while balancing the frame in her lap. In the center, Stella's favorite picture of the two of them by a giant

Christmas tree stood out the most.

"Thank you," she said, her voice soft. "Thank you for the gift and for...understanding."

"I know you loved her very much, Stell. And if we're going to be together, she'll always be a part of our relationship. I'm not saying the pain will go away, but I hope it can get better."

"I loved her so much," she said, turning slightly to meet my gaze.

"I know." I stroked her cheek.

"But I love *you* so much, too, Allie."

To say that I didn't expect to hear that wouldn't do it justice. My heart leapt so forcefully that the reverberations swirled in my stomach. A warm, tingling sensation melted down my whole body, settling in the center of my chest. I cupped her face, pulling her into a soft, perfect kiss.

She met me there, salted lips capturing each other in a familiar embrace, and she pressed me down into the pillows. The key jingled as it fell from my hand and I felt her move the photo frame from between us as she positioned herself on top of me. My legs fell around her when she settled, ending our kiss to gaze down on me. Her smile made it to her eyes, despite the shimmering tears, and I stroked her bottom lip with my thumb.

"I love you, too. And it scares me a little." I whispered the last part.

"Tell me about it." Her soft laugh settled me and I yanked her back into a kiss.

Our bodies melted together, her overheated thighs creating friction against mine. My shirt gathered around my middle and I pressed hers up over her head, tossing it aside. She moaned against my mouth when I massaged her perfect breasts, both of us moving in time together.

Stella tugged my shirt off, then reached between us, cupping my pussy and parting me with delicate, practiced fingers. A soft gasp ended our kiss and I returned the gesture, her slippery dampness surprising me. Our gaze lingered for an extra moment that spoke of a thousand *I love yous* and a million *I'm readys*.

And we were together, locked inside each other and rolling in unison. A manner different for the two of us, with less heartache and more rhythm. Of lovemaking and not just lust. Tears tangoed with us, though now they belonged to the two of us, and not just Clarissa or the pains of our pasts. Not for our losses but for our trust and growth together. Our bodies moving like we'd known each other for a millennia, and the familiar push and pull of our souls integrating in a spiritual dance.

When she broke, I crashed with her in a fluid, moan-laden ecstasy that lasted longer and rumbled deeper than an echo through a vast chasm. Stella cried out against my lips as my body arched at the same time that she squeezed my fingers. Sweat beaded her brow, dampening the canopy of her hair around us.

We calmed together, dissolving into the fluffy blankets and pillows under us. Stella lay on top of me, her head on my chest as I wrapped my arms around her, my lips pressed to the top of her head.

In a way, that night was our first night together. The first time we allowed ourselves to love each other completely, giving over our former burdens to something greater than both of us. It was the first time we found freedom in each other, and contentment in the moments that followed.

CHAPTER FOURTEEN

Stella wasn't in the bedroom when I emerged from the shower, a towel held tightly under my arms. On the armchair beside her bureau, my gun lay in its holster beside my pocket knife and bra. For the past few days, I hadn't thought about work until I saw my weapon sitting there.

"What are you looking at, Al?" Stella startled me when she entered. With her hair still damp while wearing a pair of loose-fitting shorts, and a nearly sheer tank top, she approached, sitting on the edge of the bed.

"Can I talk to you about something?" I asked, and she held her hand out to me

"Of course," she said as I took it.

I stood in front of her, taking a deep breath before speaking. "I really think I'm going to officially resign from the force."

"Okay. What's got you worried?"

"If I do that, I'll be jobless. I've never been jobless. I've been a cop for fifteen years." Again, another deep breath. "I don't know how to do anything else."

"Is that what you wanted to talk about?" she asked, tilting her head as she squeezed my hands.

"Part of it. I wanted to know what you thought about

it."

"Allie, my biggest worry over the past two weeks has been thinking about the day you go back to work. A job where bullets can fly at your head at any given moment. A job where a co-worker assaulted you. I think it's safe to say that I fully support your decision if you do want to resign." She pulled me to her, parting her knees so I could stand between them. "Although, I would support you if you chose to return to work as well. I just prefer you safer."

I draped my arms over her shoulders, stroking the underside of her hair. "I really want to leave. And with selling the building to Kari, I wouldn't have to worry about money for a little while."

"Money isn't...something to concern yourself with," she said rather delicately. "Make decisions based on what is right for you, not based on money."

"Says the woman who likes her job and has money." I smiled at her rather cheekily and she laughed, swatting my hip.

"Yes, so I know best. Come." She took my hands as she slid back on the bed. I moved with her, walking on my knees until she sat against the pillows. She kept pulling me, guiding me into her lap. Every inch of me tensed when her hands lifted me slightly so that I could straddle her legs. "I have you." My towel fell off and she brushed it away like a mildly annoying nothing, leaving me naked in her lap. "Have you ever sat like this?"

"Not completely," I admitted, gripping her shoulders as she rubbed my back.

"You're okay. It's just me. Come closer so your stomach touches mine," she said, and I slid forward into position. The contact soothed me a little and eventually I settled.

"Usually I do the holding like this…"

"Are you okay with me holding you?" she asked, her question sincere as she placed her hands on my waist.

"Yes."

"And yet you still look ready to puke."

"I'm okay," I said, not sure if I was convincing her or myself.

"You are," she said, smiling as she ran her fingers through my hair. "Do you know that you're beautiful?"

I laughed, shaking my head. "Sorry, I think you're looking in a mirror or something."

"Hush up and take the compliment. When you're wearing work clothes, you're very attractive and strong. But when you're naked, a delicate femininity emerges. And you're a doe-eyed honey-haired beauty." The grin she wore only made my cheeks heat to a near fire.

"Stella! That's ludicrous. I am none of those adjectives."

"You are, Allie." She leaned up and kissed my chin. "You're beautiful. I mean it."

"And you, Doctor Hotpants, are sexy as fuck. How's that for a compliment?" I cracked up when her eyes bugged out of her head. "Marc's called you Doctor Hotpants for the past four months since I've been swooning over you."

A playful smile melted over her pretty pink lips. "You've swooned over me?"

"As if that wasn't obvious by the sheer number of visits made to your workplace with gifts of platonic lattes," I confessed which only made her laugh.

"And here I thought you were just a *nice* girl in need of a *friend*. Or a doctor." She ran her thumb over the rectangle-shaped scar near my hip bone.

"Not sure about nice, but I definitely needed a friend and a doctor on a few occasions." I ran my thumb over her bottom lip. "Still do."

"Good, because I could use a friend, and sometimes a cop."

I laughed, caressing the space between her breasts while we talked. "A cop for what?"

"To look incredible in heeled boots and a gun?" She chuckled, her whole face bright with a light that was new to me, and to her as I've known her.

"Let's play a game."

"What kind?" She lifted a skeptical brow.

"Questions. We ask each other questions and talk about our answers."

"Is that like an ice-breaker game?" she asked, laughing harder now. "Getting to know each other?"

"Yep." I grinned and kissed her gently. "Want to?"

"Yes." She nodded and I tugged at her shirt.

"Take that off. I shouldn't be the only one naked. It's just *wrong*."

She leaned back and pulled her shirt off without batting a lash. "Better?"

"Always." I ran my fingers over her firm, perky breasts and smiled.

"Who goes first?" A shudder ran up her center and I felt it against my stomach.

"You since it was my idea. Ask me something."

"Bossy."

"I'm generally bossy."

"So am I."

"This could get interesting once we're more used to each other then."

"I expect it will." She chuckled, stroking my abdomen while contemplating her question. "Okay. I got one."

"Ready."

"Before me, when was the last time you had sex?"

"A year ago about. Maybe a little more," I answered. "With cheater number two."

"Yuck." She frowned, reaching up to place her palm on my cheek. "No more cheaters for you."

"I like that plan." I turned and kissed her wrist. "My turn. Did you swoon over me?"

"Silently. To myself." She nodded, laughing a little. "Before I even knew you were gay. But I hated myself for it. I felt like I was being unfaithful to Clarissa. When you asked me to coffee that night, I hoped it was for that reason. But it wasn't."

"But it really was." I cracked up and she joined me in it. "I didn't think you were gay either. You pretty little lipstick."

"You should talk." She swatted my thigh and I squirmed.

"Do you still feel that way about Clarissa?" I asked, rubbing my hands over her forearms.

"Sometimes," she admitted. "But not as deeply. Sometimes I wonder if she's watching me. Like when I—" She laughed, shaking her head. It made me smile.

"When you what?" I poked her stomach and it made her twitch.

"When I went down on you last night, I thought to myself, 'if she's watching, she would be loving this' because Clarissa had a raging libido." She chuckled the entire time she spoke, bringing light and joy to memories rather than sorrow.

"And you think I don't? Do you know what it's been like *not* having sex with you?" I groaned dramatically.

"Allie—" She cracked up, waving me off as she covered her mouth.

"And if Clarissa had a raging libido, I bet you weren't far behind. Because, let's be honest, Stell, I can tell you hold back sometimes." Happiness, the sounds of her happiness, filled the room and bounced around inside me like a ping-pong ball.

"What exactly was it like *not* having sex with me?" She grabbed my hands suddenly, lacing her fingers with mine and holding on tight.

"Bad." I laughed, shaking my head. "Marc caught me masturbating after that first night that I slept over while completely naked in your bed."

"Did he?" Her face was so red with her hysterics. "Allie, that's terrible."

"It was great before he interrupted!"

"Oh my God." She cracked up, dropping her head back

on the headboard. "Do you masturbate a lot?"

"New question!" I squeezed her hands. "Your turn," I said, grinning still.

"How about a more serious one?" she asked, still chuckling.

"Go for it."

She paused, pursing her lips while she thought. "How's this… Ever think about having kids?"

"Not seriously. Have you?"

"At one point. Clarissa and I talked about it, but not until I was done with my fellowship would we even consider it."

"And now?"

"Is that your question?"

"Yes," I grumbled when she caught me in my own game.

"Now, it would depend."

"On what?"

"What my partner wants."

"What if she wanted kids?"

"You're using up all your questions." She squeezed my hands again but smiled. "Then I'd want kids."

"I know. One more. What if she didn't?"

"I'd be okay with that, too," she said. "All that matters to me is that I'm in love and able to accept the love of someone else."

A smile curved my lips as I tilted my head. "Are you in love?"

"It's my turn to ask," she said though her cheeks burned bright red.

"Very sneaky." I poked her nose and she scrunched up her face.

"I know. Okay." She wiggled under me, pretending to get comfortable. "Do you think we're rushing in?"

I glanced around us, then shrugged dramatically. "I'm not sure why you're asking. I mean, making you the executor of my will, moving in, and adding my name to the deed of your house seems perfectly timely if you ask me. Four months of knowing each other is heaps of time to plan for the next sixty years."

Stella laughed, giving my hands a yank which pulled me closer. "You're horrible."

"I know." I let my proudest grin show. "But seriously, no, I don't think we're rushing in. It took us over two months to even sleep together. I spent the night several times before we did. Do you feel like we are?"

"I don't. That's why I asked you. I feel like it's on target. Maybe slower than usual."

"We're lesbians. You and I are not typical speed. Most of my other girlfriends I slept with on date number two. Some on the first date."

"You're a horny thing…"

"You're only just noticing this?" I laughed hard, tossing my head back when she tickled my sides. "And you're not so bad yourself, Stell. If you let yourself go."

"I'll take that into consideration." She bit her lip, her hands dropping to my thighs. "Just how horny are you?"

"In general, or now considering the fact that I've spent half an hour sitting in your lap while naked with my junk all exposed?"

"Hmm. Now," she said, moving her fingers toward my center.

"Well, put it this way, I'm not the most arid of deserts, babe."

"Yeah?" Her gaze met mine, sharp and strong. "Ask me a question." As her fingertips neared my lower stomach, it lurched with excitement.

"Bossy tonight."

"When I want something I am. So ask," she said, a single finger nearing the apex of my thighs. Anticipation built at the same time that the ache in my pussy grew under her affection.

"Um…" I gnawed on the inside of my cheek as I attempted to think of something to ask her. All I could think about was the dozen different ways I wanted to make her come. My hands wandered to her breasts and I brushed my thumbs over her nipples. "What's your—" A gasp caught me when she circled my clit. "Stella."

"Go ahead. I'm listening." Her expression softened to the pleasant, mild-mannered smile of her doctor face. It made me whine a little, but that only had her slipping further down my folds.

"What's it—*God*—what's it like, being a doctor who knows so much about the human body, then having sex and stuff?" I bit my tongue to hold on to the moan that threatened to escape, acutely aware of the wetness increasing against her hand.

"It makes me better for it," she said, smiling at me while she tortured me. "Or at least I'd like to think so. For example…" Without much warning, she slid two fingers inside me and my body arched toward her. My lips brushed hers but she did something to my pussy that almost had me exploding right there. The way she stroked me, hitting the most perfect spot, sent such a sharp wave of pleasure through me that I nearly shouted. "There's that." A wicked grin parted her lips and she kept doing it.

"Stella." I grabbed on to her shoulders, and any sense of modesty I had before that moment flew out the window and tangled around the Space Needle. "Oh God."

"Yeah. See? There's that." She chuckled, kissing me softly while she continued moving inside me with one hand, the other stroked my clit in firm circles. I moaned into her mouth, my nails digging into her flesh as my toes curled under the rapidly building orgasm that screamed through my core. My hips rolled against her hand, and she nipped my bottom lip when we parted. I could barely hold on to myself and it had only been a few seconds. "How fast can I make you come, Allie?"

"Stell—" And I was gone, arching hard as my body raged, bucking with the explosive orgasm she sent rushing through my system. I cried out, tensing as she held me in it, blindly and deeply with such delicious pleasure that I could barely keep my balance. When a second climax tore me to pieces, a rush left me in the heat of it. My mouth claimed hers, desperately and I brought her with me on the liquid cascade that followed the blissful ride.

Stella flattened her palm against my pussy, and rubbed in slow circles as I wrapped my arms around her shoulders, gasping for breath against her neck.

"I made you gush," she whispered, chuckling as she rubbed my back then gripped my rear. "You beautiful, sexy, thing."

"My God, Stella. That's never...I've never. What did you do?"

"Made you mine." She lifted me suddenly, one hand against the small of my back as she lowered me to the bed. "And I'm going to do it over and over, until you forget that you ever belonged to someone else…"

***

The city lights rolled to life as the sun melted away to the royal blue of the night sky. With my head on Stella's stomach, her legs against my shoulders as we both gazed out the window, we lost ourselves in an hour's worth of afterglow and tenderness. The scent and feel of her beneath me settled something so deep inside me that I didn't think I'd ever feel this way again. When I kissed the top of her pussy affectionately, she ran her fingers through my hair.

Neither of us spoke for ages it seemed, until my phone went off on the bedside table. Stella looked over then grabbed it, holding it to me.

"Thanks, babe."

"Welcome." She smiled, a dreamy almost-dopey smile as I answered the phone.

"Hey Jordie," I said, the gravelly tone in my voice startled me.

"Now that sounded sexy. Are you tongue-deep in your beautiful doctor?"

"Um…" I leaned up on my elbows which meant Stella's core was an inch from my face. "Almost." I licked her clit, grinning at her when she jumped and smacked my hand. "What's up?"

"They caught the kid who broke the window. The cops told me they didn't think it was connected to Wildrose."

"What cops?"

"Jackson."

"Well that's fairly good news then," I said. "Everything else okay?"

"Everything is good. Are you okay? I haven't heard from you in days."

"I'm really good, Jord."

"How about dinner tomorrow? Maybe just the four of us?"

I looked to Stella and asked, "Dinner with Ainsley and Jordan tomorrow?"

"Sure," she said, her eyes half lidded though her smile continued.

"We're in."

"Later, sexy."

"Bye."

"She's checking on you?" Stella asked, holding her arms down to me. I crawled up her body and hugged her, settling half on top of her with our legs tangled. She tucked my hair behind my ears while I drew figure-eights on her chest.

"She is. Jordan's a good friend. My only real one anyway, second to Marc."

"Marc hasn't called?"

"He texted me a bunch, but knows things are okay. I haven't really talked to Jordan about anything."

"You're the only one I talk to," she confessed, still playing with my hair.

"Maybe that'll change in time."

"Maybe." She bit her bottom lip in the way that I loved. "I have an answer for you."

"What's that?" My brow furrowed but I couldn't help the smile.

"Yes." She nodded, tickling her fingers over my hand.

"Yes to what, goofball?"

"Yes to...I'm in love." Her gaze never left mine, perpetuating my smile as my heart swelled with affection.

"With who?" I teased. It made her laugh softly, and swat my hand.

"*You*." She poked my nose hard and I made to bite her finger.

"You already know that I'm in love with you so don't even play around."

"Allie." Her laughter mingled with mine as she yanked me into a rough hug again. "I'm starving," she said out of nowhere.

"Me too. Want to order pizza?"

"Mmm. Yes. Pepperoni," she said, stretching a little bit.

"No way." I scowled and tickled her. "Pineapple."

"Half pineapple, half pepperoni."

"That's so gross." I laughed hard as I reached for my phone again. "But fine."

"Hooray."

"I must really love you, Stell, to allow you to deface a pineapple pizza with meat."

She cracked up and rolled me over almost viciously as we melted into a playful tickle war.

***

"So...*Stella*," Jordan said as we walked down the street together. Both of us held hot cups of cocoa between our palms. Her grin never ceased and I fought the urge to trip her.

"So...*Ainsley*."

"Don't give me that."

"I'm giving you it. You're really head over heels for her and you know it."

"She's a lot of fun and just clingy enough that I like it," she said, smiling dreamily as she brushed a smattering of snow from her black and turquoise streaks.

"And sexually adventurous."

"You know it." And there was the grin again. "And you with Stella. You love her."

"I do. She's different. Genuine. Affectionate. Emotional."

"Which is very opposite of your overbearing, *Marley*, obnoxious, *Lara*, and uncommitted, *Kari*, girlfriends of the past."

"I know…"

"Did you just have bad taste or purposefully pick women you knew would treat you poorly?" She glanced at me. "I mean, you could've had me instead."

I laughed at her as we neared the precinct, slowing our pace some. "We tried that, remember?"

"We totally sucked. Not a chance in the world. I'm too unhinged and you're too untrusting. I mean, at least untrusting in the allowing yourself to be vulnerable sense." She leaned against the brick face of the building, propping her foot back against it.

"It's not like that with Stella…" I sipped my cocoa, watching her for her reaction.

"Why not?"

"I don't know. Maybe because she's vulnerable, too. And we talk a lot. More than I've talked with anyone ever. Even you sometimes…"

"Because you're always guarded, Allie. I have to pull things out of you. You're less guarded with Marc because he's like your brother and you're used to brothers."

"That's so true. Remember when Ryan was really sick and overdosed a few times?"

She nodded. "I do. Scary."

"Stella was the on call doctor on multiple occasions. She saved him and he remembered her. He attributes her care to getting him to clean up his life, at least taking the first steps anyway. Afghanistan really fucked him up."

"Fucked up a lot of people. That's really amazing that

she was able to help him. And now she's your girl."

"She is…" I smiled at the thought of it, then glanced at the front door where dozens of people gathered with uniformed officers at the gun buyback event. "I better go inside before it gets really crowded. Thanks for walking me down."

"Want me to come in with you?"

"Partly yes. Partly no."

"Is Marc here?" she asked, her eyes following the two food trucks that drove up and parked.

"He is."

"Are you sure you're ready for a full resignation?"

"Stella and I talked about it. I'm not happy being a cop, Jord," I confessed, sighing afterward. "Part of me was happier being a beat cop."

"In that sexy uniform." She grinned and I shoved her shoulder. "But I know, Allie. You've lived a life of going through the motions. I know you like the outreach aspect of it though."

"Yeah. That I like, but I can do that in a different way. I signed the papers with Kari the other day and put the money in an account. It was way more than expected after the appraisal."

"Of course, Al. This is Seattle and the bar is popular."

"I know. So I can live off the interest or whatever for a while. I was thinking of talking to Jake about volunteering at the LGBT Center. Until I figure something out."

"Do it. That's a good idea." She smiled while she listened to me, tilting her head a little.

"What?" I cocked a brow at her.

"You sound sure and happier than I'm used to. Usually you doubt and temper your joy."

"Things've changed…"

"Good." She held her elbow out to me. "Let's go quit your job."

I laughed, slipping my arm around her elbow as my gear belt poked against her hip. "Okay."

Jordan hung out up front while I sat in Walsh's office waiting for him. Marc accompanied me, his hand on my shoulder until I sat.

"You're really going to make me partner up with Porter, aren't you?" He scowled, then gave my hair a tug. "Nice hair, by the way. All blown out and smoothed. It's almost like you have a *girlfriend*."

"Shut up." I elbowed him in the stomach, but he grabbed me into a hug as he laughed.

Walsh's grumble appeared in the hallway before he did. Marc released me and pretended to punch me in the cheek. "See you later."

"Bye."

"Goldman, let's go," Porter called out. When I peered around the doorway, he saluted me, a small, half-smile plastered on his mouth. I waved and returned to pacing around Walsh's office while waiting for him.

One wall, covered in two decades' worth of accolades, articles, and photographs, was the neatest thing in his office. Some of the pictures had people I recognized, but not all. I focused on a smaller photo in the corner of a rowdy looking group of detectives, one of which flipped the camera the bird. The woman stood about a foot shorter than Stiles and the cocky smirk that accompanied the gesture told me it must've been something she did often. Stiles had his elbow rested on her shoulder while two other men stood like cross-armed pillars on either side of them. Beside that photo, newspaper articles about the death of an elusive serial killer, coined *Four Point*, brought a flash of memory to me.

"Your cousin took him down. Damn Canadians," grumbled Walsh as he appeared behind me. I laughed, turning to face him.

"Nearly ten years ago," I said.

"Yeah. You talk to her?"

"Not much. She's a lot older than me. Who's that?" I pointed to the woman with her middle finger extended.

"Sali James," he answered simply.

"What unit is she in now?"

"Retired. She was Stiles' original partner." He moved behind his desk, gesturing for me to sit. "But that was a long time ago."

I took a seat opposite him in one of the two chairs that faced him. "Has any other serial ever come close to Four Point? Not that I know much about it, just what I've read in some articles and textbooks."

"Not in Washington State." He picked up an electronic cigarette and puffed on it. "So you're really doing this, Lange?"

"Yeah." I reached into the pocket of my jacket and pulled out the envelope with my letter of resignation. He took it when I offered it to him and set it on the desk next to my badge that seemed to be in the same spot that I left it. "I don't want this anymore."

"Are you sure you won't consider a transfer or something? Maybe work with Grant and Stiles in sex crimes?"

"No. That's worse. I really just…" I sighed, leaning back in the chair. "I'm just done."

"You're a good detective, Lange. The community responds to you."

"Yeah, well, maybe I can help the community in a different way."

"If you change your mind." He shrugged, taking the badge and letter then sliding it into the top drawer of his desk.

Somewhere in the distance, a pop sounded followed by a static silence. My body tensed, and when I looked to Walsh, his hand hovered over his service weapon the same way mine did. We both froze, listening until...*Pop! Pop!* followed by shouting.

My first thought was of Jordan as Walsh and I raced out of his office, weapons drawn as a slew of other confused, but ready, faces rushed down the hall. Every officer, every detective at the unit had their guns drawn.

I hurried forward but Walsh grabbed my arm. "My friend is outside," I told him, panic in my voice.

"Watch yourself." He pointed at the front desk where a uniformed officer stood, her weapon at the ready. "Notify the other precincts."

More gunshots rang out and shouts followed. I raced toward the front, bursting through the spinning door only to be met with absolute chaos. Pedestrians ducked behind cars and food trucks while a large group of uniformed officers exchanged fire with half-a-dozen men in ski masks. One of them held a bin of the turned-in guns under his arm.

"Drop it!" someone screamed.

"Drop your weapon. *Drop it*!"

"On the ground!"

"Get down!"

"Jordan!" I shouted her name, searching desperately in the crowd for any hint of her purple jacket. My heart pounded in my ears as Walsh raced by me followed by a wave of law enforcement hurrying into the crowd. One of the masked men hit the ground as a splash of blood spattered the car behind him. "*Jordan*!"

"Alice!" I heard her call, then spotted her huddled beside a car parked on the road. I glanced over my shoulder at the uniforms in protective vests who acted as human shields for the rest of us, then bolted toward Jordan. Bullets flew over my head and Walsh shouted my name, but I dove for her, grabbing her and shoving her lower to the ground.

"Stay down," I said as her arms wrapped around my middle.

"Oh my God. What's going on?" she cried, tears streaming her face as her entire body trembled.

"Thugs trying to steal the turned in gear. Stay down." I swung up, aiming over the hood of the car only to barely miss a bullet that whizzed by my ear. The crumbling wall behind me told me how close it came. Fifty-feet from us, the man with the gun bin approached, weapon drawn and held on its side as he fired off at anyone he could. I took two shots, clipping the bin and he shouted as the contents tumbled from his grip. The sound of metal-on-metal radiated like an explosion. Jordan screamed, her grip on me tightening.

People raced down the sidewalk behind us, cowering under purses and bags filled with post-holiday shopping. Absolute chaos rained down on us. I ducked behind the car, holding Jordan so tightly against the tire that the hubcap dug into my thigh. "Stay down, Jordan."

"Oh my God, Allie."

"It's okay. You're okay."

To our right, I saw some uniforms take down one of the masked men. Two down for sure, but how many more?

More bullets sent concrete from the building tumbling to the ground and I took my chance again, swinging up around the hood of the car and firing off a few shots at the perp closest to us. He turned, aiming at me then, and I dropped down behind the car again.

"We need to move!" I told Jordan but she nearly freaked. "Listen to me. Stay low and run the length of the cars toward the alley there. Ready?"

"No!"

"Let's go!" I grabbed her by the arm as we rolled to our feet. As soon as I stood, I yanked her back down, expecting the onslaught of gunfire which undoubtedly followed. Uniforms rushed toward us, and I fired off the rest of my clip in the direction of the masked man who now had two pistols in his palms. I pushed Jordan ahead of me, then shoved her down the alleyway.

Four people huddled behind the trash bin at the very back, one of them holding a small child, her hand cupped over his mouth. Sirens screamed in the distance as backup arrived and the units in the field undoubtedly returned.

"Stay here, Jordan." I guided her to the bin behind the others, then swapped out my clip for a new one.

"Oh my God, Allie." She sobbed, her hands grabbing at me. "Don't leave. You have to stay."

"He saw us come down here. Stay with them. All of you be quiet." I pried Jordan from me, glancing back at her as I edged my way back down the alley.

With my back pressed against the wall, I peeked out to see two men huddled over a uniformed officer who was down on the ground, grabbing at his chest where the bullet struck his vest.

"Get his weapon," an angry, muffled voice said. "Leave the rest."

When the second guy went for the gun, I fired off a round that struck him square in the neck. My stomach lurched at the sight of him hitting the ground and tumbling over the officer. Immediately, his partner shot at me and I pressed myself against the wall only to see Jordan running toward me.

"No!" I grabbed her, spun her around, and slammed her against the wall, shielding her from the rounds meant for me.

Jordan's eyes widened as she looked over my shoulder. A gun blast sounded, echoing violently down the alley. Dark red polka-dots splattered the lilac color of Jordan's jacket at the same time that a streak of blood covered her lips. Jordan screamed, her hands shaking as she grabbed me around the middle. A second gunshot sounded, followed by the squeal of radio chatter. Only then, did the burn in my chest make itself known.

"You're bleeding," I said, dizziness catching me when I made to gasp. A sharp, stabbing terribleness stole away my voice.

"Allie. Alice!" Jordan caught me around the middle as my legs gave out. "Oh God! Someone help!"

Out of the corner of my eye, the uniformed officer held his gun aimed from his perch on the ground as the two bodies of his assailants littered the area around him.

"Officer down! *Officer down!*" he screamed into his radio.

"Alice!" Jordan cried as I felt the cold concrete under me when it swallowed me whole.

The last thing I remembered was the radiant heat of the gun in my palm.

CHAPTER FIFTEEN

I floated down a luminous tunnel, white light leading me toward something greater. A bright, silver star that I wanted so badly. I ached for it, reached for it. It made me bleed with desire and I heard myself crying for the *star*.

"Right pneumothorax. One entry, no exit," an echoing voice called out. "Doctor?" The voice paused. "Doctor Corwin?"

Cries invaded the tunnel, but the star was within a finger's reach in front of me. I stretched, the heat of it tickling my palm.

The star stabbed me in the side, draining away my insides into a pool of liquid blue.

A sharp gasp had me screaming as I awoke to the sight of people racing around me. Jordan was gone and so were the uniformed officers, only to be replaced by the blues and greens of medical professionals.

"Hold her!"

Monitors blared as hands grabbed at me while wires tangled everything. I kicked at them, desperate to run for the star.

"Alice! *Allie*, easy, baby." Stella appeared in front of me, tearing off the paper mask that covered her face. Tears poured down her cheeks from her scarily wide eyes. Someone pulled me backward but the screaming never stopped. Pain. So much pain. "Push Lorazepam!" Stella shouted, then her gloved hands cupped my face as she pressed me back onto the bed. "I need you to stay still, Allie. Okay?"

"Stella," I cried when I spoke because everything hurt, everything burned. And I couldn't breathe, couldn't say the words that dangled off my lips. Metal pooled in my mouth, hot and terrible, as it trickled from my lips. Stella's eyes, nearly black from widening pupils, brought pangs of fear tangled with pain. Her desperation, and blood-covered torso brought flashes of the story she told me about Clarissa's death. *Was I Clarissa? Who am I?*

It hit me like a sledgehammer, the massive wave of comfort like a cozy down blanket tossed over us. Stella's soft sobs against my cheek remained as the fluffy bed engulfed me, sinking us deeper into its embrace. The beeps faded into the twinkling sound of an ice cream truck, rolling along the streets of summer. *Chocolate sounded perfect. With rainbow sprinkles. Gay sprinkles...*

"Doctor Corwin, she's crashing."

"Get her to the O.R." Stella's pained voice cried out.

"She's lost a lot of blood."

"Doctor Corwin…"

"Doctor…"

"Blood."

"Alice."

Allie...Rabbit.

Rabbit.

***

A pretty blonde woman stood in front of my silver star. Bright green eyes glared at me. She took a step forward, her lips moving angrily with words I couldn't hear, and she shoved my shoulders. I stumbled backward, but when I made to charge at her in my quest for the star, she pushed me so hard that I fell. Hard and fast, tumbling and spinning…

Something pressed against my hip, waking me from the ache it left in my desire to turn over. My eyes peeled open, and I looked upon the hospital room with confusion at first. Darkness filled the room save for the dim light of the lamp beside my bed. Wires connected me to everything and when I made to move, discomfort shot through me like venom in my veins. My mouth, dry and terrible, had me cringing. I lifted my right hand, tugging off the pulse monitor from my finger, but when I lowered it again, it landed in a tangle of satin strands. When I looked down, I saw Stella's head resting on my frozen hip. My stomach lurched and I ran my fingers through her hair. She didn't stir so I sat quietly as memories of what got me here assaulted me.

Walsh. Resigning. Cousin Lourdes. Gunshots. Jordan. *Jordan.* Where was Jordan? I shifted my shoulders and sucked in my breath when pain struck my back. Staying still seemed like the best plan. I closed my eyes again, continuing to stroke Stella's hair. Heat pressed my eyes as the emotions began to catch up with the memories, but when I heard the room door open, Stella's hair slipped from my fingers when the sound woke her.

"Get out," she said, her voice raspy and trembling.

"Doctor, she needs her med—"

I opened my eyes to watch as the nurse stood in the doorway with a tray of something. "I'll do it." Stella broke away from the bed and snatched something from her. "Now leave."

"Yes, Doctor." The door closed again and I watched as Stella returned to the bed. She hadn't noticed me watching her yet as she uncapped a syringe and forced the tip of it into the I.V. bag hanging beside me. I waited until she was done before drawing her attention.

"What kind of bedside manner is that, Doctor?" My voice sounded like the worst case of laryngitis to hit the West Coast this season.

She started so hard that I thought she might scream. Immediately, she broke into tears as she fought her reaction versus being a doctor. "Allie."

"Hi, babe." I smiled as she dropped down on the bed beside me when I held my untethered arm to her. She moved into it with extreme caution as I hugged her, her hot lips pressing against my cool cheek.

"Oh my God, Alice." She sobbed hard now as I grabbed a handful of her hair.

"I'm sorry, Stell. I'm okay." And I lost my shit as images of the assault flashed through my mind. I cried quietly against her shoulder. "Is Jordan okay?"

"She's fine."

"She got shot," I said, sobbing softly as she leaned back to cup my face.

"No, baby. You did." Her hand fell to my chest. "Easy. Breathe slowly with me." She glanced at the monitors and then picked up the pulse thing, clipping it back on my finger. "Jordan's fine."

"Am I fine?"

"You will be." She looked back to me, stroking my hair though she cooed gentle, soothing phrases while prompting me to breathe. Eventually the monitors stopped screaming as much.

"She had blood on her." I wasn't sure what part of me didn't believe her. Would she lie to spare me further pain?

"That was your blood, Allie. She's okay. I promise." Stella placed her hand against my cheek and I nodded, settling back into the pillows.

The longer I stayed awake, the more aware of my body I became. "I have to pee."

"You have a catheter. It's just the sensation. Allie?" She called to me and I looked back to her drawn face. "Easy."

Something tightened my chest as a wave of fear struck me. The wires tangled my neck and arms, holding me down. I reached under the blanket, but Stella grabbed my hand.

"No. I'll take it out. Okay? But you need to stay calm."

"I can't breathe." I gripped my chest, tearing at the sticky parts of the wires. Again, the monitors went crazy and that time, the door to the room opened. Two nurses stood there but didn't enter.

"Lorazepam," Stella said to them. "Now." Both of the nurses rushed in, but Stella cupped my face in her hands again. "Alice. Look at me."

"I can't breathe."

"You're okay. I got you. Don't pull the catheter." She snatched my wrist when I made a grab for it again. "I'll take it out. Okay? I'll take it out."

I nodded as hot tears streamed my cheeks. The nurses fussed around me, but I hung on to Stella, drowning myself in the sight of her. Flashes of the silver star from my dream appeared in front of me for a moment followed by a sudden lull that settled the panic in my chest. My eyelids drooped and Stella's expression shifted from girlfriend to doctor as she addressed the nurses.

"Get the cath kit," she said, and I watched as she pulled on a pair of latex gloves. The women fussing over me appeared hazy and their voices muffled.

"Are you sure you want it out?"

"She asked and when she wakes up, she'll ask again. I'll do it."

"Doctor Corwin, you have to let us take care of her," a new, firm voice said. She sounded older than the other two and not intimidated at all. "It's been several days. You've barely slept."

"I'm fine. Give me that."

"Stella, *enough*."

That was the last I heard before the comforting pull of sleep dragged me away.

When I opened my eyes the next time, the room flooded with light from the window that overlooked the city. Cool fingers pressed my left wrist and I turned to see Stella standing beside the bed. Other than the dark circles under her eyes and fraught expression, she appeared the same as she had the last time I woke up. Her eyes lingered on the monitors as she poked at the touch screen tangled within the wires. I turned my hand over then tickled the palm of hers. Immediately, she looked at me and smiled.

"Hi, baby."

"Hi." Emotions swallowed me, catching in my throat as the desire for her to hold me screamed louder than the pain that slowly worked its way to my consciousness.

"You're okay. I know it's scary." She sat down on the bed, holding my hand when I gripped hers.

"I want to sit up," I told her, my voice cracking terribly.

"I'll raise the bed, okay?" She grabbed the control and slowly did just that. "Your mom and dad just left. Evan and Ryan are with Marc in the waiting room."

"How long have I been here?" I moved my legs, but all of the things attached to me made it a fruitless effort.

"Three days now. You were unconscious for two of them. How's that?" she asked when I was almost upright.

"Better." Tears streamed my cheeks and I moved the rest of the way toward her. She caught me, her arms wrapping around me like liquid comfort, gulping me down. I sobbed against her shoulder and cried when the pain in my back made itself known.

"I love you, Alice. It's okay. You're okay." Stella's soft voice trembled a little in my ear. She kissed my neck and shoulder, anywhere she could while I nearly clawed at her.

"I love you, too. Is Jordan okay?"

"Jordan's fine. She was by this morning with Ainsley."

"My back hurts." I leaned back, attempting to reach around myself to feel it. Stella helped guide my hand into hers, holding it in my lap.

"You were shot in the back. It caused your lung to collapse and some organ damage. Surgery took care of that, but you'll be uncomfortable for a little while, baby."

"Did you do the surgery?" Sitting up made it a little harder to breathe but not terribly. In my hands, hers were ice cold.

She nodded, her eyes shimmering with the tears she stopped from falling. "Until they got another trauma surgeon in."

"I'm so sorry, Stella. I'm so sorry that this happened to you again." I squeezed her hands and she reciprocated the gesture.

"It isn't your fault, baby. None of it." She blinked away her tears, then reached up to stroke my cheek. "You saved Jordan. She's told everyone that."

"I didn't intend to—That sounded odd. I mean, I just...I saw him coming and she ran up." My heart pounded suddenly as the echoes of gunshots rang in my ears.

"It's okay. You're okay and so is she." Stella guided me into a cautious hug and I melted against her.

"Did anyone die?"

"Five of the six gang members who led the assault. Four cops were seriously wounded, but there were several others shot in the vest. A few civilians had minor injuries."

"S'what they get for attacking a police station. Idiots." I sniffled and brushed my lips over her neck.

"Agreed." She sighed, though I noticed her fingers poking around under my open gown in the back.

"Am I bleeding?"

"No, but we need to change your bandage."

"I need to brush my teeth before I die from the gross," I said, leaning back to look at her. She laughed and cupped my face, leaning in to kiss me anyway. All I wanted to do was melt into it, but we kept it short.

"Mine aren't much better. C'mon. Let's take care of that."

"Who was the nurse that yelled at you before?" I asked, shifting cautiously as she guided my movements. First, she took something off my legs, then allowed me to dangle them off the side of the bed. "Do I have a catheter?"

"Not anymore. Do you have to pee?" she asked as she

washed her hands in the small sink in the corner of the room near the bathroom.

"Not yet. This is embarrassing."

"Allie, you nearly died," she said from behind me. The way she said it sounded like a confession of sorts. "There's nothing embarrassing about it." Latex snapped faintly and the gown fell forward on me when she untied it.

"How much bandage do I have?"

"From here…" She pressed the spot near my right shoulder blade. "To here." Then ended with a poke above my right side, nearing my ribs. "Any pain?"

I heard the tape pulling away before I felt it. "More on the inside. Does that sound odd?"

"Not at all. The damage is on the inside. Tell me if I hurt you," she said, and I closed my eyes as soft fingers poked and pressed along whatever was on my back. It wasn't comfortable to say the least, but when she neared my side, I started at the sharpness of the pain.

"There."

"Tender spot but it looks okay. You're healing well."

"Did I have blood in my mouth?" I smacked my lips at the faint memory. Something cool slid along my skin and I stared at the orange socks that covered my feet.

"When you came in to the E.R., yes. A lot."

"Who was that nurse who yelled at you before?"

"When?"

"Um...I'm not sure when. *Ow*." I jolted when she poked something near my ribs again. I felt her lips brush my left shoulder with the apology that followed. Clean gauze and some tape later, and she was done.

"A few of them yelled at me," she said after removing her gloves then washing her hands again. She returned to the bed after but stood in front of me now, tying the gown around my neck again. "Want to try and stand?"

"Yeah. I feel kind of weak though," I admitted.

"It's understandable."

"I really want a shower," I told her as she unhooked a

few wires from me.

"No showers yet with that wound, but maybe a sponge bath." She held her hands to me. "You might feel more pain when you stand because of the muscle tears. Hold on."

"Okay." I took her hands, and she guided them to her waist as she gripped my middle. I stood with her help. She was right about the pain and it took my breath away, but I fought through it. My legs quaked a little but not terribly.

"Good?"

"Not horrible," I said, a little out of breath.

"You're in pain, baby."

"I can deal." We held on to each other until I was able to take a few steps. My footing found me, albeit shakily at first, until I was able to just hold her hands. "I feel like a kid."

"Remember what I said before? You nearly died, Allie. Take it easy."

"You saved me," I told her as we made our way to the bathroom with the I.V. pole tailing us as she pushed it along.

"You saved me, too, Allie. More than you know."

While I brushed my teeth, Stella stood behind me, her thighs pressed against my rear as she supported me. I brushed them twice, and then gargled some mouthwash afterward. My hair didn't look terrible, but I couldn't lift my right arm to smooth it. Stella wasted not a second before she fixed my ponytail for me while I watched her in the mirror.

"You're beautiful," I told her, and she smiled at me. "And I'm starving, by the way."

Her laughter rang out like a fresh spring breeze. "I'll get you something."

"Not *Jell-o*. Like a cheeseburger or something." I turned around, leaning against the sink as I tried to ignore the discomfort in my muscles. Stella's hands fell to my middle, her smile lingering brighter than it had. "And you need to sleep. And eat. Or something because you look about ready to pass out."

"Just kiss me with that minty fresh breath, would you?" Both of us laughed before I closed the distance between us, pulling her into a kiss so deep and perfect, no amount of pain made it to my consciousness. I let myself drown in her sweetness, and her care.

An hour, and a bland bowl of soup and toast later, my room filled with family and friends. Mom fussed over me while Ryan sat stock-still on the bench by the sink. Evan, never fearful of getting his hands dirty, sat beside me on the bed while Mom busied herself straightening up. They'd stayed with me all day, though no one said much of anything that wasn't casual. Except Evan.

"Leave it to you, Rabbit, to get shot and nearly *die* in the middle of resigning from your job," he said, grinning at me as he smooched my forehead. "And where'd Stella take Dad?"

"Very funny, and she took him to the rehab part of the hospital to look at his leg."

"He actually let her?"

"They've grown close over the past three days."

"It's the first time she's left you," Mom chimed in. "She must be certain of your recovery."

"Mommy, can you fix me some roast beef and mashed potatoes, please?" I smiled cheekily at her and she chuckled, patting my hand.

"When you come stay with us, I will."

Evan snorted.

"Mom, I'm going home when I'm discharged. I'm fine." I elbowed my brother and he just laughed.

"Nonsense." She waved me off.

"Ryan, you're quiet. Come here," I said, looking over at him. He got up slowly and joined me on the other side of the bed when Mom sat down to work on some crocheting project. "What's wrong?"

"The doctor said you died for two minutes," he said, his

dark eyes wide and freaked out.

"But I'm alive now. And I don't see dead people or have any special crazy gifts. Don't worry."

"Aw man. Here I was hoping…" Evan snapped his fingers and Ryan laughed a little.

"It's just freaky. I don't like knowing my baby sister died." Ryan hugged me suddenly and I gave him a squeeze. With my good arm because the other wasn't worthy of squeezes just yet.

"Please don't let me stay with Mom. I'll surely die from that," I whispered in his ear and it made him laugh. "I'm okay, Ry."

"Better be." He messed up my hair and smiled, finally relaxing.

The room door opened and in walked Marc, smiling at me right away. "Knock knock. Brought you someone."

"Is it a handsome blonde lawyer?" I perked up and he laughed.

"Nope." Marc held the door open and Jordan pranced in, gripping a box and a teddy bear as she bounded over to the bed. "Someone who's super happy that you're conscious."

"Allie!" She hurried over and Ryan had to duck out of the way. I laughed and caught her in a gentle hug, squishing the bear between us. "Hi. Oh my God, I'm so happy you're awake."

"I am, and please tell me that's a box of chocolates in your hand."

"It is." She set it on my lap and I grinned.

"Yay. No one else will feed me." I tore off the paper and devoured a strawberry cream one in a heartbeat. Jordan's giggle rang out, though tears trickled down her cheeks, sending black balls of mascara with them.

"Aw, Jordie, don't cry," I said, setting the teddy bear in my lap as I squeezed her hand. "I'm okay."

"You saved my life, Allie. If you hadn't gotten in front of me—"

"Jordan, you're my friend. And that's that." I hugged her when she leaned in, her body trembling a little bit.

"It was so scary," she whispered and I nodded, rubbing her back gently.

"Boys, let's go see if there's any new magazines in the waiting room," Mom said, shoving Evan and Ryan from the room. Marc got lost in the shuffle and I heard a soft, "Hey," escape him. They left Jordan and me alone which was easier, at least, to have this conversation.

"You weren't hurt at all?" I asked, looking her over, but she shook her head.

"No. Only you. I've never seen anyone die before. But the guy who shot you did after the other cop shot him," she said, sniffling a little.

"Have you talked to Ainsley about what you saw?" I asked, worried for her wellbeing more than my own at the moment.

"Yeah. I have. Eve, too. They visited a few times with me, but you were asleep still."

"I heard. I've only been awake for a day."

"Have you seen the news?" she asked, tentatively as she glanced to the television which was on but without volume.

"No. I avoid that."

"Well, Butler's case is done. The jury found him guilty. He's going to jail and so is the other guy," she said, rubbing my hand gently. "I know how badly that upset you. I know you've been upset since then, and it's made you quit your job. I'm sorry I didn't encourage you to talk more."

"Jordan, you've always been a good friend to me. It's not your fault that I didn't talk about it, and it's not your fault that I got shot. I made all of those decisions on my own, and honestly, I wouldn't take any of it back." I glanced to the door when I heard Stella's voice, then back to her. "It helped me find Stella. And I love her so much."

"She loves you, too. Like *really* loves you." She brought

my hand to her lips and smooched it half a dozen times. I laughed softly and squeezed her fingers.

"I won't break if you hug me again."

"Good." And she did, sighing deeply. "Marc told me that you told Stella what happened to you…"

"Yeah well, she figured it out herself for the most part. And she's patient with me when I need it, and bold when I need that, too," I told her, leaning back against the pillows as fatigue pressed in on me.

"You deserve her, Allie. Someone who's good and kind. And takes care of you."

"Thank you. And you deserve Ainsley, because she's head over heels for you." I smiled at the thought of the two of them.

"She's different…"

"She is and you love it."

"I do."

"Lay with me?" I asked, turning slightly on my uninjured side.

"Of course." She scooted and tucked her knees up as her head lay on the pillow. The soft smile never left her face. "Jeez, Allie, those roots."

I laughed hard and it made my side ache a little. "*Ow*. Shut up."

"I'm so glad you're okay, Allie." Jordan teared up again and held my hand while I tucked the teddy bear under my chin.

"I'm glad you're okay, too." I closed my eyes and the last thing I saw was her soft smile.

The next time I opened my eyes, Jordan wasn't there anymore but Stella was. She slept quietly, in her wrinkled scrubs and with stringy hair. I pulled the blanket over her and kissed her forehead gently before turning on my back to stretch. My body wasn't as sore, but the right side of me was much tenderer than before.

"Don't wake her," Mom whispered from her spot in the chair beside the bed. She had several magazines tucked in the cushion while her crochet project looked more like a blanket and less like a tangle of knots. "It's the first she's slept in days. At least fully."

"I know." I nodded and she stood up to caress my hair. "How come you're still here? Is it late?"

"Only seven. I promised to stay if she took a nap. And here we are." Her voice remained a gentle hush as she smiled. "Discharged tomorrow, love."

"Can't wait." I returned her smile and she squeezed my hand.

"You rest. I'll keep watch over both of you."

"Love you, Mom," I said, turning back over to face Stella. Her fingers searched for mine, even in her sleep.

***

"How did you ever convince my mother to let me stay with you?" I asked as Stella brought two mugs of cocoa to the sofa in her living room. A fire crackled in the hearth, brightening the room with a golden glow. I finally felt better after a cautious shower and dressing in my own clothes.

"Easy. She couldn't argue with the notion of her daughter bunking with a doctor who would be home from work with her for the next two weeks at least," she said, smiling as she sat on her knees beside me. She, too, now freshly showered and in a set of sweats, appeared less ragged. "Marc was easier to convince. The fact that he wanted to carry you up here..." She laughed softly, her smile broadening.

"I would've punched him." I grinned, then sipped my cocoa. "How'd you get time off like this?"

"Used some vacation time. I haven't used any in years and it accumulates. I probably have six months in the bank."

"Wow. Lucky you. Or better, lucky *me*."

"Lucky both of us." I watched as she settled into the sofa, her hand falling to my thigh. "One thing I've learned about you, Allie, is you don't tell anyone when you're in pain, emotional or other. So I'm going to ask you how you feel, but I want an honest answer."

"Kiss me and I'll tell you." I smiled at her and watched as her chuckle escaped from around the bottom lip she had between her teeth. She moved in, stroking my cheek as she kissed me sweetly. I melted into her, tracing the graceful curve of her jaw. When we parted, she rested her forehead against mine, her eyes closed.

"How much pain are you in? On a scale, one being little, ten being terrible."

"If I don't move my arm or twist sideways, a four, if I move, about a six."

"Okay," she said, setting her cup down on the coffee table and stroking my cheeks. "That's a better answer than *fine*."

"I'm so sorry, Stella. I can't imagine what you must've thought when you saw me come in the E.R. I keep playing it through my mind." The confession brought tightness through my throat and a burning bout of tears to my eyes. "How you must've felt…"

"Allie…" She took my cocoa from me and set it aside, then took my hands. "While I admit, my reaction was one laden with fear and disbelief, the outcome wasn't the same. I knew it was you. I knew what happened to you. I had answers and you spoke to me."

I squeezed her hands, sniffling a little as I continued to envision her pain. "What did I say?"

"Asking for your star and trying to get up despite the fact that you lost a lot of blood. Kept asking for Jordan. And then you lost consciousness," she told me. Her eyes shimmered with tears, but she didn't let them fall.

"Like me, Stella, you have a way of minimizing your pain until it explodes from you. Tell me the truth." I pulled her toward me as I shifted my position to sit properly on the sofa. She moved with ease as I guided her to straddle my lap.

"I was terrified that I would lose you, too." She settled

on my legs, but she moved with caution. "That okay?"

"Yes. Scoot closer," I said and she did, her stomach against mine. "Stella Corwin…" I began, pulling her arms over my shoulders as I looked up at her. "I can't promise you that I won't ever die because, let's be honest, one day we'll both leave this earth, but Stella, right now, today, you have me." Words like these had never fallen from my lips before. Stella's gaze locked on mine as a silent tear slid down her cheek. "You have *all* of me. And I love you like I've never loved anyone. You saved my life, Stella. In so many ways. *You're* my star." A smile curved my lips, unlocking me from the emotions I kept at bay. I sniffled a bit, choking too much to say anything else.

"You saved my life, too, Allie. You may not have pulled a bullet from my thoracic cavity, but you broke my heart out of a fortress of solitude bridled with darkness and pain. And I love you, too. So much. More than I ever thought I could. I'm happy to be *your* star."

I pulled her down, claiming her firm, confident lips with mine. My fingers tangled in her hair as my heart slammed in my chest, throbbing with the happiness I'd never thought would belong to me. Every part of me raged and wanted, connected and tangled with my *star* in a way so foreign and beautiful, I'd never ever let it go.

Booms and flashes interrupted our kiss when we both looked outside the wall-length window beside the fireplace. In the distance, fireworks and other incendiary blasts radiated off the Space Needle, illuminating the sky with colors and sparkles. Stella looked back at me and laughed a little bit.

"Happy New Year, baby," she said, grinning as she ran her thumb over my chin.

"We literally kissed right from one year into the next without even knowing it. Happy New Year, Stell. I look forward to starting this year with you in it." I cupped her face and brushed my lips over hers.

"And the year after that?" She nipped my lip and I

laughed.

"And the next after that," I said, slipping my hands up the front of her shirt. "And the next after that."

"And the next."

"And the…" She gasped.

EPILOGUE

~TWO YEARS LATER~

"You're not teaching them to make fruitcake are you? Because that's just *wrong*." Jake scoffed as he waltzed through the giant kitchen at the LGBTQ Center. The teens laughed at him as he gave my ponytail a swat.

"You wish. Take a hike and leave us to it." I flicked a bit of flour in his direction.

"I would, except you have a visitor, who is very demanding mind you, waiting out front," he said.

"We got it, Allie," piped Sky, her bright green eyes meeting mine with a newfound confidence.

"Yeah. We got this." Trevor clapped her on the back and the two of them returned to work.

"Looks like I'm not needed here." I smiled at them, then rinsed off my hands before ditching the apron.

Jake walked me through the uber busy center where volunteers made the whole place resemble a rainbow Christmas wonderland in preparation for our big holiday party that night.

"This place looks great, Al," he said, glancing around as we walked through to the main entrance.

"It does. You sure you don't need me at the shelter

tonight?"

"Yeah. We're good. There's just three kids staying and six volunteers." He chuckled, folding his arms over his broad chest. "So naturally, Daniel and I are inviting them all home to our place for the holiday."

"That's awesome of you guys." I paused, turning to face him. "I should've thought of that."

"For New Year's." He perked up and I grinned.

"You got it."

Some of the little kids ran amok while a brooding teenager looked on. With her half-shaved head, torn jeans, and holey shirt, she sat there picking at flecks of nail polish. I glanced from her to Jake and he offered me a half smile.

"Can you tell Stella I'll be a minute?"

"She's not here yet. Jordan was the one making a fuss, but she looks occupied." He gestured to the far side of the room where Jordan stood among a group of girls who bounced excitedly as she showed off her rainbow highlights. She set down her bag and let them watch a video on her tablet.

"Well then." I laughed and nodded toward the quiet girl. "I'll check on her."

"Good luck." He wandered off back toward one of the two Christmas trees and helped some of the young men attempting to string it from the ceiling.

Without saying anything, I dropped down to sit on the floor beside her. She lowered her eyes to her hands while resting her elbows on her knees.

"*Yo*," I said when she continued to ignore me. "What up, boo?"

That did it and she laughed a little. "Allie. So not cool."

"Like my shoelaces?" I kicked out my feet and showed her the rainbow laces in my black and white sneakers.

"Shit. You need help." She snickered, but finally looked at me.

"Tell me about it. What's got you so blue in a room full

of happy gay rainbows, Sarah?" I mimicked her posture, resting my elbows on my knees as well.

"My girlfriend cheated on me *again*. With a dude." She sighed then ran her fingers through the long part of her hair.

"Harsh. Been there."

"With a *dude*?" Her eyes bugged out of her head and I laughed.

"No! My old girlfriend cheated on me with a dude. And a few girls before that."

"It sucks." She stretched out her legs and leaned back on her hands. "I broke up with her, but part of me wishes I hadn't."

"Why?"

"Because now I'm alone. Like *literally* alone. And everyone else." She gestured to two guys in the corner who strung up some lights over one of the doorways, in between kissing. And flirting. And gentle shoves. "Maybe I could've gotten over it."

"Let me tell you something about that, kid." I turned to face her and her tentative gaze landed on mine. "When someone cheats on you one time, chances are, they might do it again. I know not everyone believes that, but I do. I also believe in waiting for the right person because…"

At that moment, a windswept Stella appeared in the doorway. She brushed some rain from her jacket while looking around the center, in search of something. It made me smile. I looked back to Sarah. "Because the right person will eventually cross your path." I pointed to Stella. "Like her."

"She's *way* too old for me." Sarah lifted both her hands up and shook her head. "Pretty though."

I laughed. "Don't even play. She's all mine."

Sarah grinned, glancing between me and Stella. "How long did you wait for her?"

"For as long as it took." I smiled when Stella found me, her gaze landing on mine as she nearly bounced in place.

"She's my *star*."

"So you think I made the right decision?" Sarah's posture straightened with her question.

"I do." I stood and messed up her hair. "Don't settle, kid."

"If you say so."

I winked at her then hurried over to my wife. She greeted me with a giant, unexpected hug, nearly lifting me from the ground. "Allie, I have to tell you something." Her words escaped her on an extended breath.

"What is it, babe?" I asked, chuckling softly at her bright-eyed expression.

A near giggle escaped her as she took both of my hands and pulled me outside. In the middle of a December afternoon in Seattle, the freezing cold rain pummeled us. "Stell, what the—"

She kissed me so hard that it took my breath away. Whistles filled the space behind us and I kicked the door closed on the brats snooping on my foray with Doctor Hotpants.

"My God. What was that for?" I asked, breathlessly when we parted.

"We need to tell Marc." She bounced on her tiptoes then covered her mouth with both hands.

"Tell Marc what— Oh?"

She nodded hard, tears welling up in her crystal blue eyes, sharper under the overcast light. I grabbed her hands and she laughed. "Yes."

"Really?" My voice squeaked.

"Yes." She sniffled and I laughed, nearly jumping on her in a crushing hug.

"Oh my God. Really?"

Stella's laugh brought me even more joy just knowing what caused it. She grabbed me hard, spinning me in a complete circle right there on the sidewalk when I lifted my feet. I squeaked and kissed her all over her face. "Allie, I'm pregnant!"

"Oh my God!" Just hearing her say it made me cry and I caught her in a heated kiss, our tears mingling with the rain that now matted our hair.

Stella's joyful cries broke our connection and I reached between us, placing my hand on her lower stomach. Her fingers squeezed mine and I kissed her again. "I love you so much," I professed, both of us sobbing like the great mushy dopes that we were.

"I love you, too, baby. Your mom is going to be *so* happy," she said, laughing and crying at the same time.

"Christmas dinner is now the lesbian's having a baby show. Get ready, love."

"I'm ready." She laughed softly, cupping my face. "*So* ready."

"Me too." I nipped her bottom lip, blinking away the rain and the happy tears. "For everything with you."

For more stories by Max Ellendale, please visit:
www.maxellendale.com

Titles by Max Ellendale

Four Point Trilogy
Four Point
Point Two
Mirror

Lesbian Romance
(*in the same universe as the Four Point Trilogy*)
Wildrose
Rabbit

Lesbian Romance
Skyclad
Midsummer
Try Pink & Indigo

The Legacy Series
Glyph
Birthrite
Sacred
Bound
Marked

ABOUT THE AUTHOR

Max grew up just outside of New York City, spending most of her formative years outdoors creating wild ghost hunts with neighborhood kids, setting booby-traps to capture unwitting family members, and building clubhouses on top of ten-foot walls. Max wrote her first story at the age of twelve and titled it *Circles of Friendship*. Through the years, Max has written several short-stories and poems, all of which met the wrath of the "Not Good Enough" monster and ended in fiery demise.

Max regained her confidence when she began writing scholarly articles and research theses on her first trip through graduate school. It took several years for her to break the habit of the formal writing that marred her creativity. An additional Master of Fine Arts degree in Creative Writing was Max's biggest support in this. Max writes primarily sci-fi/fantasy, paranormal romance, and Young Adult stories.

Printed in Poland
by Amazon Fulfillment
Poland Sp. z o.o., Wrocław

74980220R00157